THE PLUS ONE PACT

PORTIA MACINTOSH

B

Boldwood

First published in Great Britain in 2020 by Boldwood Books Ltd.

Copyright © Portia MacIntosh, 2020

Cover Design by Debbie Clement Design

Cover Photography: Shutterstock

The moral right of Portia MacIntosh to be identified as the author of this work has been asserted in accordance with the Copyright, Designs and Patents Act 1988.

All rights reserved. No part of this book may be reproduced in any form or by any electronic or mechanical means, including information storage and retrieval systems, without written permission from the author, except for the use of brief quotations in a book review.

This book is a work of fiction and, except in the case of historical fact, any resemblance to actual persons, living or dead, is purely coincidental.

Every effort has been made to obtain the necessary permissions with reference to copyright material, both illustrative and quoted. We apologise for any omissions in this respect and will be pleased to make the appropriate acknowledgements in any future edition.

A CIP catalogue record for this book is available from the British Library.

Paperback ISBN 978-1-83889-086-5

Ebook ISBN 978-1-83889-087-2

Kindle ISBN 978-1-83889-088-9

Audio CD ISBN 978-1-83889-084-1

MP3 CD ISBN 978-1-83889-745-1

Digital audio download ISBN 978-1-83889-085-8

Large Print ISBN 978-1-83889-748-2

Boldwood Books Ltd
23 Bowerdean Street
London SW6 3TN
www.boldwoodbooks.com

For Joe
The future Mr MacIntosh

1

You can't put a price on finding love. If you could, it wouldn't be £10.

I've been playing the dating game for a while now but I just can't seem to complete it – and I'm usually so good at games. No matter which level I try, there's always a hole to fall down or a monster to eat me – metaphorically speaking, of course, although with dating apps you only ever feel a few bad decisions away from ending up in someone's freezer.

Recently I have been using an app called Matcher. You know the drill, swipe left or right on singles in your area, all the while hoping not to get connected with a murderer or, worse, someone who doesn't know what punctuation is. All of my dates so far have ranged from pretty rubbish to monumentally awful. It's safe to say that the date I'm on right now is one of the worst ones.

I look down at the £10 note. Holding it out in front of me, gently waggling it to try and encourage me to take it, is Matt. After chatting with Matt on Matcher for over a week, tonight we had our first date. I've had some bad first dates recently but this is the first time there has been any discussion of money changing hands.

Matt, a twenty-eight-year-old from Huddersfield (who I matched with while he was in Leeds for the day), caught my eye with his fun-loving profile. Well, he was someone a little different from the young professionals who take themselves too seriously and brag about their latest holidays – it gets a bit tiresome when there's no chemistry to make it worth looking at that photo of them hugging a clearly sedated tiger in Thailand.

I agreed to meet Matt on his turf, which was a little out of my comfort zone, but you've got to be willing to meet people in the middle (or Huddersfield) if you want to find love. Everything about dating involves stepping out of your comfort zone. But when I turned up at the address he gave me it wasn't a bar or a restaurant, it was a house. His house, I assumed as I hovered outside on the pavement, so relieved I had decided to wear black jeans and a nice top, rather than a dress, because I would have been so annoyed if I'd shaved my legs for this. Naturally I wanted to scarper but the front door opened before I had a chance and a woman in her late fifties stepped out.

'You must be Cara,' she said warmly, spotting me on the pavement, all smiles as she hurried down the short garden path to give me a big hug. I froze in her arms as my brain tried to fit the pieces of the puzzle together. She was much shorter than me so her face pressed awkwardly into my chest. She was all dressed up as if she was heading out on a date. Her perfume was overwhelmingly strong, and definitely the scent of a more mature lady. A heavy, floral scent that reminded me of my grandma's usual go-to perfume.

Then it hit me. This woman was dolled-up to go out, she said my name, she hugged me as if she knew me... had it finally happened? Had I finally been catfished? I'd been caught out by guys who were much shorter, heavier or older than their pictures or profiles let on before. As deceptive as it felt, I got it, we all want to show our good side, I'd put filters on my photos and never upload anything where I didn't look my best, but there's a difference between being a different height and being a different *everything*.

'Matt?' I said slowly as the horror set in.

'Yes, let me show you inside,' she replied, ushering me up the steps. 'I'm Lizzie, his mum.'

I let out a sigh of relief so strong I swear I almost caused the front door to slam closed.

As soon as I realised that Lizzie wasn't Matt, I softened, ticking myself off for thinking the worst.

I felt so daft for jumping to such a wild conclusion, which is probably why I was so quick to put aside any concerns one might usually have when they turn up to a first date and it's the guy's mum who greets them.

Once inside the old, stone terraced house, I was ushered into the living room. There, sitting on a leather corner sofa in a room that was clearly too small to accommodate it, was Matt. The Matt from the photos on his profile – thank God. Tall, skinny, hair spiked up in a way I hadn't seen since the noughties. Kind of goofy-looking but in a charming way. Next to Matt was a boy of about ten.

'Cara!' Matt said with delight, jumping to his feet to give me a hug with a familiarity that you don't usually expect from someone you haven't actually met before.

'Hi,' I said. It was about all I could say. Not only was I nervous, like almost everyone is on a first date, but something just didn't feel quite right.

'OK,' Lizzie said with a clap of her hands. 'I'm going to get going. There's pizza money under the vase by the door, plenty of pop in the fridge. I'll try not to be late. You three have fun.'

'Great, bye, Mum,' Matt called after her.

'Bye, Gran,' the boy said without taking his eyes off the TV.

I didn't know what to say. I was just frozen on the spot, standing next to the door. What had I walked into? Should I just leave?

'I'm so glad you came,' Matt said. 'This is Kieran.'

'Hi, Kieran,' I said politely.

He said hi without looking at me. He was far too engrossed in the TV show he was watching. It was one of those real-life police shows where they follow officers around on car chases and drug busts. I wasn't entirely sure it was appropriate for a child of his age, but what do I know?

'Is this your son?' I asked.

'What? No! Of course not,' he replied. He seemed offended I had asked. 'Don't you think I would have mentioned that I had a son, if I had a son?'

'Sorry,' I said quickly.

'No worries, come sit down,' he said, nudging me towards the sofa, ushering me down next to Kieran.

It turned out that Kieran was Matt's nephew – his older sister's son. It didn't sound as though his sister was a very hands-on mum; it seemed more as if Lizzie took care of him. It became very quickly apparent that Lizzie had gone out on a date and that my date with Matt was taking place at the house, with Kieran on the sofa, watching his police shows.

Honestly, I was in shock. I didn't know what to do. Matt definitely should have mentioned to me that this was what the plan for this evening was, right? Unless it changed last minute but, still, he could have texted me.

'Do you have any kids?'

'None that I know of,' I joked. I love making that joke. When men make it I find it kind of gross but there's something so funny about a woman saying it.

'What?' he replied, a little taken aback by my reply.

'None that I know of,' I said again, saying it slower this time so he could tell I was kidding.

'Right... yeah...' he replied awkwardly. 'I guess we all could, when you think about it.'

We really couldn't.

So we ordered pizza and we watched old episodes of *Road Wars* and *Banged Up Abroad* because it was the only thing Kieran was interested in.

My job, which is honestly the least interesting thing I could talk about right now, given how bizarre my date is tonight, involves knowledge of different locks. This was something Matt knew about so, as we watched a young man being arrested for having a belly full of cocaine condoms (seriously, why are people letting a kid watch this kind of thing?) he leaned over and assured me that he had a pair of handcuffs that 'not even I would be able to get out of'. The look on his face was so smarmy. The unsubtle grin, the even less subtle wink – clear indicators that Matt already thought he was in there. At that point, manners be damned, and after two hours of enduring, well, whatever this weird non-date was, I knew that it was time to leave.

I opened my mouth to announce my departure when Matt's mum, Lizzie, burst back through the door with a gentleman who, based on his appearance, I could only imagine she found in the eighties. He had the big hair, the tight trousers, he even had the self-important swagger of a rock star. For some reason he had a dodgy fake tan job, making his leathery skin an intense shade of dark orange.

They kissed their way through the door clumsily. Lizzie's date was clearly going to be continuing here at the house. Upstairs. I really didn't think this date could get any more awkward but Matt's mum heading upstairs for a jump with Tan Halen certainly added a new level of cringe.

'You crazy kids can get out of here,' she told us, drunkenly stumbling forward towards the sofa, subtly handing Matt something before cranking up the volume of the TV and heading upstairs with her date.

And so, we left. We left the house, with Kieran downstairs, watching people get banged up, and Lizzie upstairs... I'm not going to finish that sentence.

'Thanks for hanging out,' Matt said to me as soon as we stepped outside. 'Family is really important to me. It says a lot about you.'

'Well, if your mum needed a babysitter last minute, what can you do?' I replied, although I still thought it was weird that he didn't tell me.

'Oh, it wasn't a last-minute thing, I just thought I could kill two birds with one stone, get the pizza paid for, you know?'

'So the date you planned was babysitting?' I asked.

'Yeah,' he replied. 'What, you think I just hang out with kids for fun?'

Matt laughed to himself obliviously before holding up what his mum had handed him – two £10 notes.

I pursed my lips, speechless. Well, of all the dates I'd been on, no one had ever tricked me into babysitting with them.

'At least we can go on a second date now,' he said. 'Now I can afford to go halves.'

I felt as if I had hit my limit multiple times over the course of the babysitting date, but this was my last straw. No more manners, no more sparing feelings.

'I don't think so,' I replied. I forwent my usual polite friendliness to be firm.

'What? No, come on,' he said. 'I'll give you half my babysitting money, seeing as though you were there too, how about that?'

So here I am, standing outside on a warm summer evening, being offered £10 to go on a second date with Matt. I can just about make out his mum's excitable giggles coming from her open bedroom window and I sincerely hope Kieran hasn't turned the TV down.

'Keep the money,' I tell him. 'Use it to take Kieran out for an ice cream.'

Or just put it towards his therapy.

'But what about our date?' he asks. 'Or our second date?'

Matt looks so disappointed. I think he thought this date had been a roaring success.

'Sorry, I just... I don't think this is going to work out,' I tell him.

This is the first time I've had a date bad enough to actually tell the guy a second date isn't going to happen while I'm still on the first one. Then again, tonight wasn't a date, was it? It was babysitting.

'What?' he says, and yes, amazingly, he is surprised.

'I'm sorry,' I apologise again, although I'm not sorry, I'm horrified. 'It's just... it's not going to work between us.'

Matt's face falls. His enthusiasm fades. I'd go as far as to say his usually goofy mask slips off.

'Bitch,' he says simply.

I feel my eyebrows shoot up with a force. I've never been called a bitch before. Sure, it bothers me as a woman, and as a human, but on a personal level I don't care what Matt thinks of me; all I care about is getting out of here.

I turn on my heel and begin the walk to the train station, which thankfully isn't far.

I just want to get home, kick off my heels, get into my own bed and just be alone.

Obviously I'm not happy being single, otherwise I wouldn't have resorted to trying to find love on dating apps, but right now, tonight, I feel lucky to be able to go home alone.

I'd rather be single than be with someone like Matt.

2

Who is the most annoying: an actor, a dancer, or a double bass player?

I'm not telling you a joke – unless you count my life as being a joke, which I suppose you could – I genuinely can't tell which one is the most annoying.

I'm not sure what woke me up this morning. I think it was the sound of a double bass, crashing, rather than drifting, its way through my open bedroom balcony door, which I opened last night because it was too hot to sleep. Now it's too noisy to sleep instead.

I rent a one bed apartment in central Leeds in a really great location. Well, at least I used to think it was. It has a small balcony off both the bedroom and a cool open-plan living space with a view across the city centre, starting at the swanky Victoria Gate shopping centre across the road, stretching across Leeds. I can see all the sights, including the Pinnacle building that stands tall in the centre of the city.

I remember the day I moved in here: after I'd spent hours and hours unpacking and setting things up, the day turned into night and I looked out of my bedroom window and saw the word 'Pinnacle' shining in big, bright white letters. Having grown up in a small village just outside Leeds, and suddenly finding myself in a super cool city-centre apartment about to start my dream job, it felt like a very appropriate message to have floating out there in the night sky. I felt as if I had finally made it.

When I got in last night, after my disastrous date, I kicked off my shoes, stepped out of my clothes and, as I climbed into bed, ready to put the evening behind me, I noticed that the lights in the Pinnacle sign were out in almost all of the letters – all of them except the L. Last night, having a big, bright, impossible-to-miss L for loser hovering outside my bedroom window felt even more appropriate.

One of the perks of mostly working from home is not only being able to go on ultimately disappointing midweek dates without having to worry about what time you get in, but also being able to sleep in whenever you feel like it. But, living where I live, I have no such luck.

Originally I thought it was an awesome, artistic place to be, sandwiched between Northern Ballet and Leeds Playhouse, and being a creative person I felt as if I was living in the heart of creativity and expression. Unfortunately, this means that my building is full of musicians, actors, and dancers, and they are a little too expressive, especially when it comes to rehearsing.

Right now I can hear the thudding of feet above me, the almost creepy sound of a double bass from somewhere below, and if I hear the person in the flat next door to me bellow, 'Ready to lower boats, sir!' one more time, so help me God...

I have managed to deduce, from what has been put on the notice board downstairs, that at the moment most people are rehearsing for either *Le Diable amoureux* or *Moby Dick*. I am literally trapped between the devil and the deep blue sea, and even when these two shows are over, there will be different plays, different ballets, new people renting the apartments that surround me. That's why I am in the process of trying to find somewhere new to live. I genuinely live in fear of *Stomp* coming to town.

While my job is a creative one, it is one that requires a great deal of care and concentration too.

My mum tells people that I lock people up for a living, which usually makes them think I'm a police officer. My dad tells people I lock people up and watch them try to escape, which usually makes them think I'm some kind of dominatrix.

I work for Houdini's Great Escape, a company that has escape rooms up and down the country. Their flagship branch is right here in Leeds and I was lucky enough to bag a job designing rooms for them.

I've always loved puzzles. Jigsaws when I was a kid, a little pocketbook of Sudoku when I used to commute, endless puzzle apps on my phone – all far easier than playing the dating game on Matcher, that's for sure.

Escape rooms are basically just a room full of puzzles of all different types. Figuring out number codes, opening puzzle boxes, finding hidden messages on the wall, and locks. Lots and lots of locks. Each puzzle needs to lead seamlessly and sensibly into another, ultimately leading up to the unlocking of a door.

I come up with themes for the different rooms, draw up blue-prints, and create the pathway that players will follow. I absolutely love it, but it's so hard to do when you can't think straight, and one little mistake could throw the whole room off.

I've known for a while that I need to move if I want to get my work done in peace, and I thought I'd found somewhere, so I gave notice that I was moving out of here. Except things fell through with the new place and my landlord had already found someone else to move in here after I moved out, so now I'm having to try and find somewhere against the clock. You'd think this would motivate me, and it does, but I do need to get on with my work too. I have a few places I'm going to look at next week. One of them has got to be OK, right? OK will work, so long as it's OK *and* quiet.

Despite it being a Thursday afternoon, today has big Monday morning energy. This week has felt like a week full of Mondays and today is dragging just the same.

I suppose I should get ready soon. I'm heading to my parents' house for dinner. They only live a short train journey outside Leeds so I see them and my brother quite often, but we make a point of having dinner as a family every other week.

The only thing that could make my day worse would be piling into a commuter train, standing for the entire twenty-minute journey, probably with my face pressed up against the dirty glass door, murky from a day's worth of fingerprints.

I'll hop in the shower, throw on some clothes and hurry for the train. Once I'm at my parents' place I can sit in front of a fan, drink lemonade and just enjoy the peace and quiet that comes with living on the edge of the moors. The only thing that could potentially ruin the nice, quiet evening of my dreams is if the subject of my cousin's wedding comes up – which it almost always does, but I'll cross that bridge when I come to it.

My phone vibrating on the desk in front of me snaps me from my thoughts. I have a notification telling me that I have a new match on Matcher. I open up the app and instinctively reject the first person it shows me with a swipe to the left. Almost everyone gets swiped away these days. I'm about to go and check my new match when I realise that it's showing me a message that I haven't seen before. I squint at it suspiciously until I realise what it says:

No more matches. Check back soon.

It turns out I have run out of people to match with in my area, meaning I have swiped my way through every vaguely eligible bachelor (plus a few married ones who, it always amazes me, are lurking on the app) in Leeds. It's official: I have run out of men. Well, you know what? Good. Good riddance to bad rubbish. This app has been nothing but trouble. I guess I'll just go back to playing Candy Crush when I'm bored, rather than swiping my way through men who just aren't worth shaving my legs for.

I place my phone on charge to give it a boost before I leave and head into the bathroom to get ready.

This escape room isn't going to plan itself but, right now, all I can think about is escaping my own room. Of course, once I'm in a room with my mum and dad, chatting about the wedding of the century, I'll probably want to escape that one too.

3

It's only now that I live in the city that I truly appreciate what a gorgeous place I grew up in. At the time, my family home just felt like a house, but it was all I'd ever known.

Growing up was like something out of *The Railway Children* – literally, my parents' house was next to the steam train line where the movie was filmed. Their back garden actually backs onto the line, which meant that we would often be able to watch as the old steam engine passed the bottom of our garden.

No one uses it to travel from A to B; there are much faster, cheaper ways. It's a tourist attraction, one that pulls in people from all over the globe. Living right next to it, we wouldn't go on it all that often. Just once a year, as kids, when we would take a trip on the annual Santa Train at Christmas time. The man who played Santa actually looked a hell of a lot like Santa Claus, with his grey beard, his rounded belly and his jolly smile, so when he would take the train for fun on a fairly regular basis, if my brother and I were playing in the back garden when he passed, he would always give us a wave through the window. Of course, we were convinced that he was the real Santa Claus, which is probably why we were such well-behaved kids. Our parents really drummed into us that Santa Claus was always watching, which feels highly manipulative, but I have to admit it's a stroke of genius.

My brother, Oliver, still lives with my parents in their three-bedroom detached house. It's a conversion of a building that is believed to date back to the eighteenth century. It looks picture perfect. Aged, but not old. Traditional, but not old-fashioned. It has always been well kept, sitting in a garden full of various plants and flowers. It's like something out of a romance movie. The kind of place you inherit (although in the movies they're usually in need of a lot of work) before falling in love with the hunky next-door neighbour. The only person next door here is a retired doctor in his nineties, and I'm betting it's been a long time since he made anyone say 'ahh'.

Oliver is younger than me. I'm twenty-nine with thirty breathing down my neck. Oliver is twenty-three with the world at his feet. Well, that's what my parents seem to think anyway.

Oliver is their most viable child, having breezed his way through his bachelor's degree, his masters, and now he's doing a fully funded PhD. I don't think they are more proud of Oliver, or that they love him more than they love me or anything like that. I just feel as if it's easier to be more conventionally proud of him, whereas I'm pushing thirty, with a kind of weird job, living my best spinster life. All of my old school friends are married with kids. You can't blame people for measuring my success against the people I grew up with, even if it's not really fair.

I decided, after my disastrous date last night, that a trip to see my family was what I needed. Real people who actually cared about me, with no ulterior motive, giving me the time of day. The four of us – me, Oliver and my parents – are currently sitting around the table in their spacious farmhouse kitchen, eating dinner. We're having salmon in a sticky honey and lemon glaze, which is my absolute favourite. I know that Oliver isn't a huge fan, so we don't have it all that often on family dinner night.

'Would you say you were in a good mindset today?' my mum asks. I shift uncomfortably in my seat. That's a strange question to ask, isn't it?

'Erm... Yes?' I reply. 'I suppose so.'

I mean, I'm not exactly in a great mood. Last night was pretty disturbing and today wasn't a very productive day. I guess I'm fine though.

'So, if I had some news that you might not be all that happy with... now might be a good time to tell you?' she continues.

My fork slips from my fingers and clatters against my plate.

'Mum, what kind of question is that?' I ask.

'The kind that makes sure you're in the mindset for potentially upsetting news,' she says.

'OK, sure, but you've already tipped me off to the bad news,' I point out. 'So whether you're telling me it or not, I know that there is bad news. It doesn't matter what it is, my brain is filling in the blanks for me – with ideas potentially worse than the thing itself. My God.'

I puff air from my cheeks. I feel in a right flap now. I pick my fork back up and reacquaint myself with my dinner. It's a shame I can't get it to takeaway or I'd be off. I'm not in the mood for a Brooks family drama.

'For God's sake,' my dad, Ted, says, clearly annoyed to be having his dinner interrupted with a woman either side of him low-key bickering across his plate. He turns to me. 'Cara, Lloyd is coming to Flora's wedding. There.'

'Lloyd?' I shriek. 'Lloyd? My ex Lloyd?'

'How many Lloyds do you know?' Oliver asks with a chuckle.

I meaningfully stab a carrot and pop it in my mouth with all the angst of a stroppy teenager.

'Don't be mardy,' my dad insists. 'Your mum worked hard on dinner. It doesn't deserve to be stabbed so violently.'

I roll my eyes. Isn't it weird how being back in your family home can make you feel like a kid again?

Ted Brooks is your classic Yorkshire dad. Honestly, he's straight off a postcard in a Yorkshire gift shop. Strong and silent – apart from when he's straight-talking – and awkwardly frugal – unless he's buying things like cuts of meat or beer. I've always found his generation of ultra proud 'Yorkshire born, Yorkshire bred' Yorkshire men to be a mess of contradictions. Simple creatures, but still somehow impossible to figure out. My dad is a fairly big bloke, but a gentle giant. My mum, especially when she's standing next to him, is perfectly petite. Reaching in on her tiptoes at just over five foot tall, Annie Brooks looks quite funny next to her husband. Once, when we were all walking up Malham Cove for 'fun' one weekend (not really my idea of fun – walking is a bit too much like exercising for my liking), my dad started chatting with a man and his family. The man, who couldn't see my mum's face behind her scarf, asked my dad how old his daughters were.

My mum does look good for her age though; she has sleek, dark bobbed hair, and almost always has a good covering of make-up on. That must be where I got it from – feeling the need to wear make-up every day. I enjoy wearing it, though, and have a lot of fun applying it. One of these days I'll take a proper class, rather than just messing around in my bedroom, usually for no one's benefit but my own. Then again, I suppose that's what my feminist brother would prefer me to say. Oliver has my mum's dark colouring and skinny frame, but it's stretched to a height to rival my dad's. I really don't know who I take after, to be honest.

I'm 5' 7", which is taller than average for a woman, but unremarkably so. All it means is that I have size eight feet, which makes shoe shopping kind of inconvenient sometimes. My height puts me about halfway between my mum and my dad, and I suppose my chest-length dark blonde hair puts my colouring at that midpoint between my dark-haired mum and my fair-haired dad.

'Sorry, Dad, I'm a little upset because you just told me that my cousin is inviting my ex-boyfriend to her wedding. I can't believe her.'

'It's her wedding day,' my mum reminds me, as though I could have forgotten that the wedding of the century is soon to take place.

My cousin Flora's long-anticipated wedding is less than two months away now. Flora, twenty-eight, is the only child of my auntie Mary, my mum's only sister. When Tommy popped the question a couple of years ago it wasn't long before Flora asked me to be her bridesmaid. We're cousins, but we're not friends or anything, so I was surprised when she asked me. We don't socialise and we're definitely not what you would call close.

We never really got on much when we were kids because Flora had that only-child mentality some kids are just cursed with. She always had to have her own way and I, being a whole year older than her, usually had to give in to whatever demands she made. In some ways that hasn't changed... well, not until a few months ago when I finally broke the cycle.

'I feel like she's punishing me,' I point out between mouthfuls of new potatoes. 'She's just being petty.'

'Well, we do all really like Lloyd,' my mum says.

'Yeah, but Flora doesn't,' I insist. 'I mean, she didn't when we were together, and even if she did, why is my ex-boyfriend still invited to her wedding?'

It's nearly a year since I broke up with Lloyd, and he didn't exactly take it all that well. It was a year before our break-up when Flora invited us to her wedding, but she only invited Lloyd because he was my boyfriend at the time, so why would that invitation stand after our break-up?

'Flora and Tommy want to honour his invitation,' my mum explains. 'They think it would be rude not to.'

'But it isn't rude to invite my ex, who I am not on speaking terms with?' I say. 'Has he said he's coming?'

'Yes. But Flora said you can still have a plus one,' my mum points out.

God, I'm going to need one now. I wasn't really feeling the pressure too much before, but if I have to go to this thing alone then I'm going to wind up saddled with my ex all day – an ex that I specifically haven't stayed friends with. Lloyd and I broke up on pretty bad terms. He was jealous, possessive and had no boundaries. The fact that he's still saying he'll come to Flora's wedding – all the way from Somerset – just goes to show how little he's changed. He's a twenty-eight-year-old man, for crying out loud. This is like something a high school girl would do.

My appetite well and truly beat, I put my cutlery down before dropping my head into my hands. I massage my temples for a moment.

'She's punishing me,' I say. 'This is because I dropped out of being her bloody bridesmaid.'

I know that it sounds bad, to agree to be a bridesmaid for someone, before backtracking, but I had a really good reason, I swear.

'Don't forget how upset Auntie Mary is that you did it over WhatsApp,' Oliver points out.

I roll my eyes. Auntie Mary is of the opinion that I added insult to injury by bowing out over WhatsApp. 'Not even a text', that's all she keeps saying, being too out of touch to know that the two forms of communication aren't really any different. The reason I sent Flora a message, instead of talking to her on the phone, is because I had already tried raising my concerns with her in person, but she kept shutting them down. I thought it best to write down exactly how I was feeling, in clear but very tactful terms – the last thing I wanted to do was upset her.

'Maybe she was looking forward to you being her bridesmaid,' my dad suggests. I can tell he's had enough of this conversation, but he isn't the only one.

'I doubt it,' I reply. 'We're not exactly close, are we? It felt like an empty gesture at best, otherwise I reckon it was just to keep the numbers up.'

I did have a good reason for not wanting to be Flora's bridesmaid, honestly. Well, I thought it was a good reason, but Flora and Auntie Mary weren't in agreement with me.

It all started when we went for our first dress fitting. The dresses were already there waiting for us and it turned out that Flora was planning on using the bridesmaid dresses from her mum's wedding (that none of her mum's bridesmaids wanted to keep, which isn't a surprise to me having seen them – they haven't aged well at all over the past thirty or so years). Somehow impossibly shiny, but still with the texture of crêpe paper, the dresses would be serving as Flora's something old (oh-so old) and something borrowed (yes, her mum wanted them back after) – and as far as I was concerned, my dress was going to be her something blue too.

You see, it just so happened that Auntie Mary had four bridesmaids – two adults and two kids. The dress that I was told to try on was actually the dress my mum wore when she was Auntie Mary's bridesmaid... but my mum was quite slim back then and I, today, am not. I wouldn't say I'm overweight, but I'm not going to be walking any Victoria's Secret catwalks any time soon. I'd say

I'm kind of average size, just with a few extra curves, and it's because of my curves up top that the old bridesmaid dress intended for me to wear just wouldn't fit. I had a little trouble after stepping into it, getting it over my butt, but as soon as it came to fitting my chest into it, it just wasn't going to happen. Hence the something blue – it would be practically pornographic if I were to walk down the aisle with my boobs out, and all because I can't get some solid-as-a-rock, eighties floral antique-curtain-looking dress over them. Honestly, it was one of the ugliest dresses I have ever seen in my life, and obviously I didn't want to wear it. But I would have worn it because it was what Flora wanted. Except Auntie Mary didn't want her old dresses 'hacking up' to make alterations so that the dress would fit me as I am. What Auntie Mary suggested to me, instead of changing the dress, was that I changed myself – by losing weight. Obviously I wasn't going to lose weight to fit into a bloody dress, and even if I did lose weight, I couldn't exactly guarantee that my boobs would shrink, could I? No one would listen when I tried to explain that I wasn't going to crash diet to fit into a bridesmaid dress, which was why I wound up having to send her a very sugar-coated version of my feelings in a WhatsApp message.

'I'll just need to find a date,' I say. 'Any date. I just need a man.'

'I can't believe, out of the two of us, I'm the better feminist,' Oliver eventually pipes up again with a laugh.

'Just because I need a man and won't wear a bridesmaid dress that shows my bra, I'm a bad feminist?' I say. 'I wouldn't lose weight for a dress, remember.'

'Yeah, there is that,' he agrees. 'You know, in *The Handmaid's Tale*...'

Oh, give me strength. My brother is writing his PhD on the male ego and female empowerment in contemporary US hip-hop, which apparently makes him the authority on feminism in this house. I am all for feminism but I don't need a lecture on how women shouldn't be calling other women bitches, because 'the patriarchy wants to set women against other women', every time I say someone is a bitch – especially not from my woke little brother.

'I can't believe he's actually coming,' I say. 'The man lives in Somerset.'

Lloyd and I were together for three years. He lived in Leeds while he was at uni, but after he finished his master's degree he temporarily moved back in with his parents – in Somerset. The plan was to figure out our next steps, but we never had the chance. The distance magnified all of the small insecurities I'd noted Lloyd having over the years. His paranoia tore us apart. Not only that though, the time apart also gave me the space to realise that we just weren't that happy together. He wasn't the one. Trying to talk to him about this only brought out an anger in him; that was when we broke up, and that was the last time we spoke.

'Is he actually going to travel all this way and stay in a hotel, just so he can attend Flora and Tommy's wedding?' I ask, although I suppose it makes sense, if he's as clingy as he was before. He'll think this is his way back in.

'Well...' My mum pauses for a moment. I watch as she shakes off the anguished look on her face, forcing it into something much softer and brighter. 'You know how much we all loved Lloyd, how he felt like part of the family...'

Oh, God, no...

'He's staying here,' my dad blurts. Ted clearly has no time for sugar-coating today.

'What?' I squeak. 'Here? Here at your house?'

'No, in the shed,' Oliver says sarcastically.

'Where is he going to sleep?' I ask, but my brain figures that one out for me a split second after I answer the question. 'You're letting him sleep in my room, aren't you?'

'Well, you don't actually sleep in it, do you?' my mum reminds me. 'You live in your own flat. I assumed you'd be sleeping there before the wedding. You're only twenty minutes away on the train.'

'It's still my bedroom,' I say. 'My childhood bedroom. I don't want him in there.'

And when I did want him in there, I wasn't actually allowed to have him in there, even though we were in our twenties, my parents have always been old-fashioned like that. This has to be some kind of horrible prank.

My mum stands up and begins clearing the table.

'It's just for a few days,' she says as she heads for the kitchen. 'I'll fetch the pudding.'

'*A few days?*' I reply. 'He's staying here for *a few days*?'

'The lad fancied a break,' my dad tells me. He leans in to speak quietly to me, while my mum is out of the room. 'Come on, it's a few days, you don't live here, you know your mum really liked him – she's just doing the lad a favour.'

I fold my arms and slump down into my chair. I can't believe it. I really can't believe it. This is classic Lloyd, muscling his way back into my life the first chance he gets. There is no way he just wants to watch Flora and Tommy get married – he never liked them and they never liked him. I get why my mum is saying that Lloyd can stay here, because she always had a huge soft spot for him, and obviously she was never privy to the reasons why we broke up. She just thought it was the distance. I didn't have the heart to tell her how intense Lloyd turned out to be after he moved back to Somerset.

My mum is just being my usual lovely mum, but Flora is something else. Her inviting Lloyd is definitely some kind of payback for me refusing to slim into a dress for her. She has no reason to invite him otherwise.

I notice my phone vibrating on the table so I snatch it up, hoping it's something that isn't going to annoy me.

Oh, it's a Matcher message from someone called Chad. I tune out from Oliver attempting to explain to my dad how the media pit Nicki Minaj and Cardi B against each other (my dad has no idea who either of these people are) and lose myself in my phone.

A few taps on my iPhone tell me that Chad was the person I matched with earlier, before I swiped away the last available man in my area. That makes Chad the last man standing. My last hope – well, my last chance to find someone in time for this wedding, at least, if I drop the melodramatics for a second.

'I know the answer to your riddle,' his message states simply.

OK, I know it makes me sound like a big nerd, having a riddle in my Matcher bio, but, well, I am a big nerd and it's important to show people that right off the bat, right?

Hello

I begin my reply.

Go on…

Almost immediately those three little dots appear, to show me that Chad is typing.

The riddle at the end of my bio says:

Jake Gyllenhaal has a long one. Brad Pitt has a short one. Drake doesn't have one. What is it?

Well, I love puzzles, and I thought that was kind of a fun question – and not an overly difficult one. People tend to ignore it, or just ask me what the answer is. No one has been all that impressed yet.

He types back:

The answer is… a surname haha. Cheeky though, I like it.

Oh, not only does he get it, but he thinks it's funny too. He asks:

What's a nice girl like you doing on an app like Matcher?

'I knew you'd come around,' my mum interrupts, pulling my eyes away from my phone for a second.

'Huh?' I reply, looking up just in time to see her placing a cheesecake on the table in front of us. A homemade passionfruit cheesecake, which is one of my favourite desserts. She really has brought out the big guns to try and offset the damage from the Lloyd crap bomb that's been dropped on me.

'You're smiling,' she tells me.

'Oh, I'm just on Twitter,' I insist.

I must be grinning like an idiot at my phone. I punch back to Chad:

A nice girl like me was just about to give up on Matcher for good. What's a nice boy like you doing here?

He replies almost instantly.

Saving you.

Damn. What a charmer. He continues:

Sounds like I arrived just in time. Give me tonight to message you my A-game and, if you like what you read, let me take you on a date tomorrow evening. What do you say?

'What are you looking at?' my dad asks me suspiciously.

'Me? Nothing,' I insist.

'Something on that phone has you grinning like the cat that got the cream,' he replies.

I shrug my shoulders. I'm hardly going to tell my dad I'm flirting with someone on a dating app, am I?

'Just memes,' I say.

'Not the foggiest what that means,' he says, but I don't think he cares.

My mum hands my dad a cup of tea, which he proceeds to put down on the dining table.

'On the coaster, on the coaster,' my mum insists.

'Bloody women,' my dad mutters under his breath – while doing as he is told, obviously.

Naturally, this statement triggers Oliver, who calls my dad out for his sexist statement.

My phone buzzes again.

Cara?

Chad prompts me.

Wow, a double message, he is keen. I reply:

Sounds like a plan

He replies:

Great. Let's see if we can't find you your happy-ever-after.

That's a kind of cheesy thing to say but I allow myself a moment of optimism. I know that I haven't exactly been winning the dating game recently but maybe it was all for a reason, all to get me to this point, so that the last man on Matcher could ask me on a date. Now I really do feel as if I'm in a romcom movie. And this little glimmer of hope couldn't have come at a better time, could it? Desperately in need of a plus one and on the verge of giving up on men altogether. I don't want to get ahead of myself but, for tonight, I will allow myself to have a little hope. The right man for me has to be out there somewhere. Maybe this is him?

4

Sometimes I feel like a shape-shifter.

To get ready for my date with Chad this Friday evening, I did a whole bunch of things to transform the way I look. I know what you're probably thinking: how can you expect anyone to love you if you don't love yourself? But I do love myself – I just love myself even more when I dress up a little.

The thing is, I really want tonight to go well, and if making an effort helps my cause, then great. I'm sure my brother would be horrified at me, saying that I'm changing my appearance for a man, but this isn't a bad feminist manoeuvre. I would hold men to the same kind of standard – if you're going on a date, you should make sure you look good. It's an attractive quality in a person: having pride in your appearance. Not in a superficial 'everyone should be a 10/10 babe' kind of way, because Lord knows I'm not that, but I know that I look far more attractive in a long black dress, a pair of tights that smooth out my curves a little, with my hair straightened and my cheeks contoured – compared to a Victoria's Secret tracksuit, a messy bun (that somehow never looks like the kind you see on Instagram) and a face with all the angles of a potato. I say all this but, don't get me wrong, I am completely comfortable with the way I look. This is me and I don't feel like I need to change my body for anything, not for a bloke or a for a bridesmaid dress, but I like to dress up a little when I can. I even enjoy the ritual of getting ready to go out. I find the step-by-step process almost puzzle-like.

I look myself up and down in the mirror on the back of the lift doors – although it's too late to change anything now I'm at the bar. I wear a lot of black – I don't know why, I just feel more comfortable in it. Tonight I'm wearing a floor-length black dress. Just a soft, strappy, summery dress I picked up in H&M. It looks dressy or casual, depending on what you wear it with. To dress it up a little, I gave my make-up more of a night-time vibe – well, that's what the YouTube video tutorial told me to do. To be honest, I feel like I've just gone on a little too heavy with my contour. In the brightly lit lift, staring into the mirror, my cheek and nose shading especially seems really severe.

I grab a tissue from my bag and blot at my face, attempting to tone it down a bit. I should have stuck with what I knew: contouring for beginners – at least I knew it worked.

Despite being on top of an office building, the bar is only accessible via a glass lift, which runs up and down the side of the building.

When the doors open I step out into the long, dimly lit corridor that leads to Thin Aire, a super-cool bar in Leeds city centre. I'm not really one for wild nights out – well, I don't really have any proper friends here in the city, and my old school friends back home have all sort of outgrown me. But, since I've been playing the dating game, I've been to a few different places for dates. I haven't been here before though and I can't quite help but feel as if I don't belong here which only adds to my nerves.

Thin Aire is a rooftop bar overlooking the River Aire. It sits unbelievably pretty at the top of an eighty-metre-tall office block, and it's almost entirely made of glass. The floor-to-ceiling, wrap-around glass windows allow for a panoramic view of the city. In fact, I can literally see my house from here.

'Hello,' a hostess greets me cheerily. I thought my contour was severe, but the hostess has me beat. I suppose it's just what is trendy at the moment, isn't it? My mum often runs a thumb over one of my eyebrows and laughs to herself about how big eyebrows are these days, but she's from a different time, a time when it was cool to pluck your eyebrows into non-existence. After years of painful plucking, my mum couldn't have big brows if she wanted to, not without getting them tattooed on. At least by embracing the trend I have lots to play with but, should smaller brows come back into fashion, I'll be in trouble. I'm too lazy to keep on top of the plucking as it is. I am so lazy, in fact, that when I was getting ready for this date tonight, I realised I was cutting it fine and abandoned shaving my legs. The problem was I'd already done a third of the job. That's why I'm wearing tights, even though it's summer. Thankfully it's a little cooler this evening.

'Are you meeting someone for drinks?' the hostess asks me.

'Erm, yes, but I think I might be the first one here,' I reply.

'Table for two?'

She gives me a knowing smile. She must see people on dates all the time. Can she tell by my nervous disposition that that's why I'm here?

'Yes,' I confirm, this time with a little more confidence. I'm not really a shy person but this just feels so awkward.

'OK, come with me. I have a table for two free on the terrace.'

I follow the hostess out onto the wrap-around roof terrace. As soon as I step out onto the fake-grass flooring I feel the cool breeze creep over my skin and it feels glorious. I take a seat at my table and order myself a cocktail – something called a War of the Roses, picked in a bit of a hurry without really looking at the ingredients. A waitress brings it out to me and I still can't tell you what is in it, but it's delicious. Now all I need to do is wait.

I can't help but think about my disastrous date with Matt the other night. You know, it might be my worst date yet. Maybe. The competition is stiff. Sure, turning up to a first date and finding out it's actually a babysitting gig isn't ideal, but is it as bad as Aaron, who was a solid decade older than the photo he was using on his Matcher profile? Or what about Felix, who seemed great at first, looking pretty dapper in a sharp black suit... but then it turned out that he was only wearing a suit because he'd met me immediately after his dad's wake, at which he got absolutely hammered...

I'm not saying that there is something wrong with all men, and that I am absolutely perfect on a date, far from it. My first date with a guy called Chris took a horrible turn when I jokily mentioned that 'coffee was my crack' – my fun way of saying that I'm low-key addicted to it. When I asked what Chris's crack was, he told me that until recently it was, well, crack. Crack-crack. Needless to say, Chris wasn't impressed with my joke, which meant that I felt obliged to spend the rest of the night listening to him talk about being a recovering drug addict. I sure do know how to pick them.

I'd be tempted to say I have high hopes for Chad though, except while I've been thinking about my recent dating history, aimlessly scrolling through my phone and sipping away at my second anonymous drink, I've realised that Chad is forty-five minutes late. I thought it kind of poor form when I realised he was fifteen minutes late. By thirty minutes I started to panic but now that we're at forty-five...

'How's it going?' a man asks me.

'Erm... Chad?' I ask, although it certainly doesn't look like Chad. From what I could gather from his photos, Chad was a skinny dude. There is no way this guy standing in front of me is the guy I saw in Chad's photos. This guy is tall... *really* tall, like 6' 2" or 6' 3". He's wearing black trousers and a white shirt with, not one, but two buttons undone. He looks impossibly cool in that way you can't replicate. Some people are cool, some people are trying to be cool, and some people are just uncool. That's it. And I'm in the third category. As far as I can tell, his chest doesn't have a hair on it – unless he shaves it as I do my legs, which is only as far as the eye can see. He's alarmingly buff – the kind of buff you only get from spending too much time in the gym. Gyms are these things I've seen in Instagram photos where people go to exercise. This guy must practically live there.

'Not Chad,' he says with a friendly but awkward laugh. He runs a hand through his longish, messy brown hair, which hangs down behind his ears. I can see his dimples as he smiles, through his stubbly beard. His brown eyes are almost impossibly dark, although that could just be because it's so dimly lit here. He's got a real Jason Momoa vibe about him. He's also definitely not Chad, so God knows why he's talking to me.

'I just thought I'd come over and say hi,' he explains. 'Can I sit?'

He places a hand on the back of the chair next to me as he waits for the go-ahead to join me.

'Look, no offence,' I start, wracking my brain for the right words, because I'm not used to having to tell men to take a hike. 'I'm sorry, but I'm not interested. I'm waiting for my date, so...'

The last thing I need is for Chad, the last man on Matcher, to arrive and find me being chatted up by another man.

'Look... he's stood you up,' the man tells me bluntly.

'You don't know what you're talking about,' I reply. 'If this is some kind of excuse to talk to me...'

'Whoa, OK, hang on a minute,' the man starts, chuckling to himself as he pulls out the chair next to me and sits down. 'Do you think this is a chat-up line?'

I glance down at the seat I had asked him not to sit in, then back up to meet his gaze.

'I'm not trying to pull you,' he insists. 'I... I felt sorry for you.'

I feel my face tighten with confusion.

'You've been here a while now, you keep looking at the door, you look anxious as hell. You're waiting for someone – probably a date.'

Right on cue, I notice the door open in my peripheral vision so I snap my neck in its direction, to see if it's Chad walking through it. It's just a gaggle of girls on a night out.

'He's not coming,' the man tells me softly. 'Has he messaged you?'

I've been keeping a keen eye on my phone and nothing has come through. I thought about messaging him, to see if he had been held up, but it's drummed into us not to seem too keen, lest we spook the men, so I decided to wait a little longer.

'Well, no,' I say. 'But—'

'So, unless the dude is dead in a ditch somewhere, he could have messaged you, right?'

I frown. This is stupid. And I'm not about to listen to some bloke who has been spying on me and has just stuck his nose into my business.

'I haven't been stood up,' I insist as I load up Matcher. I'm a grown adult, not a game-playing teenager. I'll just send Chad a message, make sure everything is OK. I'm sure there's a perfectly reasonable explanation for him not showing up.

'Oh.'

'Oh?'

I feel my cheeks warming – boiling even. There's no chance I'm not bright red right now, so no way I can style this out. I may as well be honest.

'I guess I have been stood up,' I admit. 'He's unmatched me... Unless, do you think he turned up, took one look at me and bailed?'

'Absolutely not,' the man insists. 'You look great. It's his loss. He sounds like a moron.'

I smile.

'Why are you being nice to me?' I can't help but ask.

'I *am* nice,' he replies with a chuckle. 'I was over there having a drink with my mates, you caught my eye, I twigged what was going on and thought I'd come and talk to you. To cheer you up or save you the embarrassment of sitting here alone. I'm almost offended you think I have some kind of ulterior motive.'

I feel bad, and kind of embarrassed for assuming he was hitting on me, when all he was really doing was taking pity on a girl alone in a bar.

'Sorry, sorry,' I insist. 'I've met a lot of creepy men recently.'

I sigh heavily. I can't believe I allowed myself to feel hopeful about tonight, about Chad. But these bloody men are all the bloody same.

'I guess I'll go home, then,' I say. 'Thanks for the reality check.'

'Do you want to go for a drink with me?' he quickly asks as I make a move.

I cock my head, unimpressed.

'No, nothing like that,' he says. 'My friends are heading home soon. I promised one of them I'd walk her home but then I'm heading to Hades to meet a different crowd – you been before?'

'I haven't.'

Of course I haven't. Hades is a super-exclusive nightclub with a list of impossible rules for entry that change from night to night, if not hour to hour. Hades is notorious for turning people away for pretty much any reason the doormen can come up with – they might just hate your nail polish.

'Come with me, come for a drink, have a dance. Maybe you'll meet someone better than the idiot that stood you up tonight.'

I'm not going to go to a nightclub with a man I just met in a bar, am I?

'I can put your name on the list...'

I am just about in touch enough to know that the only way to get into Hades, without adhering to the super-strict, ever-changing rules, is if you're on the guest list. I don't know who/what this man is, to have that kind of power, but if he can get me in, well, that's a once-in-a-lifetime opportunity for a girl like me, right? Everyone, whether they're into the club scene or not, who has heard of Hades would do anything to peep inside. Just out of curiosity.

'I don't even know your name,' I say with an awkward laugh.

'I'm Millsy,' he says, offering me a hand to shake.

'I'm Cara,' I reply.

'OK, now we're acquainted, what do you say?'

'OK?' I reply, although the hesitation in my voice makes my response sound more like a question than an answer.

'OK, great,' he says. 'I'll walk my friend home and meet you there?'

I pause for a second. I need to think about this carefully. This isn't a very me thing to do at all but, I don't know, perhaps the me I am now just isn't working. I can't seem to meet anyone worth hanging around with on Matcher, my friends have outgrown me and I don't seem to be having much luck making new ones as an adult. Maybe I do need to take a few chances. Try to make some friendly relationships and maybe I can meet new people that way, rather than through apps.

'OK... OK, sure.'

I keep saying OK, but I'm not sure that it is. Is it OK? Am I making a huge mistake?

'Cool, I'll meet you by the bar.'

'OK,' I say again. God, I sound like a broken record.

'What's your last name?' he asks. Quickly adding: 'For the list.'

'Brooks,' I reply – I want to say cautiously, but if I were being that cautious I wouldn't be telling him at all.

'Cara Brooks,' he repeats back to me.

'What's your surname?' I ask, levelling the playing field.

'Mills,' he says with a laugh, as though he thinks that I think that Millsy is his first name. I haven't ruled it out. 'Joe Mills, but my friends call me Millsy.'

'Am I your friend?' I ask as a bemused smile spreads across my face.

'If you don't stand me up, sure,' he replies. 'See you in a bit.'

I watch as Millsy heads back over to his friends. He helps a cool-looking blonde girl with her jacket before they head to the door together. Am I supposed to believe that's just his friend? That he wants to be just friends with me? I mean, I'm pretty sure he's way out of my league, but why would he be nice to me? Perhaps I've been online dating for too long, but I struggle to believe that genuine men exist at the moment.

You know what though? I am going to go to Hades. I'm not going to sit here moping about Chad, wondering what he might have thought was wrong with me to put him off dating me. I'm going to seize the day, go to Hades, hang out with Millsy and see what the night brings. You have to understand, though, I never do things like this. In fact, I've never done anything like this. My idea of a wild Friday night usually involves being locked in a fake jungle, solving puzzles to try and escape.

I hate phrases like 'you only live once' but, you do, right? I'd be mad not to go to Hades and see what it's like. And if anything bad does happen to me, well, at least it will get me out of going to my cousin's wedding with my ex.

5

'What do you mean I can't come in?' an angry brunette in a barely there dress asks the doorman angrily.

'No selfies in the queue,' the doorman insists.

'Can I still come in?' her friend asks.

The first girl practically hisses at this betrayal, but then laughs when her friend is turned away too.

'No, you were dancing in the queue.'

I feel my eyes widen with horror. The list of rules really is super strict here. I've been queuing outside Hades for a little while now, and so far I've seen people turned away for dancing, smiling, nodding their head to the music, being too enthusiastic about getting in, wearing pastel colours and even for wearing dangling earrings. As I approach the front of the queue, I feel my palms start to sweat. What if Millsy was full of crap? What if there's no way he could have got me on the list? What if he was exaggerating or messing with me? Why did I just trust him like that?

With no turning back now, I step up to the two doormen. All I can do is give my name, hopefully before the onslaught into my appearance kicks in, and hope that Millsy was telling the truth when he said he'd put my name on the list.

It's only when I get to the front of the queue that I realise there is a second roped line, at the other side of the door, where people on the guest list are breezing through.

I am just about to open my mouth when the doorman, the shorter of the two (although he's still at least six foot) nods me through. I hover on the spot for a second, thinking I'm misunderstanding the situation. I mean, what are the chances I can get in on my own?

The man narrows his eyes at me.

'You're in,' he says. 'Chop-chop.'

'Oh, right, OK,' I babble as I hurry past him.

Just like that, I am inside the most exclusive nightclub in Leeds, and completely on my own merit too. I might not have been good enough for Chad, but I'm good enough for Hades, and the validation from that gives me a surge of self-confidence.

As the name suggests, Hades exudes wealth. Actually, does the name suggest that, or am I just being geeky, knowing that Hades was the God of hidden wealth? The wealth in this place is absolutely not hidden; everyone here is literally wearing their designer logos on their sleeve. I imagine the place is also called Hades as a reference to the underworld, and the potentially devilish goings-on that take place here.

As soon as you walk through the door you are greeted by an overly bronzed, buff bloke wearing very loose-fitting white robes that don't leave much to the imagination. He carries a sceptre, just like Hades himself, but it only seems to prevent him from doing his hosting job properly.

As I walk through the large golden gates that lead into the main room I am thrown straight into the heart of the action.

Despite it being a dimly lit room, with dark, almost black

walls, the sheer volume of golden furnishings and the fire machines pushing out real flames dotted all around give the place a warm and unusual brightness. There is a woman going around in a gold bikini, swigging from a container before breathing fire in the direction of patrons who seem surprisingly indifferent about her presence. I'm in awe but I don't show it, just in case it's against the rules.

I wade through a sea of beautiful people, finally reaching the large circular bar in the middle of the room. I have a look around for Millsy but he's nowhere to be seen. Then again, I came straight here and he was walking his friend home first, so I can't realistically expect him to be here just yet.

I squeeze my way to the front and try to look at the menu on the bar top. Yet another cocktail menu that means nothing to me.

'You doing OK there?' a friendly barman asks me over the music.

'Oh, yes,' I say, pleasantly surprised. I don't know why but I wasn't expecting him to be friendly, I imagined the staff here being as hostile as the doormen. 'Just wondering what to have.'

'First time here?' he asks.

'Does it show?' I reply.

'Nah,' he says. 'Shall I surprise you?'

'Sure.'

'I'll pay for this,' I hear a dreamy-sounding Australian man's voice next to me.

I look right, to make sure it's me he's talking to.

'My drink?' I say.

'Sure,' he replies. 'I'm buying a round for my mates. I might as well pay for yours while I'm here. You look a little nervous...'

'Oh, thank you,' I reply with a smile. 'That's very nice of you.'

Is everyone in here so rich they're just throwing their money around? Everyone but me, obviously.

'I'm Jackson,' he says.

'I'm Cara,' I reply.

As Jackson and I shake hands we have a few seconds where we just stare at each other and smile. Jackson is tall and muscular, he has quite short, dirty-blond hair that looks effortlessly but intentionally messy, and a pair of eyes so blue they send a chill down my spine.

'You're not from around here,' I say, rather pointlessly. I'm sure he knows.

'What gave me away?' he asks in the strongest Aussie accent I've ever heard in real life.

I just smile.

The barman places my drink down in front of me as the hot Aussie hands over his card. I look down at my drink, which is served in a golden cup, and inhale the strong fruity scent. I can't resist having a sip straight away. As always I have no idea what it is, but it tastes like champagne with some sort of mango jelly inside. It even comes with a cute little golden spoon.

'I'm over from Australia, for work,' the man explains.

'Oh, what do you do?' I ask curiously before taking another sip of my drink. It's incredible.

'I play rugby,' he tells me. 'I'm here celebrating with my team-mates – we won today.'

Jackson gestures behind us, to a table overflowing with large-framed men.

'Congratulations,' I reply. I'm not really into any sports. I have a basic understanding of football to the extent where I could watch a game, but with rugby, I have no idea. I wouldn't have a clue what was going on, even if I did watch a game.

'Thank you,' he replies. 'You here alone? You wanna join us?'

'Oh, I'm meeting someone,' I reply, wondering if I shouldn't have accepted a drink from him, knowing that.

'Perhaps I could take you out for a drink another evening, then,' he suggests. 'One that we could actually drink together.'

'I'd really like that,' I reply.

We swap phones, adding our numbers to each other's contacts. Is this actually happening? Am I swapping numbers with a man in a bar? A real one – not one from a dating app – with friends and a job. Why on earth is he talking to me? Is this what happens when you go to bars, or is this a thing that happens in nice bars? Perhaps, because the entrance policy is so strict, people feel as if their fellow patrons have been sort of pre-vetted, so it's safe to just strike up a conversation with whoever you feel like talking to. So the opposite of Matcher, I suppose, where my general rule was to assume everyone was a murderer until they proved otherwise.

Jackson heads back over to his friends' table. I hug my cocktail with my hands, grinning from ear to ear, because I can't believe a man just approached me in a bar, but I have no one to tell.

I was in a WhatsApp group chat with the four other girls I was in a clique with at school until a couple of months ago, when I was unceremoniously kicked out by my old friend, Christina. Things started changing after school was over. I went to university while the rest of the gang gravitated towards getting married and starting families. As far as I was concerned, both routes were perfectly valid life choices, each to their own... My friends didn't quite feel the same way, often excluding me from meet-ups because I was missing one must-have accessory: a baby. It's great that they love being mums, and doing mummy things, but they made it impossible for me to join in. The same goes for the group chat. I didn't have a baby to post daily selfies with, or pregnancy complaints everyone understood but me, and without being able to join in, it got harder and harder for me to talk. Christina decided I wasn't being chatty enough, or that I thought I was better than them, or some rubbish. She pulled the trigger, but I think they all decided they had outgrown me.

'You're not allowed to look so glum in here,' Millsy tells me, sidling up next to me at the bar.

'I saw a girl get turned away for smiling,' I tell him.

'Yeah, there's a sweet spot somewhere between the two emotions we're all expected to maintain.'

I laugh.

'Sorry, I got lost in my thoughts,' I explain. 'I'm actually in a really good mood. A guy bought me a drink – and he gave me his number.'

'Ooh, check you out,' Millsy teases. 'I didn't think you were here. Your name wasn't crossed off.'

'Erm, yeah, I guess I just got in,' I say with an awkward chuckle.

Millsy's eyes widen.

'It's safe to say your day has turned around, then. I'll drink to that.'

My new friend orders a drink. As I watch him chatting with the barman as if they're old friends, I can't quite believe I'm here, at this bar, with a stranger.

'Let's sit down,' Millsy suggests, picking up our drinks, nodding towards a seating area.

'OK,' I reply. I still feel like a rabbit caught in the headlights.

We head over to a large area of the room dominated by massive white sofas. Somehow, the music is just a touch quieter over here, making it easier to chat.

'Are you OK?' he asks me. 'You look a little...'

'Oh, no, I'm fine,' I insist. 'I don't usually do things like this.'

Millsy just laughs.

'Is it weird that I find it weird that you're being nice to me?' I ask honestly.

'It sounds like maybe you've been let down by people,' he reasons. 'Although, in hindsight, maybe this does make me look like a creep. I don't know. I didn't really think about it that way. You just looked like you needed a friend. I promise I'm not up to anything although, the more I insist I'm not, the more I fear you'll think I am.'

I laugh. Somehow this puts me at ease.

'Was that your girlfriend who you walked home?' I ask.

'My friend,' he says, with extra emphasis. 'My best friend. Well, yeah, I guess we are still best friends, but I don't see so much of her any more. She's getting married soon.'

'Oh,' I say. I suppose that makes sense. If he has female friends, he probably wouldn't have thought twice about chatting with me. 'No girlfriend, then?'

Why am I even asking?

'Are you trying to work out if I'm gay?' he asks with a cheeky smile. 'Just because I have female friends and get my eyebrows threaded?'

I hadn't noticed his eyebrows were so well groomed, which I suppose is testament to the beauty therapist's work. As part of the bigger picture, they just add to his general good looks.

'I wasn't getting at that,' I insist.

'I have lots of respect for women,' he says. 'I just don't want a girlfriend.'

'Fair enough,' I reply.

It must be hard for him, if his best friend has drifted away from him. I totally get that. I feel bad for questioning his motives now.

'What do you do for work?' I ask him.

'I'm an actor,' he replies. 'I've done a lot of theatre, and I have a few random gigs I do now and then.'

'Oh, God, you're not famous, are you?' I blurt. It would be so like me to meet someone famous and be totally oblivious.

'Not really, no,' he says. 'I do a lot of local theatre. I made my small-screen debut recently, in a toothpaste advert. I was the man who used the electric toothbrush though, not the before guy.'

'God forbid you would be cast as the person who uses the manual toothbrush,' I reply sarcastically.

'Not with these pearly whites. Check them out,' he insists, leaning in.

Millsy flashes me an enormous, flawless grin.

'Nice,' I say.

'I'm trying to break into movies,' he tells me. 'It's a long game though. What do you do?'

'I design escape rooms,' I say.

'You design what?'

'Escape rooms. They're like puzzle rooms. People do them for fun. Did you ever watch *The Crystal Maze*?'

'I remember it, sort of, from when I was younger,' he replies.

'Not a million miles off that,' I say. 'It's just lots of puzzles in one room.'

'That's pretty cool,' he says. 'You must be pretty smart.'

'Naaah,' I reply – I've never been great at taking compliments. 'Just a bit dorky.'

'Well, everyone loves a dork,' he says with a big, reassuring smile. I'm sure that can't be true and yet somehow he has me convinced.

'Tell that to everyone in my life,' I reply. 'I'm persona non grata in my family. The last man standing on Matcher stood me up.'

'Ah,' he says, a knowing look in his eye. 'Yeah, I gave up on those apps a long time ago. I don't think you'll find anything meaningful on there.'

'I see that now,' I say with a half-hearted laugh. 'I was kind of amazed that someone spoke to me at the bar here. No one approaches me – not ever.'

Millsy looks at me thoughtfully. I can practically see the cogs turning and I wonder what on earth is going through his mind.

'Do you always wear a lot of black?' he asks me.

'Yeah, pretty much,' I reply.

'Always covering a lot of skin too?'

He nods towards my tights.

'Kind of,' I say. 'But this is just because I haven't shaved my legs.'

Oh, God, why on earth did I tell him that?

Millsy laughs.

'Perhaps, in the context of this place, you seem like a cool, gothic, artistic type. Some guys are really into that. I think you look good.'

I'm sure he's just being polite.

'What are most guys drawn to?' I ask. 'You can tell me honestly.'

'Honestly... most guys are drawn towards bright, shiny things. Bold clothes, skin... I'm just as bad sometimes.'

'You're not telling me anything I didn't know already,' I reassure him. 'Thanks for being honest.'

'Not that you should change yourself for anyone,' he insists. 'You're obviously a cool person.'

Do I look unapproachable? Are my dark clothes, combined with my lacking-in-confidence demeanour, putting men off me? Jackson did say I looked nervous...

I always thought I was happy with who I was but, I don't know, maybe I've just been settling. Perhaps there is some middle ground, somewhere between refusing to diet to fit into a dress and actually looking like a friendly, approachable person.

'Maybe I should force myself out of my comfort zone, buy some colours, shave my legs and burn my tights. Maybe I'll watch a few more daring YouTube make-up tutorials, get my hair done...'

'I could help, you know,' Millsy says. 'I haven't paid for a haircut in years. I have friends who work in hair, beauty, styling – all desperate for models for portfolio work. You could wake up in the morning and go to bed a whole new person. Worst-case scenario, you'll look hot. Best case, it will give you the confidence boost you're after.'

I just stare at him for a moment.

'I'm not gay,' he insists again with a laugh. 'Or trying to have sex with you. I've always had a female best friend. And, truth be told, I'm a bit bored at the moment.'

'Is that why you're looking out for me?' I laugh. 'Because you're bored?'

'I... don't know why I am,' he replies, equally bemused. 'But, well, are you free tomorrow?'

Tomorrow is a Saturday – *of course* I'm free.

'I am,' I say after a couple of seconds. I need to at least pretend that I'm thinking about whether or not I have plans rather than just knowing I don't as default.

'OK, well, meet me tomorrow and... we'll see.'

'We'll see?' I reply.

'Are you one of those people who doesn't like surprises?' he asks.

'Well, there are two kinds of surprises, right?' I start. 'There's: "Surprise, here's a birthday cake you knew nothing about!" and then there's: "Surprise, this is Dr Whatever, he'll be performing your Brazilian butt lift today!"'

Millsy laughs.

'A makeover is a lick of paint on the walls. It isn't knocking a wall down here and bricking up a window there,' he says.

'Yeah, I just want to refresh my look. I'm more than happy with my body.'

'So you should be,' he tells me. 'You look great. So, makeover tomorrow sound good?'

'It does,' I reply. 'OK, sure, let's do it.'

'Great,' he replies. 'You don't need to worry about it. I have a couple of friends with a pop-up studio, who do drop-ins. They do a lot of portfolio work. They do a lot of stuff for me – usually just in exchange for photos. I need some waxing anyway.'

They might want photos of Millsy – he'll look great in their portfolios – but I doubt pictures of plain old me are any use to them.

'Are you going to be my girly best friend?' I ask playfully.

'Don't knock it until you've tried it,' he insists. 'And, if meeting people to date in real life is what you want, I can steer you in the right direction there too. Acting aside, it's maybe the thing I'm best at. Just do as I say, you can't go wrong.'

I don't know what it is about Millsy but I feel so good about myself right now. It's nice, being around him. He's obviously a really good-looking guy and he has this way of making you feel so important. He somehow makes you spend every second questioning why he's even talking to you, but it's not because of anything he's doing.

I didn't think it was possible to be this comfortable around a man I didn't know well. Well, it's a sign of the times, isn't it? I've spent my entire teenage and adult life being told how to keep myself safe, given rape alarms – even Matcher has guidelines on how to stay safe when meeting people. And I'm not saying everyone on Matcher is dangerous but I'm not not saying that either. You never really know who people are. With Millsy, though, I just don't feel any bad vibes, I don't see any red flags – unless, of course, a man being normal and nice is a red flag, which, given my recent experiences, seems pretty unusual to me.

If Millsy has a female best friend and she's getting married, then it makes perfect sense that he feels a bit pushed out. I know all about how unimportant you're made to feel when someone close to you is getting married. It's as if the entire world revolves around that one day, and *everything* is all about them. Perhaps he saw a bit of what he's feeling in me and that's why he's taking me under his wing.

Whether he's just bored, or a saint, or cares about me specifically for some reason, I'm not about to turn down a free makeover.

We sit and we chat and we order more drinks. We talk about makeovers and life choices and movies and everything in between – in fact, we chat so much, Millsy doesn't even make a move to go and hang out with his friends until I decide it's my bedtime. Millsy is a lot of fun to talk to – way more fun, and much sharper, than any of my Matcher dates. Perhaps meeting people in real life is the way to go and, with Millsy on my side, I might actually stand a chance.

6

Luca, Millsy's hairdresser friend, looks as though he's about to cry.

'When was the last time you had a trim?' he asks me. I suspect he knows the answer because he has a face as if every single word he says tastes bad.

'Oh, I don't know really,' I lie. I kind of know. It's been a while. 'I'm trying to grow it a bit but it never seems to get any longer.'

'It's breaking,' he snaps at me. 'Do you straighten it?'

'Yes...'

Luca says something in... I think Italian? Whatever it is, I don't imagine it translates into anything positive. His hair is, of course, absolutely perfect. Longish on top, swept over to one side. It's possibly the sleekest black hair I have ever seen in my life. So perfectly shiny I can almost see things reflecting in it.

It's just me and Luca in the small training salon. Millsy is off somewhere getting *something* waxed. I dread to think what. I do kind of wish he were here though, to defend me against this moody stylist.

Luca puffs air from his cheeks before relaxing into something calmer.

'OK, we can fix this... So, you want longer hair?'

'Yes... Well, that was what I was working towards...'

'Are you in a hurry?'

'Nope, no hurry. I just really appreciate you taking the time to do this for me.'

Luca bats my gratitude away with his hand.

'And I can do whatever I want?' he confirms for maybe the fourth time.

'Yes...' I reply, although every time I have to answer the question, I sound a little less like I mean it.

'*Allora,*' he says. 'Let's do it. You want me to do it away from the mirror, so you can have a big reveal?'

'OK,' I reply brightly, instantly wishing I hadn't said that. At least if I were watching, I could tell him to stop.

To start with, Luca starts snipping away at my chest-length, dark blonde locks. I have no idea how much he's taking off, but it seems like a lot, from the hair I can see gathering on the floor.

Eventually Millsy joins us.

'Oh my God,' he blurts, a look of terror on his face. Before I have chance to ask what's wrong, but not before I panic, Millsy starts laughing.

'He's quite the prankster, isn't he?' Luca says with a laugh. 'Such a lad.'

On face value, Millsy does seem like a 'lad, lad, lad' type but... I wouldn't have thought that type would be so thoughtful.

'So, what are you doing?' Millsy asks Luca.

'Something completely different,' he replies. He squeezes my shoulder. 'Whose hair do you like?'

I flick through one of the hairstyle magazines in front of me. I spot a photo of Brie Larson with bright blonde long locks and side parting that I sort of fancy.

'How about this?' I suggest.

'Captain Marvel?' Millsy says. He doesn't look impressed. 'I was thinking more Poison Ivy – remember that bright red colour Uma Thurman had when she played her? You'd look just like her if you had the hair. You've got the body for the outfit too.'

I blush because Millsy has noticed my body shape. I didn't think he looked at me as a woman. A potential friend, at best, if not just a charity case.

'Oh, I don't know about that,' I say. 'I've been blonde all my life.'

'Well, you should be comfortable,' Millsy insists. 'But I can totally see it.'

'Do you want to see some colours?' Luca asks me, dashing off before returning with a book full of locks of hair in varying colours. 'So, this shade of blonde right here, that's probably what I would go for. Over the page... this deep pinkish red is more daring. I think both would look gorgeous.'

'I'm not sure I'm ready for hair that is shorter, *and* a different colour,' I say, anxiously reaching up to check the length of my hair. He's taken off less than I thought.

'I'm not going to make it shorter, darling, I'm giving you hair extensions,' he replies. 'So either way, you can have the hair you want. Blonde is your girl-next-door look, playful, cute, et cetera. Red is your hot, wild child, siren look. It all depends on the vibe you want. So, what's it going to be: blonde or red?'

I bite my lip, as I always do when I'm thinking hard or concentrating. Long, bright blonde hair sounds like everything I've been trying to achieve on my own. I could get the length (which I guess was never going to happen without professional intervention) before getting some highlights put in. It sounds nice, but it wouldn't be that different for me. If I want to shake up my look I need to do something drastic.

'Red,' I blurt nervously. 'Let's go for red.'

'Yes, that's what I'm talking about,' I hear Millsy say behind me. 'I take risks all the time – they always pay off.'

'Until one day, when you get a specific kind of infection the antibiotics can't quite shift,' Luca teases him.

Oh, so Millsy is a ladies' man. That's what it sounds like.

'You're just jealous,' Millsy claps back.

'Hello, hello,' a high-pitched woman's voice squeaks behind me. 'I'm Dani, I'm here to do your make-up.'

'Oh, wow, hi,' I say. 'This really is a makeover.'

Dani plonks herself down on a stool in front of me. She asks me questions about what kind of make-up I wear, what sort of look I'm into and so on. I tell her that I want a much bolder, stronger look. That I want perfectly chiselled cheekbones (or at least contouring to make them look that way) and a highlight that would make an influencer jealous. Dani laughs, but says that not only can she make it happen, but she can show me how to do it myself moving forwards.

Honestly, I'm expecting to wake up any second; this can't be real life. Sure, I have to pose for a few photos for their portfolios, but I can't believe Luca and Dani are doing this for free. All of it. Transforming me into a completely different person. I want to be more confident in my look; I want to be someone who feels worthy of love. I'm sick of being cast aside by men, by my cousin and my auntie treating me as if I'm not good enough. I don't just need an image makeover, I need an attitude makeover too. And it's coming. With every length of deep red hair I see Luca bring towards me, and with every sweep of make-up Dani applies to my face, I feel my confidence growing.

'Do you fancy going out again tonight?' Millsy asks me. He's patiently waiting for me, chatting with everyone as he thumbs through old copies of *Cosmopolitan* magazine. 'We could try out your new look at Hades, see if any more men give you their number.'

'I'd love to,' I reply. 'Although, should I not contact the guy I swapped numbers with first? Before I go trying to bag others. The guy last night seemed awesome. Friendly, handsome...'

'Nah, dating is a numbers game,' he tells me. 'You can't waste your time on one person – and you better believe he isn't putting all his eggs in one basket. If he's so great, all the more reason to practise your flirting game. See, if I had been flirting with you last night, well, all you did was tell me how you'd been stood up.'

'Erm, you kind of inserted yourself in my jilting, but I take your point,' I reply. 'So, I'll practise talking to guys tonight and then I can give this guy a call, see what happens...?'

'Exactly,' Millsy says, clapping his hands together. 'That's exactly what you need to do. Be more man.'

'Be more man,' I say to myself with a laugh.

'If you're going to take dating advice off anyone, take it from this guy,' Dani tells me. 'He's been on *a lot* of dates. Do not, however, take relationship advice from him. He has no experience with actual, meaningful relationships.'

'Oi,' Millsy laughs. 'I didn't realise it was Bash Millsy Day.'

Millsy hops up from his seat and squats down in front of me.

'How against telling me your dress size would you be?' he asks. 'I know men aren't supposed to ask, but I could go and grab you a dress for tonight. You're going to be stuck here for hours, getting your hair done.'

'Oh, erm... yeah, I guess I could tell you. It just sort of depends on the shop and the style... Like, on a good day, in the right shop, I'm easily a twelve, but if there's no stretch in the chest...'

Wow, Millsy is really invested in this makeover, if he's willing to go out and pick up a dress for me.

'Stand up for a second,' Millsy says, while Luca is off getting more hair and Dani is cleaning her brushes.

I do as he says before he places his hands on my waist. He runs them up and down my sides before giving me a sort of strange hug that feels as if it is exclusively for sizing me up. I feel my body stiffen in his hands. I'm clearly not used to men touching me. Last of all, he checks my height against himself. I barely reach his shoulders.

'What are you, some kind of curves whisperer?' I joke.

'Something like that,' he replies. 'Shoe size?'

'I'm an eight, so good luck with that,' I reply. 'Are you actually going clothes shopping for me?'

'I have a friend,' he tells me. It sounds as if he has a lot of friends. 'She'll hook you up.'

'OK, sure,' I say. 'Thank you so much.'

'Probably an ex still pining after him,' I hear Luca say to Dani quietly.

I don't care if Millsy is a ladies' man, he's really going out of his way to help me, and, from what I can tell from the stories, it sounds as if his insincere encounters are far briefer. Assuming I like my new look, of course, because the more time that passes by without me seeing what I look like, the more nervous I get...

7

I don't know who I am any more.

Millsy dropped off my dress before dashing home to get ready while Luca finished off my hair. By the time Millsy got back it was time for me to slip into my dress, ready for the big reveal. I knew I was in for a shock, but I didn't realise how different I was going to look. Boy, do I look different. So different it was as if I were looking at a picture of stranger, not in a mirror. Luca said I looked like the real, authentic me, which sounded great, but I never would have thought my authentic self had so many bits stuck to her, like hair and eyelashes. Dani was so proud of her work, constantly telling me how great I looked, taking so many photos. As for Millsy, it took him a few seconds to say anything. He just stared at me, expressionless, and for moment I was worried that he thought I'd made a terrible mistake... but then he smiled.

So here I am, the new, authentic me, out again, this time in a short, bright red dress, an impossibly high pair of black heels, with my long red hair cascading down, framing the curves high-lighted by my dress, and then my make-up... the make-up that gives me an almost completely different face. Honestly, when I saw it earlier, I wanted to cry, but Millsy said I wasn't allowed to, lest I ruin my make-up.

My makeover has had the most fabulous effect. I feel so amazing, so confident, and still somehow a bit like a fraud, but I'm pushing that feeling to the back of my mind. I don't feel as if I'm me right now, but right now I'm kind of into it.

Millsy looks great, with his wild curls tamed, in yet another perfectly fitted shirt with the sleeves rolled up a quarter of the way. He's so effortlessly stylish, I don't know how he does it. It took a whole team of people to make me look like this.

Another reason I don't recognise myself is because I am at Hades for the second night in a row (also the second time in my life, but we don't need to dwell on that part).

It turns out Millsy is somehow 'in' at Hades. I'm definitely interested to find out how but right now I'm just loving the attention my new look is getting me. It isn't that everyone is checking me out, and it's not that I want everyone to fancy me or anything, it's just that... I don't know, it finally feels as if people can see me. We've only just got here and a large group of Millsy's male friends are already gathered around one of the super-VIP tables. Every single one of Milly's friends is a big, buff dude, just like him. I wonder whether or not they're actors, but I don't recognise anyone.

Standing at the edge of the VIP area, checking his phone, is a man with short brown hair and a neat brown beard. He laughs at something on his phone, which showcases his gorgeous smile.

'Who is that?' I ask Millsy.

'Why don't you go and find out?' Millsy suggests.

'What, just go over and talk to him?'

'Yeah,' Millsy says.

I take my phone from my clutch bag. Something I often do

when I'm nervous; it's as if I hide behind it. Millsy takes it from me and puts it in his trouser pocket.

'You need to practise – flirt up a storm with him, see what happens. It will be good for your confidence. In fact...'

Millsy gives me a nudge in the man's direction. Because I'm still so unsteady in these sky-high heels I'm not used to, I stumble over to him a little too enthusiastically, catching his attention as I present myself in front of him. While I might feel more confident because of my new look, I cancel this out by stumbling into the man.

'Hi,' I blurt.

'Hi,' the man replies. His face is void of any kind of emotion as he stares at me, waiting for me to say something.

'Erm...' I wrack my brains for something to say. Damn, Millsy was right, I really do need to work on my flirting. 'Do you know where the toilets are?'

The man glances next to us, where two neon signs shine brightly. A blue one for the men's and a pink one for the ladies'.

'Oh, right, of course,' I say.

I feel butterflies in my tummy – no, not butterflies, they feel more like bats. Big ones, desperately trying to find a way out.

'Can I help you with anything else?' he asks through a grin.

'No, no, just the loos, and now I've found them so, I'll go there...'

I make a move to head to the loos, even though I don't need to go.

'I like your hair,' he says.

He stops me in my tracks.

'Oh, thanks,' I reply. 'I just had it done today. It's a bit different from what I'm used to.'

'I used to have longer hair,' he tells me. 'I got it cut last year, grew a beard – people think I look like a different person. A better one. I looked like an ugly girly before.'

I laugh. Cute, charming, funny, doesn't take himself too seriously. So Hades is where all the decent men have been hiding, huh?

'Do you want to grab a drink, have a chat?' he asks me.

What I need to do right now is to put the old me out of my head. I need to be the new me. Cara 2.0. The one who is full of confidence. The sex kitten. I'm going to have this guy eating out of the palm of my hand. I just need to do what Millsy told me: be more man.

'I would love to,' I reply, in my most flirtatious – yet still quite subtle – tone. Wow, is this how easy it is, to be cool and sexy? Is everyone else just pretending too? I thought maybe some people were sexy and some were dorks but... I really feel as if I'm doing it.

He fetches us a couple of glasses of champagne and, as we sit down in one of the booths in the VIP section, Millsy gives me a subtle thumbs up before getting back to chatting with his mates. I suppose this guy is one of his mates too.

'I'm thinking of getting a pug,' he tells me.

I laugh.

'OK.'

I can't help but smile. Of all the things we could talk about, he's talking about dogs.

'I've been to see a few, and obviously I want them all. But there's this black pug, I think he's the one for me. The problem is that, while my flatmate is happy for me to get one, he takes issue with the fact that I want to call him Count Pugular.'

Why did I have to be taking a sip of my drink when he said that? I laugh so hard I start to cough.

'Did you just say Count Pugular?'

'I did,' he confirms, talking about this stuff as if it's completely serious. 'There was this kids' show…'

'Oh, I remember it,' I tell him. 'I remember it well. *Count Duckula*? I absolutely loved it growing up. I remember Nanny and Igor. Gosh, I haven't thought about it in years. Decades, maybe.'

I don't worry about sounding old because, if we both watched it growing up, we're probably around the same age.

'It's a classic,' he insists. 'But my flatmate, he grew up in another country where they deprived him of *Count Duckula*, so he's dead against it. I suggested a few other names. I thought about Mr Puggy – of course, my flatmate grew up without *Noel's House Party* on TV, so he has no idea who Mr Blobby is.'

'Do you want it to be something from your childhood?' I ask.

'I do,' he replies. He smiles at me. 'Don't psychoanalyse me, but my parents would never let me have a dog so I really want to give him a name that I would have given him back then.'

'Is Captain Pugwash too obvious?' I ask.

He narrows his eyes as he smiles at me.

'How on earth did I miss that one?' he asks. 'That's a great idea. I'll run it by my flatmate, see if he can live with it.'

'It's on-brand with your other suggestions so I'm not sure he'll be a huge fan,' I point out. 'Did you ever watch *Doug*? You could just call him Pug… You'd know it was a reference to a kids' TV show but to everyone else, it just seems like a cool, meta name.'

'You're good at this,' he tells me.

'We always had dogs in our family home. After the last two died recently, with me not being around any more and my brother being busy with uni, my parents decided to wait a while before rushing into getting any more. They were both so amazing, such a huge part of my life. I really miss having a dog around now. But one thing you will quickly learn is that, once you've got one, you'll probably call him twenty completely daft names for every time you use his real one. Names that rhyme, names that describe the way he looks... And, by the time you're calling him nicknames, he'll already be a part of your family, and I remember my dad saying that he'd never get a dog, never wanted a dog. And every dog we've ever put in front of him, he's instantly fallen in love with it. I'm sure your flatmate will feel the same before he even realises.'

Oh, God, why did I just talk about dog names for a solid five minutes, barely stopping to take a breath?

'Wow, someone who likes dogs as much as I do,' he eventually says with a smile. 'That's it, you've convinced me. I'm definitely going to get one.'

'Glad to be of service,' I tell him.

'So, you live alone now?' he asks.

'Yes, in the city centre. I love being in the heart of the city. I grew up in a village, so it's a completely different vibe.'

'I grew up in a village too,' he replies. 'So I get exactly where you're coming from. I live in Headingley now. It's not quite the city centre but it's alive with students pretty much 24-7. And it's near work, so it's perfect for me.'

'I went to uni in Leeds so I know Headingley well,' I reply.

'How many times have you done the Otley Run?' he asks.

'Oh, God, a few,' I reply. 'But not for a long time. I don't think I could handle it any more.'

'We all still do it, at least once a year,' he tells me. 'We dress up, do it for charity.'

The Otley Run is the legendary pub crawl starting in Headingley and finishing in Leeds city centre. Participants will usually wear absolutely ridiculous fancy dress costumes to visit sixteen pubs along a one-and-a-half-mile route. Back when I was at uni, when I had uni friends, we did it a few times. I was the only local in my friendship group though, and everyone else moved back home after they graduated. I haven't had anyone to do it with since.

I don't know how long we chat for – it feels like forever. I don't remember the last time I met someone and just hit it off with them like this. He's so funny and charming. I certainly didn't feel a genuine attraction like this towards any of my Matcher dates.

As I stare into his dark eyes, Millsy's words ring in my ears: be more man. I do feel a lot more confident for my makeover, but not completely. If I'm going to do something bold, it isn't going to come naturally, I need to act as if I'm confident and hope that the real deal isn't far behind.

Without really thinking about it, and yet somehow still completely overthinking it, I do something completely out of character for me. I place a hand on either side of his face, lean in, and give him a kiss. It's just a peck, before I quickly pull away, but it feels like progress.

'Wow,' he says.

I smile. Although I don't think it was the kiss that blew him away so much as the surprise.

'I realise this isn't the best time to do this but I've just realised we never swapped names.' He laughs, still sounding a little flustered.

'Yes, we're doing this in the wrong order, I think,' I reply with a super-awkward, half-hearted chuckle. 'I'm Cara.'

I offer him a hand to shake, which seems ridiculously formal considering I just planted a kiss on his lips.

'I'm Johnny,' he says, shaking my hand politely. 'What are you doing tomorrow?'

'Oh, not much,' I reply. Of course, the real answer is absolutely nothing. 'You?'

'Well, I have work first thing in the morning.'

'Work first thing on a Sunday – are you a priest?' I joke.

Johnny laughs.

'Nothing like that,' he says. 'I'm a rugby player. I've got some sponsorship meeting, nothing that means I can't stay out a bit late.'

'Oh,' I blurt. 'You know, I just need to go find my friend quick.'

'OK,' he says, not detecting my alarm. 'Come back after.'

'Mm-hmm.'

As I push my way through the crowd to find Millsy, suddenly all the big, muscular dudes make sense. Shit.

I find Millsy chatting up a petite brunette, which I suppose is on-brand for him.

I tap him on the shoulder. He does a double take.

'Oh my God, if I don't see you for a while, I forget that you look so different. I think you're just a chick in a bar.'

I frown.

'You know what I mean,' he says.

'Can I have a quick word with you?' I ask.

'Of course,' he says. 'Be right back, babe.'

My nose scrunches at his use of 'babe' – I guess this is the first time I've seen Millsy, the ladies' man everyone keeps hinting at.

'What's up?' he asks me when we're alone.

'Are you a rugby player?' I ask him.

'No,' he replies.

I breathe a sigh of relief. I was worried for a second that everyone knew each other because they all worked together – and that they all knew Jackson too. I'm not exactly an expert at talking to men in bars, but I don't imagine it's a good look, seemingly flirting your way through a friendship circle.

'I used to be their mascot.'

'What does that mean?' I ask, cocking my head curiously.

'I was Leo the Lion,' he says. 'The Leeds Lions' mascot. It was one of my first acting jobs – it's a long story. I don't do it any more but they still treat me like part of the team.'

'So these are all Leeds Lions' players?' I check.

'Yeah.'

'So Johnny plays for them?'

'Yeah,' he confirms again. 'Ooh, how did practising flirting with him go?'

'Erm, fine, really well, actually. I kissed him.'

'Oh, no, no, no, no,' Millsy says. For the first time he looks a little worried, ushering me even further away from the crowd, towards the side of the room. 'You weren't supposed to kiss him, you were supposed to practise flirting with him. Everyone on this team who isn't married – as well as a few who are – just sleep with as many girls as possible. I knew Johnny would hit on you, that's why I encouraged you. To practise.'

'But he was so sweet, and funny, and—'

'Talking about his dog?'

'He said he was getting a dog...'

'Yeah, that's just what he does, that's how he pulls,' Millsy explains. 'That's why I suggested practising on him.'

'I'm starting to think I shouldn't be taking dating advice from you,' I say with a sigh. I tug at my dress, as though it's going to make it longer. 'Or fashion advice.'

'No, you look incredible,' he insists. 'But, yeah, OK, maybe I'll lay off dishing out the dating advice. I don't think what works for me is going to work for you.'

'Anyway, I have bigger problems. Is there a player called Jackson?'

'Yeah, Jackson Wolfe. Aussie fella.'

'He's the bloke I met at the bar yesterday.'

Millsy's face falls.

'Oh, God, no, don't go near him,' Millsy says. 'Even the other players hate him. He's a weird deviant. You say he approached you last night?'

I nod.

'Yeah, he likes timid women, he's not a great guy.'

'Right, OK, fuck it, I don't want a man at all. The makeover is great, if not slightly obscene, but no more men.'

'No more rugby players, at least,' he jokes. 'You're working your way through the team.'

I allow myself a little laugh.

'So everyone in here is just looking for someone to shag?'

'Basically,' he says. 'But I don't want to shag you.'

He says this in a tone of voice that suggests he's intending this as some kind of comfort.

'Back at you,' I reply. 'It doesn't seem like membership is all that exclusive.'

Millsy laughs.

'Maybe just stick with me for the rest of the night, OK?'

'OK, sure,' I say. 'But, moving forward, perhaps the club scene isn't for me.'

'Well, let me get you a drink, before you retire,' he suggests.

In the VIP section of Hades, the champagne flows freely. Scantily clad servers float around in robes, popping corks, topping up glasses. Millsy grabs us a couple of glasses from on top of a gold grand piano that seems to be entirely decorative.

'To your retirement from the club scene,' he says, raising a glass.

'I'll drink to that,' I reply, clinking my glass with his.

'Cara,' Johnny says as he approaches us. 'Oh, hey, Mills. You two know each other?'

'We're friends,' I reply.

'Met at the STD clinic,' Millsy says. I think this is supposed to put Johnny off me but he takes it as a joke.

'I just wanted to see if Cara wanted to get out of here,' he says – to Millsy, for some reason. Surely you'd ask a person something like that directly? Not that I want him to ask me at all. Suddenly all the men in here feel like predators and all I can think about is getting myself to safety.

'Hey, guys,' a familiar Aussie accent chimes in. 'Sorry I'm late, I...'

As Jackson claps eyes on me, his voice trails off. I think it's my new look that catches his gaze but it's the familiarity in my face that keeps it.

'Did we meet last night?' he asks me. 'We did, didn't we? Wow, you look so different. I was going to give you a call... Can I get you a drink?'

'Oh, I have a drink, thanks though,' I blurt. I don't really know what else to say.

'We were actually just talking about getting out of here,' Johnny tells him.

'Yeah, well, we made plans to see each other again some time last night,' Jackson says.

'Well, she kissed me, did she kiss you?' Johnny asks him.

I watch as Jackson's blood boils. I feel as if there's this pre-existing competitiveness between them that has nothing to do with me.

'Is this revenge for Frances?' Jackson asks him.

'I thought you said nothing happened?' Johnny replies as his eyes grow wider and his jaw visibly tightens.

'Well, at least we'd be even, if that's what was going on...'

'Except I definitely slept with Lucy,' Johnny points out with a smug smirk.

Yep, I'm definitely just a pawn in all of this.

Jackson picks up a champagne bottle from on top of the piano and launches it at Johnny, who dodges it before tackling Jackson to the floor.

Oh, God, how the hell have I got myself involved in something like this? I'm just a nerd who works from home and doesn't really have much of a social life. The most controversial thing I've done as an adult is refuse to be a bridesmaid. I don't cause fights.

The pair of them roll into my feet, giving me a knock that causes me to drop my drink and my clutch bag. Millsy quickly pulls me out of the way.

Soon enough the bouncers are here, pulling the two of them apart. No one says anything to suggest this, but you can just tell from the bouncers' body language that they know who they're pulling apart, and they seem to treat them with a greater degree of care than they would two lads scrapping in a Wetherspoons.

'Now then, what are you two fighting about?' a painfully Yorkshire-sounding bouncer asks.

'It's her fault,' Johnny says, pointing towards me.

I suppose now he thinks I'm not going to sleep with him he doesn't really want me around.

'OK, you, out,' the bouncer tells me.

'What?' I say, not that I care too much. I don't really want to be here.

'You heard,' he says.

'OK, just—'

'Nope, out,' he says again. This time he grabs me by the arm.

'OK, wait a second,' Millsy intervenes.

'You can get out too,' the other bouncer adds, grabbing Millsy.

As the pair of us are frogmarched out of Hades, in front of a sea of people who all think they're super-cool and chill, all looking down their noses at us, I babble about needing my bag, but the bouncers don't care.

'Come back for it in the morning, when you're sober,' one of them tells me. 'I'll hand it to the office. You're not getting back in tonight.'

'Can you bring it to me now?' I ask him. 'I've not even had that much to drink.'

He doesn't listen. Instead, they just shove Millsy and me out of a back door, into an alleyway, closing the door straight after.

I glance around the dark, wet, dirty alleyway. I hug myself self-consciously. Suddenly I feel quite vulnerable.

'Don't worry, the front is just around this corner,' Millsy reassures me.

As I take a step to follow him my heel wobbles uneasily on the uneven floor.

'Come here, take my arm,' Millsy says, before carefully escorting me back out onto the busy, well-lit road.

'I'm sorry,' he says. 'I feel like that might have all been my fault. My intentions were good, but...'

'Oh, I'm not bothered about that,' I tell him. Well, I am, obviously, but I'm not mad at him. I'm disgusted at men. Honestly, I think I'm better off on my own. 'I'm more bothered about the fact that my flat keys were in my bag.'

'At least I have your phone,' he says, pulling it from his pocket.

'Thanks.'

I glance at my watch. Far too late to get the last train to my mum and dad's, and God knows what they would think if I turned up at this time, looking like this.

'Where do you live?' Millsy asks me.

'The City Heights building,' I tell him. 'You can't even get into the lobby without a fob or I'd go sit in the gym until morning.'

'Oh, you're on my side of town,' Millsy says. 'Do you want to just come and stay with me?'

I pull a face.

'I have two bedrooms,' he tells me. 'One of them is all made up, ready for a guest. I've been showing it to potential flatmates, so it's flawless, has its own bathroom too.'

'Are you sure?'

'Of course,' he says. 'This is all my fault.'

'OK, thanks,' I say sincerely.

'You can keep hold of my arm if you like,' he says as he leads me in the right direction.

'Thanks,' I say again. 'I have a question... how did you become the Leeds Lions' mascot?'

'Well, when I was at school I was good at two things: acting and rugby. I was crap at everything else. My dad wanted me to be a rugby player – he's been a Lions' fan since the day he was born. Much to my dad's annoyance, as I got older, I gravitated more towards acting. When I saw the job advert for someone to dress up in the Leo the Lion costume and dance on the sidelines I jumped at the chance. I got to be part of the team, all the while twerking on the sidelines once a week. It was lots of twerking back in my day – recently it's all dabbing and flossing and pretty much anything you'd find on Fortnite.'

'I always wondered what kind of person is inside animal costumes. Does it require an actor?'

'No, just a vaguely athletic, reasonably good dancer. I think it was being able to do the worm that got me the job. You should come with me to a game some time.'

'I would, but I fear it might end up in a brawl,' I remind him. 'Maybe, next time you see them, tell them you weren't really my friend.'

'I'd never denounce you like that,' he jokes. 'Don't worry, they won't hold it against me.'

'Ah, good, I wouldn't want it getting in the way of your pulling game,' I tease.

'I'm not going to lie, the lion suit did bag me a lot of women's phone numbers,' he says.

'I'm no expert, but isn't your face completely covered in the costume?' I ask. 'Are you not just a massive fluffy lion?'

'I think women are into it,' he tells me. 'I think some girls think there's something kind of hot about the anonymity that comes with the territory. They would see these little glimmers of my personality, my funny dance moves. They could tell I was a big bloke and that I'm fit... I think it's the danger.'

I feel my cheeks warming, just a little.

'I'm not attracted to danger,' I say quickly. 'If tonight has taught me anything, it's that dating is terrifying. I wouldn't be surprised if I took my ex back out of fear.'

'A specific ex?' Millsy asks.

'Yeah, I...' I stop at the top of a flight of steps that leads down next to the river. Millsy must realise I'm hesitating.

'I'm not bringing you down here to kill you, honest,' he insists.

I glance down into the darkness.

'Are you sure?' I ask. 'Because right now I look exactly like the kind of body they pull out of a river at the start of *Law & Order*.'

'Promise,' he says. 'My flat is down here.'

I exhale before taking hold of his arm again. I have no reason to think Millsy is going to kill me, not when he's been so generous. His advice might not be great but his intentions are good. Anyway, I don't lead an interesting enough life to get murdered.

We walk along the edge of the river for less than a minute before we're outside Millsy's building. It's a small apartment building, consisting of five floors. The higher ones have wraparound balconies with incredible views of the River Aire and the stunning Royal Armouries Museum building across the water at Leeds Dock.

'You've got one hell of a view,' I tell him. 'Do you rent?'

'No, I own mine,' he says. 'I used to live in my uncle's flat, a couple floors down. When I got a decent payday, I had enough for a deposit on the top-floor apartment.'

Does dancing in a lion costume and flashing your teeth in an advert really pay that well?

'Impressive,' I admit.

'You were saying about your ex,' Millsy prompts, clearly interested, as he lets us into his building and steers me towards the lift.

'Yeah... Well, I'm just being dramatic. I have no intention of getting back with him. My cousin has invited him to her wedding though. Some crap about how he was my plus one when she invited me so she should honour his invitation. I'm allowed a plus one but my quest to find one isn't going all that well. I think I'm going to give up, to be honest.'

'Man, that's rough,' he says. 'Your cousin must really hate you.'

'I wonder sometimes,' I reply with a sigh. 'She's just a bit spoiled, likes everything to be on her terms. If she doesn't get her way, you better hope you're not the reason why.'

Millsy unlocks his front door, holding it open for me to walk in first.

'Oh, wow, this place is great,' I tell him.

Millsy's flat is very much a bachelor pad, but a super-cool one. It's bigger than I thought it was going to be. His decor is simple: white walls, wooden floors. His sofa, curtains, cushions and rug are all various shades of grey. The only colour comes in the form of LED lighting he has running around the room. He cycles through different light patterns before landing on something warm, with shades of red and orange glowing around the open-plan living space.

'Shall we sit out on the terrace for a bit?' he suggests. 'I'll grab us a couple of drinks.'

'That would be lovely, thanks.'

'What can I get you?'

'Surprise me,' I say, unwilling to give up cool, easy-going Cara 2.0 just yet.

I head outside, making myself comfortable on one of the inviting-looking patio chairs. I plump up the cushions and plonk myself down, taking in the view while I wait for Millsy to join me. The Royal Armouries might be closed, but the Hall of Steel, a stunning glass tower with various weapons on the walls, is still lit up. This really is the life, sitting out here on a summer night. I'll say one thing for this obscenely small dress – it's nice and cool.

'Here we go,' Millsy says, handing me a can of something cold before sitting down next to me. 'You know, I get where you're coming from with the plus-one drama.'

'Oh, yeah?'

'Yeah. Ruby, the friend who I was telling you about, the one who is getting married. We've been best friends ever since we were babies, but she still won't let me bring a plus one to her wedding in however many weeks away it is.'

'How come?' I ask nosily as I play with my new fake hair between my fingertips.

'I haven't really been looking to settle down with anyone serious,' he tells me, which I imagine is quite a tactful explanation. 'Ruby says she doesn't want me bringing one of my "floozies" to her wedding. She thinks I'll turn up with some girl I pulled the night before, both probably still drunk. I guess I've done that before, which is why my family won't let me bring a plus one to family stuff either. They all say that if I find someone I can get serious with, I can get my plus-one rights back. It's crap though. I don't want to go to these things alone. I've got a bunch of lame family stuff coming up. I hate being the only person not in a couple when it's all everyone bangs on about.'

I think to myself for a moment. Millsy has done so much for me, perhaps I can return the favour...

'Ruby was the one in the bar last night?' I ask. 'Do you think she'd recognise the new-look me as being that girl?'

'I doubt it,' he says. 'You look more like my usual type now.'

'Interesting,' I say. I swig my ice-cold drink and relax into my chair as much as my short dress will allow. 'Very interesting.'

'What are you thinking?' he asks.

'I'm thinking, you need an acceptable plus one for Ruby's wedding, and whatever the lame family stuff you mentioned is. I've got a summer full of events too. My bosses' wedding, my cousin's wedding, my school reunion... I don't want to go to these things alone, but I definitely don't want to do any more dating for a while. You don't want to go alone, but you need a regular girl to go with. I have a job, I don't drink too much, I can talk to adults, I'm polite. And you said yourself, I look more like your type now. People will think you've just found the best of both worlds. I don't think people will struggle to believe that the right person could make you have a change of heart, do you?'

'I mean, I know me, so that doesn't sound right, but to the normal folk...' he jokes, '... that could actually work.'

'We don't have to go too hard, pretending to be a couple who are madly in love or anything like that, we're just the appropriate plus one the other person needs. We can get each other through the summer.'

'I'll drink to that,' Millsy says, clinking his can against mine. 'How do we do this?'

'I guess we can give each other a list of dates in the morning?' I suggest. 'See which ones we can make.'

Millsy laughs.

'You've got your shit way too together to pull off claiming you're dating me,' he says.

'And you're way too cool for anyone to think you're dating a puzzle nerd,' I point out. 'But you're an actor, right? And, like I said, we're not pretending we're in love. We're just plus ones.'

'Just don't go falling in love with me for real,' Millsy playfully warns.

'Wouldn't dream of it,' I reply.

I think we can safely say there's not much chance of that. Well, he's far too cool for me and I'm far too dorky for him. Cool has never been my type, and I suspect I'm nothing like the kind of girls Millsy usually goes for either. We're not even close to being each other's type. I do like hanging around with him though, and I can't think of a better person to be my plus one for the summer.

8

I'm one of those people who is quite fussy when it comes to beds. It's not so much that I have especially high standards, I just never seem to get a good night's sleep unless I'm in my own bed.

But last night, when Millsy showed me into his spare room, I couldn't wait to get into the bed. He told me that he's currently showing the room to potential flatmates, so I guess that's why it's so neat and tidy, and why he's put so much effort into making it such a nice room. It doesn't quite have the chilly bachelorness of the rest of the apartment but it's still super cool. And with the king-size bed, with lovely soft microfibre sheets, along with the Goonies T-shirt Millsy gave me to sleep in, I pretty much drifted off the second my head hit the pillow. I've never felt so at home somewhere that wasn't my home.

It's Sunday afternoon now and I'm almost at my parents' house. I couldn't face going back to Hades to fetch my bag but Millsy said he'd go for me. It does mean that I can't get back to my apartment until tonight though, so I wasn't able to go home and get changed. Millsy did offer to pop to town and pick up something a little more daytime friendly for me, but he's already done so much for me. I thanked him for my makeover over coffee this morning, and he downplayed it, but I really can't thank him enough. I feel like a different person.

I decided that the easiest thing to do would be to pop into town on my way to the station to buy some clothes and some make-up myself. Well, I definitely want to keep my new face, so I need to get the right items to recreate the look Dani gave me. My hair still looks amazing, in that way that it always does after a professional hairstylist has dried it for you – I'm dreading washing and drying it myself though. As for my new style, well, even if I could completely get on board with my tiny red dress being right for me, I definitely don't think it's the best idea for Sunday dinner with the family; do you?

I popped into the Trinity shopping centre, hurriedly buying make-up before whizzing around a few clothes shops. The fitting rooms in H&M were not that busy so I rather cheekily applied my make-up while I was in there. It must have been so weird for the assistant, seeing me go in there looking like a caricature of the morning after the night before, with my crudely removed old make-up and my peculiar outfit consisting of a red dress with a Goonies T-shirt over the top. After paying for my new outfit – careful not to go over the contactless payment limit – I nipped to the toilets to get changed. Another miraculous transformation. I look half decent now.

I don't remember the last time I went to my parents' for dinner in anything other than my comfy clothes. Usually super-soft tracksuits, off-the-shoulder tops – almost always in black or shades of grey. But today, starting as I mean to go on, I'm rocking up to their front door in a red and white floral mini tea dress, the likes of which probably hasn't been seen on me since I was a toddler, when my mum could dress me in whatever she wanted without protest.

I'm walking along the street towards their house, enjoying the delicious combination of the sun on my skin and the cool breeze, when I notice something that stops me in my tracks. On the driveway, sandwiched between my mum and dad's cars, is a baby-blue Mini Cooper, and I only know one person who drives that car: my cousin Flora.

I hover on the spot for a second. I'm not sure I'm in the mood for Flora, especially when I'm so very clearly still in her bad books, no matter how hard she tries to pretend otherwise.

Before I get a chance to even think about making a break for it, a black Ford Fiesta pulls up just in front of me and out pops Oliver from the passengers' side. I recognise it as his friend's car.

Of course, my brother doesn't recognise me, not with my new makeover. We both reach the end of our parents' driveway around the same time. He glances at me, in that way you do with people when you cross paths so closely. He looks away before snapping his neck back in my direction.

'Cara?' he says, his eyes wide with... something. I can't read him. 'Is that... is that you?'

'Of course it is,' I say with a laugh. 'I had my hair done – what do you think?'

'I like it,' he replies as his initial surprise relaxes into a smile. 'It suits you.'

I wrap an arm around my little brother, giving him a squeeze before we head for the front door together.

'I see Flora is here,' I say.

'Yeah, and Auntie Mary,' he replies. 'Mum just told me on the phone.'

'Fabulous,' I say sarcastically.

Auntie Mary is nothing like my mum. My mum is warm and affectionate, kind and generous – almost to a fault. She's the rational person in our family, who keeps everyone together. She's a great cook with a lovely house, but she isn't going to rain hellfire down on you if you leave crumbs on the worktop or wear shoes on the carpet.

Auntie Mary, despite being raised by the same parents, in the same house, is nothing like my mum. She isn't warm or friendly. Her house is like a museum, where you're terrified of knocking things over or spilling your drink – if you did either, you would never hear the end of it. She's not one for showing positive feelings or emotions, but an angry scowl or a harsh word of displeasure comes easy to her. Perhaps saddest of all is that I don't have any positive memories of her, despite her being around me for most of my life. I have loads of memories of doing fun things with my mum and Flora – they are really close – but none involving my auntie. It's just the way things have always been though, so I'm not all that bothered by it, and she's the same with Oliver, so I know that it's not me, it's her. It's never mattered until recently. The cold, reluctant hugs at Christmas and silent indifference at family gatherings were all I knew. It's only since I decided I didn't want to be Flora's bridesmaid that my auntie has upped from indifferent to hostile.

'Hello,' Oliver calls out once we're through the door.

'In the living room,' my mum calls back.

I let Oliver go first, following just a few steps behind him.

'Have you had fun?' my mum asks him, but Oliver doesn't get a chance to reply before she notices me slinking into the room behind him.

'Cara!' she shrieks, jumping to her feet. 'Oh my God, Cara! Is that you? I thought Oliver had brought a girl home for a second.'

Oliver seems to shudder at the thought. I'm sure he can't think of anything worse than bringing a girl home to meet his female relatives.

My mum hurries over to me.

'Oh my God, look at you. You look so different. What happened?'

Thankfully my mum is smiling widely, so I can tell she approves.

'I just decided my look needed a bit of a refresh,' I explain. I notice my dad enter the room. 'What do you think, Dad?'

'Yeah, very nice,' he replies. He wouldn't think that if he'd seen me last night, in my little red dress, with rugby players fighting over me. He'd probably lock me in the cellar and throw away the key.

'Stunning,' my mum says, touching my hair. She lowers her voice. 'Wow, it feels so real.'

Bless her, for even thinking twice about outing my new hair as fake, even if no one in this room thought my hair grew several inches since the last time they saw me.

'Thanks,' I reply. 'I'm so relieved you like it.'

I glance over at my auntie and my cousin.

'Hi,' I say, in an attempt to bring them into the conversation. Sometimes I think my cousin has inherited her mum's aversion to pleasantries.

I give them a sort of half-wave as I greet them. Well, we're not on hugging terms.

'Hi,' Flora replies. No word on my new look.

My auntie gives me one of her famous tongue clicks.

'What have you done?' she asks me, but she doesn't wait for me to reply. 'I suppose this is all for Flora's benefit?'

'Of course it isn't, Mary,' my mum says, jumping to my defence.

'You just want to upstage her at her wedding,' Mary persists. 'Why else would you change the way you look to something so... so... Kardashian?'

There's a really snobbish, judgemental tone to her voice. My auntie is clearly not one for *Keeping Up with the Kardashians.*

'The Kardashians are symptomatic of a toxic culture,' Oliver chimes in. 'But they've managed to cheat the system, to profit from it. That's really quite smart. Plus, you know, women have the right to do whatever they want.'

My auntie rolls her eyes.

I smile at Oliver. I know I joke about how 'woke' he is, but it's honestly such a breath of fresh air being around a male with a healthy take on feminist issues.

'It's just hair dye and a not-black dress,' I point out. 'It's not a big deal.'

'Cara might not even be coming, Mum,' Flora tells her. It sounds as if she's ticking her off, but this is just another dig. She knows I'm coming, she's just making out as if I think the day isn't important, for dramatic effect. Well, she isn't getting a floor show from me.

'Of course I'm coming,' I say, sitting down on the sofa with my mum. 'In fact, I have a plus one.'

'What?' Flora says. 'Really? What about Lloyd?'

'I know you're still inviting him,' I say, although I can still never quite believe my ex is invited to her wedding. 'But you did say I could still invite a plus one.'

'Yeah, but I didn't think...' Flora doesn't finish that sentence. 'So, who are you bringing? What's his name?'

'M... Joe,' I quickly correct myself. Probably best I use Millsy's actual name, rather than his nickname.

'And what does Mjoe do for a living?' my auntie asks nosily. 'Does he lock people up too?'

'No, he's an actor,' I reply.

My auntie scrunches her nose. I don't think she's impressed.

'What, like on TV?' Flora asks excitedly. 'Am I going to have a famous person at my wedding?'

'Oh, no, he's a theatre actor,' I reply.

'Oh, OK,' she says. 'Never mind.'

You've got to laugh at Flora's priorities. Now that she's realised there's nothing in this for her, she isn't at all interested.

'Anyway, we'll get off,' my auntie says. 'Let you get your dinner.'

My mum sees them to the door. To be honest, I'm glad they're leaving. At least I can relax now.

'Bye,' I call after them.

I get half-hearted replies.

I pull myself up and wander into the kitchen. It smells just like Sundays. Beef, vegetables, Yorkshire puddings, gravy. I didn't even tell my mum I was coming, but she does this every week without fail, and there's always plenty for everyone.

'Everything's ready,' my mum says, joining me in the kitchen. 'You timed it just right.'

'Not just right,' I remind her. 'Your sister was still here.'

'She's a little ray of sunshine, isn't she? Just ignore her, your hair looks amazing.'

'Thanks, Mum.'

As she removes Yorkshire puddings from the oven, placing them on the same plate she uses every week, I pinch one. It's almost too hot to hold, but I'm starving.

'You might look more sophisticated, but you haven't changed.' My mum chuckles. 'Although you didn't tell me you have a boyfriend.'

'Oh, I don't have a boyfriend, I just have a plus one.'

'Joe the actor,' my mum says.

I raise an eyebrow.

'He's a real person,' I insist. 'I'm not so desperate for a man that I'm imagining one.'

'I didn't think that, don't be silly,' my mum reassures me. 'I thought maybe you were paying an actor.'

'Hilarious,' I say sarcastically. 'You're lucky your Yorkshire puddings are good, or I'd be off.'

'There's baked Alaska for dessert.'

'Well, I guess I'd be off after that, then, wouldn't I?' I joke.

'Well, I look forward to meeting this Joe,' she says. 'Fancy carrying some food to the table?'

'Sure,' I reply.

It's weird, because obviously I want Millsy to be my plus one for the wedding, but I don't think I've actually processed what that will entail. I'm going to have to introduce him to my family. My actual family. And while I'm certainly not going to be trying to pass him off as my boyfriend or anything, he's still *with* me. Millsy, as generous as he has been, and as much fun as I have with him (I know I've only hung out with him for a couple of days but I can't stress how boring my days are usually), seems as if he has the potential to be a bit of a wildcard, and then there are his womanising ways I've heard all about. I suppose, at least, I don't have to worry about him trying to pull me. Well, even if he is the ultimate womaniser everyone else claims he is, he still managed to hold down a female best friend, didn't he? It's definitely a relief to know that he does form sincere bonds with women, but it does niggle me, just a bit, because if he will supposedly sleep with anyone, I have to wonder what's wrong with me that made him immediately usher me into the friend zone.

Is this a terrible idea? Have I really reached that level of desperate, where I'll take a near stranger to all of my big events over the summer? I really want to say no but, now that I've told my family that I'm bringing Millsy with me as my plus one, I've somehow made things even worse. Now, if I turn up without him, I'll look even more tragic than if I'd just turned up alone. At least we've got a few events to go to before Flora's wedding, so I suppose we can get in a lot of practice. I really don't know why I'm getting cold feet all of a sudden; surely now the worst thing I could do would be to back out of our plus-one agreement. Millsy hasn't steered me wrong yet... well, I guess he has, but only as far as dating advice goes, but I guess he's just programmed differently from the way I am. As a friend though, I can't fault him. Who knows? We might even have fun at these things. It's too late to turn back now, we'll just have to wait and see...

9

'Look at you,' Millsy says as I meet him outside my apartment building. 'You're sticking with the new look, then?'

I can't exactly change the hair in a hurry but I don't know if he believed I'd keep up the new clothing style and bolder make-up.

It's weird – if I haven't seen my reflection for a little while I forget that I look different at all. I forget about the daring (for me, at least) outfits, the make-up that completely transforms the shape of my face – I even forget about the long red locks.

'Yeah, I love it,' I tell him. 'Even my family loved it... for the most part.'

'You can't win them all,' he replies with a shrug of his broad shoulders and a flash of his cheeky smile. 'I have your bag.'

'You do,' I say, almost surprised as I take it from him. He notices the look on my face.

'What, did you think I was going to let myself in with your keys?' he asks.

'No, no,' I reply quickly. 'But I can't say I'm not surprised every time you're just a nice, normal person.'

'Does my reputation precede me?'

'A little,' I admit. 'Plus, you know, how often do people just... do nice things for people they don't really know, just to be nice?'

Millsy shrugs and smiles again.

'Do you want to come in?' I ask. 'See if you pass the not-murdering-me test?'

I feel as if a joke might dispel a little of the potential offence I might have just caused, even if he isn't letting on.

'Yeah, sure,' he says. 'We need to plan, don't we?'

'We do,' I reply. 'We definitely do.'

'After you, then,' he prompts.

It's safe to say that no one ever comes back to my flat, and my family don't visit all that much, so I spend the entire lift journey wondering what I need to quickly kick under the sofa or swipe from the worktop into the sink. I like to think I'm a reasonably tidy person but I'm no stranger to leaving my tea mug by the sink or kicking my tights off on the sofa. I suppose because Millsy's flat was so amazing, and so tidy, I feel a little self-conscious about mine.

Thankfully, once we're inside, it turns out I actually left the place quite tidy – with the exception of a few papers on my coffee table.

'Can I get you a drink?' I ask.

'Please,' he replies. 'Anything cold.'

I'm with him on that one. It's such a muggy evening.

Millsy looks around the room before cocking his head curiously.

'Do you have a leaky pipe or something?' he asks me. 'Not that I know what a leaky pipe sounds like, but...'

'Oh, just give it a few minutes,' I tell him as I gather up my papers.

As the rhythmic tapping turns into more of a banging, followed by the clash of cymbals, Millsy realises what the noise is.

'Oh, God, do you live next to a drummer?'

'A drummer, a saxophone player, singers, dancers, actors with lines they need to practise until the early hours. It's driving me mad, man.'

'Is that why you're flat-hunting?' he asks, gesturing towards the papers in my arms.

I look down at them. The flat listings the estate agent gave me, none of which feel right. They're too far outside town, too small or too expensive. They are almost all too expensive.

'Yeah. I work from home and it's impossible to get anything done with the noise. I'd found somewhere new but it fell through so I'm looking a little more urgently now.'

I stuff the papers inside a folder on my desk before heading to the fridge.

'You rent?' he asks.

'I do.'

'Furnished?'

'Yeah.'

'Interesting,' Millsy says thoughtfully. 'Did I mention I was renting out my spare room?'

I laugh.

'I'm serious,' he insists. 'You're looking for somewhere to live, I'm looking for a roommate. It sounds like you're going to be homeless soon. We're basically working together. Move in with me.'

'This relationship is moving a bit fast,' I point out with a chuckle. 'Thanks for the offer though.'

I grab a couple of cans of Coke from the fridge and hand one to Millsy. I swipe the other one across my brow in an attempt to cool myself down.

'Are you sure?' Millsy asks.

'I'm...'

Right on cue, potentially the loudest bass drum of my life is beaten. I feel it rattle right through my body. I really don't know how much longer I can take the noise here. I don't know if it seems worse than ever, or if I'm just so annoyed by it that it seems even more intrusive. And I really am going to be homeless if I don't like any of the flats I view next week. I have to admit, none of them are as central as I am now, and they certainly aren't as nice as Millsy's apartment – not without flat-sharing with someone who would be an actual stranger I know nothing about. At least I've known Millsy for a few days, I know things about him, I've seen his place and know that I could make myself at home there. My only other option, of course, would be to move back in with my mum and dad...

'Well, maybe if I could temporarily, while I look for somewhere more permanent?'

'Yeah, whatever you want,' he says casually.

'You're so nice to me,' I point out.

'I really need a plus one.' He laughs. 'But, honestly, it's no big deal. And we can just have the one lair where we do all our plotting.'

'Are we going to have a serial-killer wall, with maps and photos?'

'Absolutely,' he replies. 'What's our first gig?'

'My bosses are getting married next weekend,' I say. 'It would be good to have a plus one. It's only the evening do, so nothing too formal. They keep telling me I can bring someone if I want to.'

'Sounds great,' he says. 'But can we talk about this at home, please? Between the sweltering heat and the banging of the drum, I'm getting a right headache.'

At home. I laugh.

'I'll grab a few things,' I say. 'I can come back for the rest later… if you're sure?'

'I'm sure,' he insists. 'I'd rather rent to a friend.'

'OK, well, let's go plan this wedding,' I tell him.

'I thought you'd never ask,' he replies with a cheeky smile.

10

My two bosses, who run the escape rooms I design, and tying the knot today, always make me think of that age-old question: what came first, the chicken or the egg? And it isn't because she has fluffy yellowy blonde hair, and because he has a smooth bald head – they are just happy coincidences.

The actual reason they make me wonder about the question is because they have a background in magic. He used to be a magician and she used to be his glamorous assistant (although anyone in the industry knows the assistant is basically a magician too). The thing is, their names are Paul and Deborah. This instantly makes me think of the famous magician Paul Daniels and his assistant/wife Debbie McGee. I mean, what are the chances they would have the same first names, the same jobs, and now they're getting married?

Deborah, like Debbie, is younger than Paul (the age gap isn't nearly as wide though). They've been together a while but now they're finally tying the knot. Most of the people who work at the escape rooms are students or young actors, but I guess they work more closely with me, designing rooms together, and I suppose I am a decade older than students, which, now that I've realised it, is a truly terrifying thought because I hadn't realised how quickly time had passed. Obviously I know that I'm twenty-nine but things still seem as if they weren't that long ago. It's only when you stop and think about time that you realise how much has gone by. Look at it this way, it's been sixteen years since the last episode of *Friends* aired – that's over half my entire lifetime ago. What the hell? How can that be right?

I'm close enough for Paul and Deborah to invite me to their wedding, but only close enough to be invited to the evening do. That's the best part though, right? No boring ceremony, no need to worry about whether or not the food is going to be any good. Just turning up for the party. It's a big hotel just outside Leeds so thankfully we can get a taxi there and back.

I was worried the red dress might be a little bit much (or not enough, technically, I suppose) for my bosses' wedding, so I went out and bought yet another new dress. This one – a mauve maxi dress with embroidered detail and long mesh sleeves – is more family-friendly. Millsy has scrubbed up well too, in a blue suit jacket teamed with smart black trousers and brown shoes. We haven't been here long and we've just bumped into Keith, the only other person from work I can spot. He's here with his wife, Sarah, who I haven't met before, and, despite our rehearsing in the car, I still feel terrified of introducing Millsy to people.

'How long have you two been together?' Keith asks. 'I didn't realise you had a boyfriend, Cara.'

I'm about to awkwardly tell him Millsy isn't my boyfriend-boyfriend – just my plus one – when Millsy gets there first.

'Six months,' he says, wrapping an arm around my waist, squeezing me tightly.

I always stiffen awkwardly when he touches me, not because I don't like him touching me, but because I'm not used to casual physical contact from attractive men.

This boyfriend angle isn't something we discussed at all. In fact, I was very quick to say the opposite.

'You sure kept that quiet,' Keith says with a smile. 'Well, good on you, I'm really happy for you.'

'Thanks,' I say with my best fake smile. 'Joe, shall we go and get another drink?'

It feels so weird, calling Millsy by his first name.

'Sure thing, babe,' he replies.

We excuse ourselves and head in the direction of the bar, weaving our way through the large round tables. Only a few people remain seated, mostly older relatives and friends. The tables are laid with cream and gold tablecloths and are littered with used plates, bearing the remains of the bacon sandwiches they're serving and half-eaten bits of cake.

'What the hell are you doing?' I ask him through the fake smile that is still cemented in place on my face. My teeth are clenched so tightly, it's hard to release them, and as I talk through them, while pushing Millsy from behind, I look a little bit like I'm working a ventriloquist dummy.

'What am I doing?' he asks, surprised. 'They totally bought that.'

'I don't want them to buy it,' I reply. 'I told you, I wanted a plus one, not a fake boyfriend.'

'What's the difference?' he asks, taking a bite out of another bacon sandwich.

'Where did that come from?' I ask, baffled because I didn't notice it in his hand before. 'Anyway, it doesn't matter. The difference is, a plus one is a plus one, but if they think you're my boyfriend, then I'm going to have to explain where you go.'

'Where I go?'

'Yeah, when all this is over, and I all of a sudden don't have a boyfriend any more.'

'Oh,' he says. 'Oh-h-h. Yeah, OK, that makes sense, I guess... So, I'm single at these things?'

And there he is, the Millsy that I was warned about.

'Yes, Millsy, you're single at these things,' I say with a sigh.

'You sound like you're bothered,' he says with a bit of a grin.

'I'm not,' I quickly insist. 'Just because we're plus ones for the summer, doesn't mean your love life can't carry on as normal so, go ahead, crack on with whoever you want, don't let me stop you.'

'OK,' he replies slowly, clearly picking up on something. I do seem to be insisting a little on the hard side, which must have him puzzled. 'On that note, I'm going to the loo... If I'm allowed?'

'I'll get the drinks in,' I reply, unimpressed by his attitude.

I order our drinks before leaning back against the bar to take in the room. Most of the chairs have jackets on them, which I suppose people have taken off before heading out onto the dance floor. It's interesting how, as weddings go on, standards go down. Everything perfect at the start but by the end, as messy as the room may be, everyone is way more relaxed and having more fun than they were eating a sit-down dinner in their formal wear. My favourite part of weddings is when the ties come off, the heels are discarded, and everyone lets their hair down.

There are small pockets of people dancing to the music – a folk band covering popular songs. There is a gaggle of young women dancing together. There's a man, who I'd guess is a groomsman from his outfit, doing the worm to impress the crowd gathered around him. My favourite, though, is the seven- or eight-year-old boy who has stolen one of the gold sashes from one of the tables, and is currently dancing with it, in the centre of the dance floor, all alone, dancing as if no one is watching. That's a mood. We'd all do well to be more like that kid.

I glance over at the photo booth area. I've never really understood their presence at weddings. Well, why would you want to remember the happiest day of your life by looking at a snap of your drunk friends in feather boas and pirate hats? I watch as an elderly man discards the pair of fake glasses he just had his photo taken in. He's wearing a fedora, which I think is actually his own, not a prop. He deposits it at his table before shuffling onto the dance floor with an energy that puts mine to shame. I don't think it would hurt me to be more like this guy too.

Paul and Deborah are quite cool people so naturally their wedding is too. Flashes of shimmering gold aside, everything in the room is earthy and natural. In fact, I do believe the bacon sandwiches are made with vegan-friendly bacon, the wedding cake is vegan... I haven't told Millsy because you never know who is going to be the type of person to have a meltdown because Greggs have started selling vegan sausage rolls.

The bride and groom catch my eye, chatting with Keith and Sarah at the side of the room, so I decide to pop over and say hi now, while they're not too busy and Millsy isn't with me. It will save me having to keep up his story about us being a couple. Ergh, why did he say that? I suppose now I'll have to go to the trouble of fabricating a fake break-up so that people stop asking me about him. I'll say I broke up with him, naturally. If the point of this whole thing was to make me look better, saying he dumped me isn't exactly going to achieve that, is it?

It's only as I get closer that I realise something is wrong. Deborah doesn't look like a joyful bride on the happiest day of her life, she looks upset.

'Erm... hi,' I say, with no time to pull a U-turn and come back at a better time.

'Oh, hi, Cara,' Paul says. 'Thanks so much for coming.'

'You're welcome. Con... congratulations.'

'Sorry, I'm just a bit annoyed,' Deborah says to me quietly as she leans forward to hug me.

Other than looking a little upset and a lot angry, Deborah looks absolutely gorgeous in her stunning, floor-length cream lace gown. Her hair has been plaited on both sides before being pinned to the top of her head, forming a gorgeous crown braid, full of flowers. She's nailed the bohemian bride look.

'Cara brought her boyfriend,' Keith sings.

'You have a boyfriend?' Deborah squeaks. 'And he's here?'

'Yes,' I reply awkwardly. This is exactly what I didn't want to happen. 'He's around here somewhere.'

Deborah ushers me a few steps away from the others.

'Quick, tell me all about him before he gets back,' she demands excitedly.

'OK, but are you OK?' I ask, partially changing the subject, but also because I'm concerned. No one should be miserable on their wedding day. 'You looked really upset when I walked over.'

'Oh, I'm fine,' she insists. 'I'm just a bit annoyed because I just nipped to the loo, and on my way back I crossed paths with a man and... well, he hit on me.'

'He hit on you?'

'Yeah, can you believe that? At my own wedding.'

'What kind of person would try to chat-up the bride at a wedding?' I ask angrily, but the words have no sooner left my lips when the answer hits me.

'I know, right?' she replies. 'And the worst thing of all is that, I think he's a wedding guest, not staff or someone just staying in the hotel. Someone actually brought someone like that to my wedding.'

'Are you sure he's a guest?' I ask.

'Yeah, well, this is a private area and he was dressed like a guest. He was wearing a blue blazer. I told Paul all about it. He's keeping an eye out for him. He's going to ask him to leave, and God help whoever brought him.'

I feel as if I'm frozen on the spot.

'Anyway, enough of that, where's this fella of yours? I can't wait to chat with him,' she persists.

Somehow I doubt that's going to be the case.

'Erm, yeah, he's around here somewhere... Actually, I'll go find him. Back in a bit.'

'OK,' she says with a smile. 'No rush. I had no idea getting married meant talking to so many people.'

I laugh politely, walking away calmly, only picking up the pace once I'm out of her eyeline.

Shit! Shit, shit, shit. What are the chances that it wasn't Millsy who just tried to chat-up the bride at a wedding? He's only been out of my sight for a matter of minutes!

I hover outside the men's toilets for a few seconds before marching straight in – my gaze firmly fixed on the floor, of course. I know the men's room doesn't have the same level of privacy as the ladies' loo does.

'Millsy?' I call out.

'Yes?' he replies casually. He sounds as if he's only a matter of inches away from me. 'Did you miss me so much you thought you'd come in here to find me?'

Now isn't the time for laughing at his jokes.

'Just... come out here,' I insist.

You know how public toilets often have two doors, with a small, pointless corridor between them? Well we're standing in that, so I'm still technically in the men's loos, but not actually in them.

'I can't believe I'm about to ask you this,' I start in hushed tones, 'but... you didn't try to hit on the bride, did you?'

'Absolutely not,' he says. 'What kind of man do you take me for?'

'Sorry,' I say. 'It's just I was talking with the bride, and she said someone in a blue jacket tried to chat her up by the toilets.'

'Well, it must be some other dude in a blue jacket,' he assures me.

'Oh, that's such a relief,' I reply, leaning back against the wall. 'It's just, well, she's my boss, and she's really upset so... it would have made me look bad, you know?'

'I totally get that, but no, not guilty. I did try and chat one woman up, just a bit, but she wasn't the bride. She wasn't wearing a white dress.'

'Well, that's... Wait, she wasn't wearing a white dress? Was she wearing a cream dress?'

'Yeah... Why, do you know her?'

'Millsy, that's the bride,' I whisper angrily.

'How am I supposed to know that, if she's not wearing a white dress?'

'Was she wearing a wedding ring?'

Millsy runs a hand through his brown hair that is neatly slicked back for the occasion.

'I've never really paid much attention to whether or not people are wearing wedding rings,' he says by way of an explanation.

'Why not?'

'In my experience... it's never posed much of a problem. Oh, I did notice something though – she had flowers on her head.'

'Oh my God, I'm going to lose my job,' I say to myself.

I quickly step out of the way as a man opens the door on his way to the toilets. He gives us both a look of acknowledgement but doesn't seem to be overly concerned with my presence here.

'Well, I can just sneak out and leave,' he suggests. 'That way, they won't even see me.'

'Except Deborah is waiting to meet you. It's going to make me look bad, if you disappear from her wedding... admittedly not as bad as you trying to shag her on her wedding day, but still...'

I puff air from my cheeks as I wrack my brains for a solution. My job is all about problem-solving. I come up with problems with step-by-step solutions for people to figure out the answer to, so if I could just flip that process on its head... I've successfully made it out of every escape room I've ever tried. I should be able to problem-solve my way out of this one too.

So, if this were an escape room, I would be looking for objects to help facilitate my escape. And now this has occurred to me, I've cracked it.

'How long did you talk to her for?' I ask.

'Oh, seconds, just in passing. I barely said a word to her before she stormed off...'

'Hmm...'

And it is quite dimly lit in the area outside the toilets. Perhaps the only thing that caught her eye was the blue jacket... this might just work!

'OK, you wait here, I'm going to nip out there and... we're going to borrow a few things that will make her think you're someone else. You're an actor, right? Can you do a different accent?'

Millsy sounds very much like a Leeds lad and, with Deborah being from down south, I'm sure she'll remember Millsy's accent as well as his blue jacket.

Millsy, presumably not taking this all too seriously, launches into the 'is this a dagger?' monologue from *Macbeth*.

I cut him off.

'Marvellous, but can you do something a bit more subtle?'

'Received pronunciation,' he says, toning it down. 'I can speak without an accent.'

'Fab,' I say semi-sarcastically. 'Wait there.'

I hurry from the doorway of the men's toilets, back into the main room where the wedding is. First of all, I snatch up a jacket from the back of a chair. A black jacket – absolutely nothing resembling blue. My next port of call is the photo booth, where I swipe the black thick-rimmed fake glasses that are used as a prop for the photos. Finally, I borrow the old man's fedora from the table he left it on. And I do mean borrow, I hasten to add. I am taking these things temporarily, to try and reverse Trojan horse Millsy out of this wedding, and by doing so I will be escaping with my job and my dignity still intact. Although I did just semi-steal a hat from an OAP...

I find Millsy exactly where I left him, sheepishly hanging out in the pointless void between the two toilet doors. 'So, what's all this?'

'Put this jacket on, and these glasses, and this hat. I'll leave your jacket on the back of a chair and, once you've said hello to Paul and Deborah, we'll return this stuff, grab your jacket and bail. She's waiting to meet you now but, once she has, there are a lot of guests here. She won't notice if we leave.'

I sigh. It's not great but it's the best plan I have.

'Sure,' Millsy says with an awkward laugh. 'I am sorry though, I just think... after you were so firm about me chatting other people up, it seemed like a good idea. Obviously I never would have done it if I'd realised she was the bride.'

'One would hope,' I say, helping him on with a black suit jacket that thankfully fits him well enough to pass off as his own. 'So we go see her, you say hello, you channel every acting ability you have to just try and seem like anyone but yourself and then we run away, sound good?'

'I'm uncomfortable with how good at this you are,' he points out. 'But yes, sounds good.'

I peep out of the toilet door, making sure there is no one around to see me sneaking out. I don't feel out of the woods yet, even if this does work. If someone were to see me and Millsy slinking out of the loos, they would probably think we had just snuck in there to get up to no good, and that's not a great look either, is it?

With the coast clear I hurry out with Millsy close behind me. The seemingly new and improved Millsy.

'OK, let's go order more drinks, because I kind of abandoned our others, and then find the happy couple,' I say.

The drinks are more of a prop, really. Something to show that everything is normal and fine and we're just having fun, nothing dodgy going on... Alcohol feels like a mistake though, so I grab us a couple of orange juices.

With everything in place I call action, before we walk over to the table where Paul and Deborah are currently sitting, chatting with guests. It just so happens to be the table where I swiped the jacket from, and a few of the men sitting at it are currently without jackets. I don't know what the chances are of someone recognising a black jacket, in a sea of black jackets, but I don't want to take any chances.

'When we sit at the table, take the jacket off and just leave it on the back of the chair, OK?' I whisper.

'OK,' Millsy replies dutifully.

'Deborah, hi.' I beam. 'This is Joe.'

We take a seat opposite them at the table.

'Oh, Joe, hello, I've heard a lot about you, so lovely to meet you,' she says, greeting him with a big, warm smile.

'It's lovely to meet you too,' he replies politely – and in the voice of a BBC newsreader. 'Congratulations on your wedding. You both look amazing.'

I smile to myself. It's not often that men compliment other men on how they look, is it? It says a lot about Millsy, that he feels secure enough to do it.

They both thank him.

'You're not the only one who thinks my wife looks good,' Paul points out.

'Yes, I was just telling everyone how someone came on to me, near the toilets,' Deborah adds.

'What did he say?' Millsy asks.

It takes me every facial muscle I have to stop my eyes widening. As if it's not risky enough, hiding him in plain sight, but he's flying really close to the sun now.

'He says, "Hey, baby, can I buy you a drink?"' Deborah says. You can see how embarrassed she feels, telling the story. I can feel my own embarrassment pumping through my veins.

'That's despicable,' Millsy 2.0 says. 'Did you get a good look at the guy?'

I literally bite my tongue, to stop me from saying anything that could make this worse (although what the hell could I even say?), and to try and keep myself from cringing so hard I bare my teeth.

'Kind of,' Deborah starts, her eyes narrowing as she looks over towards him. 'He had longish hair, a blue jacket, he was built quite a lot like you, actually...'

I have to put a stop to it right now. Millsy is playing with fire. I don't know if he's trying to make sure she doesn't suspect him, or if he's just flexing, but inviting any kind of comparison is more than I can handle. With a seemingly careless dip of my wrist, my glass of orange juice tips to one side, the entire contents spilling out over Millsy's white shirt and his trousers. He immediately jumps to his feet.

'Oh my gosh, M... Joe,' I say, perhaps a little too theatrically to be as sincere as I'd hoped, and I really do need to try harder to call him Joe in front of real people. I'm still messing it up every now and then. 'So sorry, clumsy me. We'd better go sort you out. Sorry, guys, lovely to see you though.'

I grab Millsy by the hand and drag him outside, snatching up his infamous blue jacket from where I hid it on our way out.

'I'm not sure that was completely necessary,' he points out, sounding just a little bit annoyed with me.

'I needed to shut you up somehow. She was basically describing you, to you.'

'I was making sure she wasn't on to me,' he replies. 'I was trying to help.'

'Well, I think we got away with it,' I reply, finally relaxing a little. 'Sorry for covering you in orange juice, I'll have your suit cleaned for you.'

'Ah, don't worry about it,' he replies.

I root around in my clutch bag until I find a packet of tissues. He smiles as I hand them to him. I know they're not really going to make a difference, but now I'm thinking that I may have over-reacted, just a little.

Millsy almost entirely unbuttons his shirt before using one of the tissues to dry his stomach. As he takes off his fedora it disturbs his hair. By the time he's taken off the black-framed glasses too, and slicked his hair back into place, I get strong Superman vibes. I quickly glance away.

'I'll take these back inside,' I say, before clearing my throat. 'We should probably just go home.'

'We'll do better next time,' Millsy reassures me.

'Hmm,' I reply.

'You're not going to bail on me, are you?' he asks, suddenly sounding worried. 'We've got my sister's gender-reveal party coming up. You can't expect me to go to something like that alone – it sounds horrendous.'

That's exactly what I was planning on doing. I can't help but feel as if this whole plus-one pact was a stupid idea. We tried it and it didn't work – the obvious thing to do is sack it off. As Millsy stares at me with his dark, puppy-dog eyes, I reach for the words to tell him that we should call this whole thing off, but I can't find them. Well, I suppose I do owe him one event, at least, just to even things out. But after that, that's it. No more.

'Of course, I'm still coming with you,' I reply.

Millsy relaxes in an instant.

'Phew,' he says. 'I've seen gender reveals on Facebook – they always look cringey as hell. But my sister is excited about it, so... you've just got to turn up, right?'

I think about my cousin's wedding, that my life would be so much easier if I didn't attend, but I know I have to.

'You do,' I agree.

'At least I'll have you with me,' he reasons.

I smile.

'You will.'

For a few seconds we just exchange glances. It almost feels as if we're having a moment. A moment I am far too self-conscious for.

'Right, OK, well,' I babble. 'You book us a taxi, I'll go back in and return these items to their owners and then we'll get you home, and you can get your pants off.'

The second the words leave my lips I realise how dodgy they sound. Millsy just laughs. There's something kind of nice about how easy-going he is. It's infuriating when he does something insane like flirt with a bride at a wedding but doesn't freak out over the consequences. But it's quite nice, like now, when he doesn't care about much more than the smile on his face. If I'm going to enjoy a gender reveal with anyone, it's going to be Millsy. More than anything though, I'm just really intrigued to meet his family...

11

There's something about Millsy that is a little... I don't know. I can't quite put my finger on it. He's kind of elusive. He seems to know so many people, but from nights out, not from work. And then there's the matter of how he makes a living. He owns a swanky flat, dresses well, goes on lots of nights out. And he's so generous too. But while I've been living with him I haven't seen him do a scrap of work yet. I've been doing loads, now that I'm living peacefully by the river, rather than in *La La Land*. I feel so settled there already, making myself at home in the spare room, utilising the kitchen as much as my skills allow. It's just so easy to get so much work done, before chilling, then enjoying a peaceful night's sleep.

Millsy never works though, as far as I can tell, which makes me wonder where his money comes from...

I've been floating a few ideas with my wild imagination. I quickly dismissed any thoughts of him being something bad, like a drug dealer, because I really, truly haven't seen him do anything resembling work at all. Even drug dealers have to put some graft in.

Then I thought that maybe his family have money, but now that I'm walking down the driveway to his dad's house – the house that Millsy grew up in – I can immediately tell that his upbringing must have been similar to mine, and there's no way my parents are buying me swanky flats and funding my lifestyle.

The houses on this street are nice. Really nice. Detached, but not mansions or anything. I can't help but notice how perfect everyone's garden is – and I mean *perfect*. Perfectly cut grass, neatly trimmed hedges. There are no footballs knocking around, no bikes. I'm getting mad Wisteria Lane vibes, and we all know what that picture of perfection had going on behind the scenes.

I'm so glad I made an effort, in a floral floor-length summer dress. I'm getting pretty good at styling my fake hair now and I'm even nailing my make-up. It all feels like second nature now.

'I really appreciate you coming with me to this thing,' Millsy says as we approach the front door. 'Ruby will be here, but she'll have her fiancé, Nick, with her and... well, he isn't my biggest fan. Ruby's parents live next door, so they've known my sister all her life.'

'Your sister is Fran?' I double-check.

'Yes. Quick refresher: my sister is Fran, Dad is Rod – short for Rodger, but only my stepmother, Mhairi, calls him that.'

'Do you get on with her?' I ask curiously.

'Yeah, she's all right. I would have preferred my mum and dad to stay together but, you know. Mum lives in Australia now, so she won't be here. She's coming over for the birth instead. Mhairi is from Scotland, but she's lived in England since she was in her twenties. She's got a pretty heavy Glaswegian accent still, so good luck with that if you're not used to hearing them. I'm decent at translating now, unless I've upset her...'

I do wonder if there might be a story there, but before we have the chance to say another word, the front door opens.

'Joe, I thought I heard voices,' a man who looks just like an older version of Millsy says as he pulls him in for, what I'd call, a manly hug. It's stiff, and almost reluctant, but you can tell there are affectionate intentions behind it.

'All right, Dad,' Millsy replies.

As his dad releases Millsy he notices me standing behind him. I'm carrying a reasonably big white box with a red velvet cake inside it. Millsy volunteered to bring a cake to the party, as a gift to his sister, and he had arranged it a while ago, so it was just to pick up today. Not only a very sweet gesture but exactly the cake I would have chosen myself.

'Oh, who's this?' his dad asks. 'I didn't realise you were bringing anyone.'

'Dad, this is Cara. Cara, this is my dad, Rod.'

'Hi,' I say brightly, but I feel awkward as hell. As if he didn't tell them I was coming with him. I feel like an intruder. 'Can you hold this, please, Joe?'

I hand him the cake box to offer his dad a hand to shake, to show him that I am a polite human and I'm not just one of Millsy's bimbos that it sounds as if everyone has grown tired of meeting.

'So lovely to meet you,' I say, offering him my hand. Rod isn't interested in shaking my hand though, instead he pulls me in for a hug, wrapping me up in his arms, giving me a squeeze.

'And it's lovely to meet you, Cara,' he says. 'Come on, let's head outside. We're having the party in the garden.'

As we pass through the hall I can't help but notice baby and childhood photos in frames on the walls. Some of them must be of Millsy, which I'd love to see. I make a mental note to have a good look at them later.

We reach the kitchen where a petite blonde woman, who I'd

guess is in her fifties, is loading ice into a cool box full of bottles of beer.

'Mhairi, Joe has brought a girl with him,' Rod says. 'Well, not a girl, a lady.'

I'm not sure anyone has ever called me a lady before. It really does make me wonder about the kind of girls he usually dates.

'Hello, hen, it's nice to meet you,' she says.

Mhairi shakes my hand. Hers is freezing from the ice but it's welcomed on a hot day like today.

'Joe, is that the cake?' she asks excitedly.

'Yes,' he replies. 'Where do you want it?'

Mhairi glances around the messy kitchen. It seems to be in a state of temporary chaos thanks to the party. It looks as if she's making all the food herself, so every inch of worktop space is currently occupied.

'Just outside the back door there's a table with presents on it – can you pop it on there for now, please? It's in the shade, at the side of the house. I'll make some space and be right out for it. All the action is in the back garden.'

'No worries,' he says before turning to me. 'OK, let's ditch this and go introduce you to everyone, shall we?'

'OK, sure,' I reply, hoping my nerves aren't obvious. Why do I feel as if I'm 'meeting the family'? I mean, yes, obviously I'm meeting Millsy's family, but we're just friends. I feel about as nervous as I would if I were meeting a boyfriend's family for the first time.

We walk out of the kitchen side door where, sure enough, there is a table, hiding in the shade, covered with presents.

'Oh, wow, there are a lot of people here,' I say quietly.

'Most people are all right. There are only one or two you need to worry about.'

I'm almost certain he's joking.

I don't know nearly enough about plants and flowers to identify them, but there is one, or a combination of a few, in Millsy's dad's back garden that give off the most amazing smell. I don't quite know how to describe it, but it smells like summer out here. The plants, the barbecue – I can even smell the creosote on the fences, which for some reason reminds me of the long six-week holidays as a child. It makes me think of playing out in the garden at home, playing Swingball with my brother, watching the steam trains pass by at the bottom of the garden.

There really are quite a lot of people here – at least fifty. I don't even think I would know fifty people to invite to a thing. My parents, my brother – Millsy now, I guess. I try not to think about whether or not my auntie et al. would RSVP because I don't know what's worse, if that lot didn't turn up, or if they did. Of course, this is an entirely fictional event I'm pondering. I'm not going to have anything to invite anyone to any time soon.

'Oh, look, there's Ruby,' Millsy points out. 'Don't worry, I told her you were coming.'

I remember her from the night I met Millsy. I recognise her long honey-blonde hair and intimidating smile. She seems like such a happy, bright person. She's sitting on the lawn, on a blanket with a man either side of her.

'Hey, Rubes,' he says.

'Hello,' she says, pulling herself to her feet. She hugs him before turning to me. 'And you must be Cara!'

'Yes, hello,' I reply.

As Ruby reaches out to hug me the first thing I notice is the sunlight bouncing off her massive rock of an engagement ring. It's gorgeous.

'It's nice to meet you. I've heard a lot about you,' she informs me. 'This is Nick, my fiancé, and Woody, my brother.'

'It's nice to meet you both,' I tell them.

Ruby must not recognise me from the night I met Millsy, but, while I might look more his type now, he has insisted that he wants me to be myself. He says the only way Ruby will let me come to the wedding is if I seem 'normal', so I suppose it's a compliment that he thinks of me as normal, even if normal isn't his type.

'So, where did you two meet?' Nick asks curiously.

Millsy has told me a lot about Nick. He's a doctor – a gynae-cologist, no less. When Millsy first met Nick he was just Ruby's annoying, boring, uptight flatmate. Millsy really didn't like him and, apparently, neither did Ruby. Millsy told me that Nick had a horrible girlfriend – someone he'd met when he delivered her sister's baby – and I don't know what happened but, somewhere along the way, Ruby decided she didn't hate Nick, she loved him, and I guess all is well that ends well because they're engaged.

'We met at my work,' I say quickly, before Millsy has the chance to tell the truth.

'What do you do?' he persists.

'I design escape rooms,' I tell him, relaxing a little for knowing I'm switching back to the truth.

All three of them seem taken aback by this.

'What were you doing at an escape game?' Ruby asks him in disbelief.

'Erm, escaping,' he tells her, sounding almost offended. 'And, it was so much fun. I was talking to the staff after and they intro-duced me to the designer... and it was Cara.'

'Isn't that a bit like Stockholm syndrome?' Nick jokes. 'Bonding with the person who held you captive?'

I watch Millsy force out a polite laugh and do the same. Nick seems all right, but if he's the opposite personality type to Millsy then I'm not surprised they're not exactly best friends.

'Wow, I feel like I hardly see you these days, with all the wedding planning going on and stuff, and suddenly you're doing escape rooms and dating intelligent women – maybe *I* was the bad influence?' Ruby jokes.

'I'm still me,' Millsy insists.

'Unfortunately, for all of us,' a pregnant woman jokes as she creeps up behind him, hugging him the best she can with her bump to contend with.

'Oi,' he replies, giving her a squeeze, before introducing us.

It's quite overwhelming, meeting so many people at once. With so many names and faces I'm terrified I'm going to start getting them confused.

'Cara, this is Fran, my sister. The one who is going to let us know if she's having a boy or a girl by, I don't know, what? Smashing up a piñata full of pink or blue glitter.'

'Oh, aren't you hilarious?' she says. 'Hi, Cara, so nice to meet you.'

'You too,' I say. 'Congratulations.'

'We've been guessing,' Nick starts. 'We think you're having a boy.'

'Doesn't matter if it's a boy or a girl, it'll drive you mad,' Woody adds, hopefully only semi-seriously.

'Oh, yes, you seem like your kids really stress you out,' Fran replies in a sarcastic tone. 'And yet here you are, lying here on a blanket in the sun, while your wife is trying to get out the ketchup your Robbie just massaged into his and his sister's hair.'

'She'll have it under control,' he replies, making himself somehow even more comfortable than he was before.

'Honestly, the men in this family,' Fran replies.

I must look puzzled.

'Well, not that we're all actually related,' she continues for my benefit. 'But we've all grown up together, living next door to each other, our parents joking that they would often mix up the babies – especially Joe and Ruby – without noticing for days at a time...'

I've been wondering, this past couple of weeks, if it might be possible that Millsy is in love with Ruby. Well, given the rumours I've heard about his romantic (or not all that romantic, as the case may be) relationships with women, I did wonder how he's managed to have a female best friend all this time. But the more I hear him talk, and the more time I spend around members of his family, I realise that Millsy does love Ruby, but it really is like a sister. He isn't in love with her. They grew up together, they've been best friends all of their lives, and now that Ruby is getting married, I suppose Millsy just feels a little lost without his best friend. It really does seem like they were inseparable until Nick came along. I suppose that's what happens in any friendship, when the other person settles down. It's certainly how I seemed to lose all my friends.

This is probably how I got such an easy in with Millsy, him being abandoned by his bestie, but at least I know that I can trust him, that it is possible for a man and a woman to be just friends.

'OK, well, I'm going to drag this one away to get a drink before you tell her anything about when I was a kid that might embarrass me,' Millsy says as he ushers me away from the group.

'It's the adult Millsy stories that are the most likely to embarrass you,' Nick calls after us.

'Ergh, his jokes,' Millsy says to me quietly. 'I never get his jokes.'

Nick's voice isn't the only thing that follows us. Fran is hot on our heels.

'Joe, I need a favour. I'm trying to play music through the Bluetooth speaker you bought Dad and none of us can get it to work. Can you sort it out, quick?'

'Wow, you're not even a mum yet and you're like a grandma,'

he jokes before turning to me. 'Do you wanna go grab us some drinks? I'll be back in two seconds, just as soon as I've got whatever cringey boyband this one wants playing coming through the speakers.'

I smile.

'Sure thing. Beer?'

'Please,' he says. 'Back in five.'

As Millsy goes off with his sister, I head up the narrow garden path, towards a table laid out with drinks.

So far everyone seems absolutely lovely. Just a nice family with a lovely house and a beautiful garden, with a perfectly picturesque pond...

I'm so busy taking in my surroundings I don't see the person in front of me. I feel my body collide with his. That will teach me to look at the scenery when I'm walking on a path that runs alongside a pond. He somehow manages to grab me by the hands, steadying me on the spot, keeping me upright on the path instead of laid out in the pond. The water probably isn't deep but I would have wound up very wet and even more embarrassed if he hadn't caught me.

'Oh, God, I'm so sorry,' I babble. 'My fault completely, I... I...'

I finally look up at the person I just bumped into.

'Partially my fault too,' he insists in an accent that I can think of no better way to describe than: Hugh Grant. 'I wasn't really looking where I was going either.'

For a moment I just stare at him. He's around six foot tall, slim built, with chiselled good looks and big dark green eyes. His light brown hair is short, apart from on the very top of his head where the slightly longer ends are just edging into intentionally messy. He has a very short, very neat beard to match, one that sits flat to his face and stops just past his jawline. He's wearing jeans and a neatly pressed white shirt. I feel like a sweaty mess but he looks perfect, as if he should be on the cover of *GQ* magazine.

'You saved me from ending up in the pond,' I point out.

'Erm, I saved you from ending up in prison,' he corrects me with a playful grin.

I just stare at him.

'There are great crested newts in there. If you landed on one, and killed it, that's six months in prison. I suppose you could be out in four with good behaviour.'

'And you would have called the police, would you?' I ask, safe in the knowledge he's joking.

'I would have to,' he informs me in a faux-serious tone, attempting to mask his smile. 'It's my job.'

'Pond nark?'

'Ecologist. But I'll let you off the hook this time, so you can get on with...'

'Going to get a drink,' I reply. 'Also important work.'

'Well, why don't I walk you there?' he suggests with a smile. 'Make sure you don't kill any endangered species on your way.'

'I'd like that,' I say with a smile of my own.

'I'm Jay,' he says as we stroll up the garden path towards the makeshift bar in the garden.

'I'm Cara,' I reply.

'What's your drink, Cara?'

I cast my eye across the table. There's something for everyone here – most of it alcoholic.

'Ooh, an elderflower cider would be lovely.'

'Coming right up,' he says before grabbing one and popping the cap off for me.

'Mum or dad?' he asks me.

'What do you mean?' I ask, swigging my drink from the bottle as delicately as possible.

'Oh, sorry, would you like a glass?' he asks.

Perhaps I'm not doing it as delicately as I thought.

'Oh, no, I'm fine,' I insist.

'OK. Well, you know when you go to a wedding and people ask you if you know the bride or the groom...'

'Oh, right, yes.' God, why do I always sound so awkward. 'Mum's side, then, I suppose. What about you? Are you on the clock? Are they using rare butterflies to announce the baby's gender?'

'Yep, I've got a box full of large blue butterflies waiting in the wings, if you'll pardon the pun,' he jokes.

'Oh, see, now you've spoiled it for me,' I insist with a playful pout.

'OK, but I did save you,' he reminds me. 'And hold your hand at the same time.'

'Hmm, that's true.'

God, I must be smiling like an idiot. I've got butterflies in my tummy – and it's been a long time since I had butterflies in my tummy. Never mind the large blue butterflies, these ones are even rarer.

'I don't even know how you did,' I admit. 'I bet you couldn't do it again if you tried.'

'OK, I like a challenge, pop that drink on the table,' he insists. 'Without warning me, flail your arms like you're falling and I'll try to grab them to save you.'

I pause for a few seconds as Jay stares at me. For someone waiting to react quickly, he still looks cool as anything.

I quickly throw my hands out, only for him to catch them.

'See, I'm a regular Superman,' he tells me.

We both spread out our fingers, clasping each other's hands as we playfully sway a little on the spot.

'Erm, what is happening?' Millsy interrupts us.

Shit, I was so captivated by Jay, I'd managed to forget there were other people in the garden. I'd definitely forgotten about Millsy, who went off to try and get the music sorted fifteen minutes ago. It's only now that I'm thinking about it that I notice he succeeded.

I quickly snatch my hands from Jay's.

'Hey, I was just getting a drink,' I say. 'I nearly fell, and this man saved me from landing in the pond.'

'Oh, did he?' Millsy says, unimpressed.

'How are you doing, Joe?' Jay asks him.

'Yeah, I'm good. Just came to get Cara.'

'Oh, you two know each other?' Jay says.

'We came together,' Millsy says.

'We're friends,' I say at the same time. Bit awkward.

'How do you two know each other?' I ask.

'We're brothers,' Jay says with a smile as he wraps an arm around Millsy, giving him a playful squeeze.

'Stepbrothers,' Millsy corrects him. 'He's my dad's wife's son from a previous marriage.'

'I'm sure she knows how stepbrothers work,' Jay teases him with a light-hearted laugh.

'Cara, we need to go sort the cake,' Millsy tells me, ignoring him.

'Oh, OK. Well, it was nice chatting with you, Jay. Thanks for not arresting me.'

'Any time,' he says with a smile.

Millsy practically pulls me back down the garden path, towards the house.

'Oh, God, was he using his job to flirt with you? That dork.'

'Erm, I thought it was kind of charming,' I reply.

I think that's what I like about Jay, after only spending fifteen minutes with him. He seems like he's a dork. I'm a dork. We're not cool like Millsy; we have our nerdy jobs and our dorky interests and we're proud of them.

'He's an absolute dick,' Millsy insists. 'And, anyway, what's with this double standard? I get in trouble for flirting at your thing, but you can do whatever you like at mine?'

'Erm, you flirted with a bride at her wedding – I wasn't flirting with the baby's dad, was I? And how was I supposed to know you had a stepbrother? You never told me you had one. And where are we even going?'

'Fran wants to see the cake. I said we'd go get it to show her, before they do the big reveal. And I didn't tell you I had a stepbrother because I wish I didn't. Everyone thinks he's so perfect – well, he isn't.'

We're at the side of the house now, away from the crowd, retrieving the red velvet cake so we can show Fran. It's probably best I get it. Millsy seems really annoyed I was talking to his stepbrother; I don't want him to drop the cake because he's in a bad mood. Then again, I'm the only person to show her clumsy side so far today.

'Why doesn't he have a Scottish accent like Mhairi?' I ask curiously.

'Oh, God, you're into him, aren't you?'

'I'm just asking!'

'Because he grew up in London, where his dad is from, and only moved up here with his mum when he was like eighteen or something.'

I reach for the white box with the cake inside.

'Oh, wow,' I say. 'Well, I couldn't have known, could I? He doesn't sound related to you, or to his mum. He just seemed like a guest.'

'Yeah, so probably don't flirt with people until you know who they are, as a rule...'

As Millsy rants, clearly horrified at the idea of me and his stepbrother, I lift the lid off the cake box. It all happens so quickly, it takes me a few seconds to realise what's happening. Millsy too. A baby-blue helium-filled balloon is floating up past our faces. It's too late to grab it. It's heading for the clouds.

'Oh, shit,' I blurt. 'Shit!'

I look down inside the empty white box – the box I thought the cake was in. I quickly return the lid, although it feels a little bit like shutting the gate after the horse has bolted.

Right on cue, Mhairi walks out of the kitchen side door with the cake in her hands.

'Joe, Cara, this cake is gorgeous. I'm just taking it to show Fran,' she tells us. 'Then it's reveal time.'

'Can't wait,' Millsy calls after her before dragging me into the kitchen.

'Please tell me that wasn't the gender-reveal balloon,' I say pointlessly, because of course it was. No one has a box with a balloon that says 'It's a boy' on it lying around, do they?

We stare at the sky helplessly as the balloon gets smaller and smaller.

'Cara, don't panic,' Millsy says firmly. 'We can fix this. I'm going to fix it and it's all going to be fine. Mhairi always has balloons and crap like that in a junk drawer in the kitchen. We just need to swap it out before she comes back.'

'OK,' I reply, puffing air from my cheeks.

I watch Millsy rifle through a kitchen drawer before pulling out a packet of balloons.

'These will have to do,' he says.

'Millsy, they're white balloons.'

'So?'

'So they know that much already,' I say. 'How can you do a gender reveal with a white balloon?'

'You blow it up. I'll think of something,' he replies.

I blow up the balloon as he rifles through the drawer again. This time he pulls out a blue marker pen before quickly scribbling the words 'It's a boy' on it. It looks awful – especially because it's just full of air, rather than helium – but it's better than nothing.

'Outside,' he says. 'Quick.'

We bolt for the door, placing the balloon in the white box before joining the party again. We go sit down next to Ruby and Nick, making polite conversation, pretending everything is fine. It must be nearly showtime.

'OK, everyone, gather round,' Rod calls out.

He's carrying the box with the balloon in so carefully, you'd think there was an actual baby inside. Little does he know, it's not worth the effort.

Fran and Dennis, her husband, stand in front of the box, waiting for their audience. Once everyone is ready they open the box together, stepping back, expecting the balloon to fly out. When nothing happens they lean forward and peer inside.

'Oh,' Fran says, reaching to lift it out, staring at it almost suspiciously. 'Erm, it's a boy.'

She seems confused – so much so, the words leave her lips so casually. Then it hits her.

'Oh my God, it's a boy,' she squeals. 'It's a boy!'

'A boy!' Dennis says, squeezing her.

Everyone cheers and coos and absolutely no one cares about the crappy balloon.

'Amazing news,' Rod says, hugging them both. 'Although it would have been amazing either way.'

'Congratulations, sis,' Millsy tells her. He looks so relieved that she's too happy to care about her rubbish balloon.

Rod leans in towards us.

'You know, I thought these balloons would be much fancier,' he tells us.

'At least it's better for the environment.'

I jump a little at the sound of Jay's voice. I hadn't realised he was next to us.

'*The environment,*' Millsy echoes, mocking Jay's voice.

Millsy pulls me to one side, away from all the excited congratulations.

'Crisis averted, no one really noticed or cared,' he reassures me.

'Thank you. Thank you, thank you, thank you. Honestly, I don't think I've ever felt so guilty in my life. Such a stupid mistake.'

'Well, you don't need to worry about it. Let's just enjoy the party.'

'That was some quick problem-solving,' I tell him.

'Yeah... maybe I would be good at escape games,' he muses.

'We'll have to test that theory some time,' I reply with a smile.

'OK, let's go get some drinks. Don't think I didn't notice you didn't get me one before, when you were flirting with *Jay*.'

'Is he really that bad?' I ask, noticing the mocking tone he said his name in.

'Honestly, everyone thinks he's so perfect. He's such a dick to me – but no one seems to notice.'

'Well, you've got me around to keep an eye on things now,' I tell him. 'I owe you after today.'

'Actually, I suppose today makes us even,' he reminds me. 'After the whole bride thing, which, I swear, was just as accidental. It's nice to know we have each other's backs though.'

'Yes, it is,' I reply.

It really is. I'd been thinking that, after today, we might call this whole plus-one pact off but, I don't know, stress aside, it's kind of nice to be here now. I'll stick it out for a few more events, see what happens.

'Oi, Joe, come here,' Rod calls.

'What's up?' Millsy replies.

'You're still on for next weekend, right?'

'Yeah, yeah,' he replies. 'Even though Fran doesn't have to go.'

'She's very pregnant,' his dad reminds him. 'She can't be doing six hours in the car to Scotland.'

Millsy sighs.

'Where are you going?' I ask, trying to dispel a little of the awkwardness.

'Pitlochry,' Rod tells me. 'It's Mhairi's mum's birthday. She has a house up there, on the edge of a loch. Gorgeous place.'

'Oh, cool.'

'And I actually like my stepgran,' Millsy tells me.

Rod pulls a face.

'And all the others, obviously.'

'Obviously,' Rod echoes with a chuckle. Then he has a brainwave. 'Cara, you should come! Are you free next weekend?'

God, I'm free every weekend. I'm so free, so many weekends, that I can't even quickly come up with a convincing lie.

'Erm, yeah, I'm free...'

'Come,' Rod insists. 'You'd love it. And Joe will have more fun if you're there, I'm sure.'

'I absolutely will,' Millsy tells me. 'If you fancy it?'

'OK, sure,' I reply. 'Sounds great.'

And just like that I've gone from trying to ditch Millsy to going on a mini-break with him.

I'm sure I'll have a laugh, so long as I don't mess up again. It would feel so on-brand for me to accidentally destroy his step-gran's birthday cake, or something. More than anything, though, I really hope Jay is going too. I know that Millsy might not like him but, I don't know, it just feels as if there's this connection between us, and I can't wait to talk to him again.

12

Working at Millsy's apartment – well, my apartment too, I guess, I do live here now, *for now* at least – has completely changed my working life.

Unlike the high-rise I used to live in, Millsy's building is much smaller, meaning there are far fewer people living here, and the ones who do live here are silent. I haven't heard so much as a ringtone since I moved in, never mind a double bass.

Not only is it quiet inside the building, but, for some reason, even though we're still in the city centre, it's a completely different vibe outside. Where I lived before, I was surrounded by life. Activity around Leeds Playhouse, BBC Yorkshire, the bus station, a bingo hall, restaurants... it was always alive outside. Here, the only thing consistently alive outside is the river, and the noise of the water is so gentle and relaxing. I think it acts like white noise, drowning out any irritating sounds. I feel as if I'm living inside a relaxation app.

Not only is this place more peaceful, but it's far more comfortable too. I love working at Millsy's big desk, sitting in his ergonomic desk chair, drinking coffees from his fancy machine.

And he's actually out this morning, for some kind of work meeting, so I have the place completely to myself.

I've done my washing, ironing, and tidied my things away. Everything in my room is in place now – I'm actually starting to feel at home here, although weirdly I've felt this way since the first night I slept here. With the room nice and tidy again, it's time to get some work done.

I'm currently designing a jungle-themed escape room, drawing up blueprints, plotting out the route participants will take through the three rooms it is set inside.

I drain my cup and stretch my back before picking up my pencil and getting back down to work. Right on cue my phone rings.

'Hello, Mum,' I say brightly as I answer. 'Having a nice day?'

It's Wednesday which means it's my mum's day off. She usually spends it with her friends and then calls in the evening for a long chat.

'I'm about to be,' she says. 'I'm outside your flat. Thought I'd pop to Leeds to find some shoes for Flora's wedding. Fancy helping me?'

'Oh,' is about all I can manage to blurt.

'Sorry, are you busy with work? I should have called first.'

When you work from home people often think that you can just stop what you're doing and do other things whenever you feel like it. Luckily, because I've been getting so much work done here, I actually can.

'No, no, it's not that, I'd love to go shopping with you,' I insist. 'It's just that, erm, I don't live there any more.'

'You moved?' she replies in disbelief.

'Erm, yes. I suppose I would have told you this evening when you called me.'

I mean, I like to think I would have, but there must be a

reason, other than just being busy, why I haven't told her yet. Perhaps it's because my roommate is a man – maybe I'm worried she'll be worried about me, or, even worse than that, that it might get her hopes up.

'OK, are you far from here?'

'Not at all,' I tell her. 'Do you want to pop in?'

'That would be nice,' she tells me. She's being polite but now I think she feels as if she needs to scope this new place out. 'I was going to drag you straight to the shops, but I'd love to see the new place.'

I give my mum directions to where I am now. It shouldn't take her much more than five minutes to get here. Just enough time for me to tidy away my work and run a brush through my hair. It turns out that very long hair is very hard work. Most days, if I have nowhere to go, I just pile it up in a bun on the top of my head.

I walk out onto the terrace just in time to see my mum taking in her surroundings outside.

'Oi, Mum,' I call out. I don't think I've ever sounded more northern.

'Cara!' she calls back. 'Look at you up there! Hello!'

'I'll buzz you in,' I call back.

I'm quite excited that my mum has turned up. I thought today was going to be otherwise uneventful (and life does seem to be a bit more eventful for me at present). It will be nice to go shopping, have lunch, have a chat.

'Oh, Cara, wow,' she says as she twirls in the centre of the open-plan living space. 'Haven't you gone up in the world!'

'I'm technically on a much lower floor than I used to live,' I joke. 'But I take your point.'

'I invited your auntie Mary to join us today – imagine her face, if I'd brought her here!'

'She said no, I take it?'

'She did.' My mum sighs. 'You know what she's like.'

'I do. I don't know why you try so hard with her.'

'Oh, you know. She's my sister. I know she's not very nice but she's the only sister I've got.'

My mum says this so casually. I guess my auntie has always been quite cold and stand-offish. If she's always been this way I suppose my mum is just used to it. I appreciate her realistic approach to the complexities of families. Life isn't a movie. You're not always going to like the people you're related to, and you're probably never going to have some big meaningful moment when things change. Sometimes horrible aunties are just horrible aunties. I have a lot of respect for my mum, though, for always trying with her no matter what.

'Oh, look at this kitchen,' my mum says as she runs a hand across the black worktops. 'Stunning! Have you had a pay rise or something?'

'I haven't... I'm sharing the place with someone else.'

'Oh, really? Well, that will be nice for you, living with someone else, sharing the costs.'

'Yeah, definitely. He owns the place, pays all the bills, and so on. The rent on my room is *so* much cheaper than I was paying for my flat in the City Heights building so it just made sense.'

'*He?*' my mum says.

Wow, nothing gets past her, does it? She was like this when I was growing up too but luckily, back then, I was just as boring as I am now. I never really got in trouble. Neither did Oliver. I would say they were lucky, to have a boring puzzle-nerd daughter and a woke feminist son, but it's probably not luck – I think they just did a good job raising us.

'He?' my mum prompts again.

'Oh, yeah, sorry. I'm living with Joe... the one I told you about.'

'You're living with him? We haven't even met him yet!'

'Well, I'm living with him, but I'm not *living with him*. I'm renting a room from him. We're just friends, Mum.'

'I'm making dinner for the family on Sunday. Your gran is coming – why don't you bring Joe over for dinner, so we can meet him, make sure he's good enough for my baby?'

I smile.

'That's very sweet of you, Mum, but I'm actually busy this weekend. I'm away.'

'Away? Away where?'

'Pitlochry. In Scotland.'

'What are you doing in Scotland? Is it for work?'

'Erm... I'm going with Joe.'

My mum furrows her brow.

'Oh, Cara. I don't know, this all sounds so fast.'

'We're just friends, honestly. I promise you. He's a really great guy, he's always got my back. I'm having a lot of fun with him.'

My mum's eyebrows shoot up.

'*Not* like that. Never like that.'

'I just want you to be safe. I don't want you to get hurt.'

'Thanks, Mum. Well, I feel the same way about you, so if we don't get you a pair of heels you can keep your balance in, who knows what will happen to you?'

'OK, love,' she replies. 'But I do want to meet him.'

'Well, you'll see him at Flora's wedding,' I remind her. 'Unless I somehow get myself uninvited.'

'You never know,' my mum says with a sigh. 'Anyway, let's go shopping.'

'I'll go make myself decent,' I tell her.

'Probably for the best,' she replies as she finds a pair of my knickers on the floor by the sofa.

Shit, I must have missed them when I was sorting out my washing earlier.

I take them from her and retreat to my bedroom.

I know that she's only looking out for me, but I really do feel as if I've got everything under control. I know how it looks though, as if it was my mum who had it good all those years, when I was a good child. Now that I'm closing in on thirty it must seem as though I've finally decided to go off the rails, moving in with a man at the drop of a hat, but I know that it's not like that. I just need to show my mum that everything is OK, that I'm much happier now. And it's true, I am much happier now – it turns out all I needed was a Millsy in my life. I know I might be getting older, I should be getting married, thinking about having kids, blah blah blah. Can't I have a little time to just be? It's hard not to feel as if I've been left behind a little, when everyone else is growing up around me, overtaking me – lapping me, in some cases. I already have old school friends who have been married *twice* while I haven't even got close to once. But I'm fine with that for now; that's to worry about at a later date. I'll go shopping with my mum, buy some more 'new me' clothes to take to Scotland with me, and I'll go and have fun.

I think I'll worry about growing old another day, thank you.

13

_____

The drive from Leeds to Pitlochry takes just over five hours, in no traffic, with no stops. Of course, road trips rarely go so smoothly so we're already over the six-hour mark. It's pretty late, and very dark, but we're almost there.

Millsy, who it turns out is a lot of fun to go on road trips with, is driving, but he doesn't actually own a car. He says there's no point, living in central Leeds, with everything on his doorstep and a train station nearby. However, neither of us fancied being cooped up on a train for at least five and a half hours so Millsy decided he would hire a car. Not just any car though, he said he was going to hire a cool car, and, boy, has he delivered.

We cruised north in a brand-new convertible Mercedes C-Class. On paper that meant nothing to me but, now that I've been in it, I can definitely see the advantages. I knew I was onto a good thing when I got in the car, closed the door and a little motorised arm popped out to hand me my seat belt. It has heaters in the headrest (which were sadly no use on a hot summer's day) and amazing air conditioning (which was very welcomed today), super-comfortable seats, and one hell of a sound system. Seriously, on a road trip is there anything more you could ask for than someone who is not only willing to stop multiple times, but will also sing along to cheesy pop songs with you?

'OK, let's get down to it,' Millsy starts.

'To what?' I ask nervously.

'To the real music,' he suggests. 'The music that shows who we really are. The guilty pleasures. What's your ultimate guilty-pleasure song?'

I bite my lip. I know the answer to this question but I'm not about to tell someone as cool as Millsy that my guilty-pleasure song is 'Escape' by Enrique Iglesias. I really should come up with a cool fake answer to this question.

'After you,' I insist with a cheeky smile. He's not getting it out of me that easy.

'Chicken,' he says with a chuckle.

Millsy calls upon the digital assistant in his phone and asks it to play none other than 'Escape' by Enrique Iglesias.

'Wow, are you kidding me?' I practically cackle.

'OK, come on, I did say it was my guilty pleasure,' he says quickly, seeming ever so slightly less sure of himself.

'No, it's not that,' I say. 'This is my favourite guilty-pleasure song too. I was just too embarrassed tell you.'

'What? I'll turn it up, then,' he replies. He seems as surprised as I do that we have such a specific song in common.

Millsy turns up the volume and starts to sing along. I actually feel comfortable enough to do the same.

'It's a shame we haven't been able to drive with the top down,' Millsy says once the song has finished. 'We just weren't on the right roads for it before it got dark. We can really make the most of it tomorrow though, driving around, enjoying the sunshine, admiring the scenery. It's so beautiful up here.'

'Looking forward to it,' I reply. 'I suppose that's one of the cool things about driving somewhere in the dark. You get there, go to bed, wake up and you're in the heart of it.'

'And it's about to get a whole lot darker,' he says as we turn off the well-lit main road onto a much darker, narrower one. 'Honestly, it might look like nothing but walls of darkness outside but you won't believe what's hiding behind them.'

The road is narrow with absolutely no lights on it. The only light we have is from the car headlights but, other than seeing trees that line the winding road, I can't see a thing. It's kind of scary.

'Don't worry, I know this road well and I'm taking it slow,' he reassures me, reading my mind. 'What you can't see on your left is just loads of trees. What you can't see on your right is Loch Faskally and the River Tummel. The road runs alongside the river all the way to my gran's house. My gran's house is cool. It's pretty big, right on the edge of Loch Tummel – the loch is at the bottom of her garden! And she lives there all alone. There are farms about ten minutes away in both directions, and some kind of massive, castle-looking house across the loch – not exactly easy to pop over to in an emergency. My gran does have a boat though.'

'Sounds like a gorgeous place,' I reply.

It's interesting, isn't it? Millsy talks about his stepmum, and his supposedly evil stepbrother, but when it comes to his step-gran, I'm starting to notice he just calls her gran. I suppose, when he said he really liked her, he meant it, and you can tell by the way he talks about her that he thinks she's great. She's just his gran, as far as he is concerned. That's so lovely.

'What's your gran's name?' I ask.

'Iona,' he replies. 'She's turning eighty-five this time.'

'My gran is eighty-eight,' I tell him. 'She still lives in her own home too, on her own. She's such a cool, sweet lady. I'd do well to grow up to be like her.'

I pause for a second.

'Well, I say that... I'm nearly thirty. Funny that I want to grow up to be like her – she'd had both my mum and my auntie long before she was my age.'

'Do you want kids?' Millsy asks me.

'Yeah, but not tonight,' I reply with a smile. 'One day, biological clock permitting.'

Millsy nods thoughtfully.

'You already got a couple knocking around?' I tease.

'Sadly not,' he says. 'But I'm firmly of the opinion that – oh, shit, Cara, look!'

I only have a split second to wonder where Millsy was going with that sentence before I realise what's made him change the subject so quickly. In the centre of the long, winding road, in the light of our headlights, there's a deer running in front of us, straight down the road, like a car. We follow it slowly, as if we're in traffic behind it.

'I've never seen anything like it,' I reply.

'Neither have I,' he says.

'How many cars do you think are actually using this road after 11 p.m.?'

'Not many,' Millsy says. 'But, don't worry, we're sticking with it. It's safe in front of us.'

For a few minutes we just marvel at this deer leading us along the road to Iona's house. Eventually, as the forest on my side of the road lowers to the same level as the road, the deer darts to the side before disappearing into the darkness.

'That was cool,' Millsy says. He glances at his satnav. 'And now, we are... here.'

Right on cue a house appears on the right-hand side of the road – you can only spot it once you're alongside it, when the lights in the windows aren't being hidden by the trees that surround it.

As we pull onto the driveway a security light comes on. It's still too dark to see much, but I can tell that there are two cars parked outside, and although I can't see the house properly, I can tell it's quite big from how many lit-up windows I can spy.

'Who's here?' I ask.

'That's my gran's car,' he says, nodding towards a small red, old-looking car. 'And my dad's next to it, so he and Mhairi are here too.'

'No siblings, then?' I ask.

'Nah, Fran wasn't up to the drive,' he replies.

I mean, obviously I'm only really asking to find out if Jay is going to be here. I guess he isn't.

Millsy presses a button on the car remote, which pops open the boot.

'So cool,' he says to himself. 'It's making me want a car.'

He grabs our bags and we head to the front door. Millsy's hands are full so I press the doorbell. It only takes a few seconds for Mhairi to appear.

'Oh, you're here! Hello,' she says. 'We were starting to think you might have stopped somewhere for the night.'

'Ah, you know what the drive is like,' Millsy says. 'A few hold-ups and you're hours behind. And then, as we were driving along this road, we had this deer running in front of us. We had to crawl behind it.'

He's so cute, telling the story like an excitable little kid.

'All right, Joe, you don't need to make excuses,' she says. She seems a little grumpy, but I imagine it's just because she's tired. 'Your dad was tired from the drive so he's gone to bed. Mum said to let her know when you were here, but she's in her bedroom, so I won't disturb her. Is that OK?'

I imagine Mhairi is just a little bit annoyed about being the person who had to sit up late to let us in, but it really knocks the wind out of Millsy's sail.

'Yeah, no worries,' he replies. 'You get to bed.'

'Thanks,' she says almost sarcastically. 'You're in the bedroom off the lounge. Goodnight to you both.'

'Night,' we call after her, perfectly in sync.

Millsy shrugs it off.

'Well, fancy a quick tour of the house?' he asks. 'We'll probably avoid upstairs, if people are up there sleeping, but that leaves two other floors – and that's where all the best bits are.'

He seems as if he's perked up again, now that Mhairi has left us.

'I'd love that,' I reply.

Immediately on our left is the kitchen. It's a large, L-shaped room that wraps around the front driveway. From there we go through to the open-plan living/dining room. It's an absolutely massive room, with a fireplace smack bang in the middle of it that you can walk around. Two of the long walls are made entirely of glass, looking out over what Millsy tells me is the back garden. He told me that, if it were light, I'd be able to see the loch, which is so strange because right now it's like looking at black wallpaper.

Millsy takes me downstairs, to a lower level. It's below the ground floor at the front of the house, but it isn't a basement – not that I can tell right now, given how dark it is outside. Apparently the back garden slopes down towards the loch. I can't wait to see it in the daylight.

'So, this is my favourite room,' Millsy announces as he leads me through. 'This is the party room.'

'Oh my God,' I blurt. 'This is just... wow.'

It's a large room – it seems as if it's the only room on this floor – and it's full of fun stuff. There is a large pool table in the middle of the room, and, while I don't know much about pool tables, I'm going to say this is a full-size one, because I didn't actually realise they were so big. There is a large flatscreen TV on the wall, and a bar. And then there are the books. One corner of the room has a big, comfortable-looking chair, and two walls with shelves that are absolutely stuffed with books.

'Wow,' I say again. 'Wow, wow, wow.'

'I know that it might seem a bit weird, for a granny to have a room like this in her basement, but it used to be the family's summer house, where they would all go for holidays a few times a year. Last year my gran decided she wanted to live here full time. Enjoy the rest of her retirement somewhere beautiful.'

'Your gran sounds seriously cool,' I tell him. I'm sure he already knows.

'She really is. OK, last but not least of the rooms I can show you without Mhairi murdering me...'

We head back up the stairs, through the living room and along a short corridor. At the end there are two doors, one on each side.

'On the left is the downstairs bathroom,' he tells me. 'There's a toilet, a sink and a shower in there. The bath is in the upstairs bathroom. Then here, on the right, is our room.'

In the centre of the large bedroom stands a four-poster bed. The frame is made from dark, twisted wood, which someone has wrapped fairy lights around. It's not just a wide bed, it's a tall bed, too. So far off the floor, in fact, that there is a little stool at each side that you use for climbing into bed.

Opposite the bed is yet another large window. The curtains are open but there's nothing to see.

'I'm sure it goes without saying now,' Millsy starts, 'but there is one hell of a view out there. Whenever I come here, I always want to stay in this bedroom, but I rarely get to. I guess, because you're with me...'

'About that,' I start. 'People know we're just friends, right?'

'They do,' he tells me. 'I keep telling them but I'm starting to get the impression that they think I'm lying, so that they think I've changed. Like I'm pretending we're platonic, just to look good, so...'

I nod thoughtfully. That makes sense, I suppose; I'll just have to be more obvious about the facts.

'Don't worry though. I usually wind up sleeping in my gran's old recliner chair in the living room. I'm sure I would have been if you weren't here with me. It's no trouble at all – you should have this room.'

I think for a second as I watch Millsy rifling around in his bag on the bedroom floor, before removing a pair of shorts, a T-shirt and his toothbrush.

'Wait, you don't have to do that,' I tell him. 'We're adults, we're friends... we can share a bed.'

'You really don't have to do that...'

'I know I don't but, come on, this isn't a movie. We'll be absolutely fine. We're not going to fall out – or fall in love – just because we sleep in a huge bed together, without building a pillow barricade down the middle, or sleeping at opposite ends, or whatever the cliché says we're supposed to do.'

He laughs.

'Are you sure?'

'Positive,' I reply.

Millsy uses the bathroom first, returning in his shorts and T-shirt. I'm being mature about this but, for some reason, I don't want to actually watch him get into bed, so I hurry off to get changed and brush my teeth. By the time I get back to the bedroom Millsy is already in bed and I don't know why I thought it would be any less awkward this way.

I pull back the covers and use my little footstool to climb in next to him. Thankfully the bed really is big enough for us to be nowhere near each other – in fact, you could probably fit a third person in between us, although that's hardly going to make this less awkward, is it?

'You OK with the light off?' he asks.

'Sure,' I reply.

It isn't until Millsy flicks off the light on his bedside table that I realise why he was asking. It's dark. Not just dark, pitch black. I can't see my own hand in front of my face. I don't remember the last time I was in such deep, empty darkness. Living in the city, there are always lights somewhere, but even at home, living in a village, there were still plenty of things outside giving off light.

'Sweet dreams,' he says.

I was so lost in the darkness it gives me a little jump scare.

'Yeah, see you in the morning,' I reply.

It's so strange, being here in the darkness. On the one hand, it should be very easy to pretend that I'm here all alone – well, unless I turn on a light or roll over three times, I can't even tell that Millsy is next to me. But... I don't know... there's something about knowing that he is there, next to me, in bed with me, that gives me this feeling that I can't quite put my finger on. I feel as if I'm blindfolded. I remember what Millsy said, about women wanting to sleep with him when he had his Leo the Lion costume, because they found something sexy about not being able to see the person inside the costume, the anonymity, the danger... I quickly push those thoughts out of my head. That is absolutely not what is happening here. It's just creepy, being in a room with someone you can't see. It's not a sex scene, it's more like something from a horror movie, right?

Anyway, we're only here for two nights, and I'm sure tomorrow night things will seem more normal. And then it's back to Leeds, where we have separate bedrooms, so it's going to be fine.

The sooner I fall asleep, the sooner I can wake up, and then I get to see this place in the daylight. I'm looking forward to that more than anything. That's far more my scene, and my kind of mystery, than hooking up with people while blindfolded.

Still, if that's true, I wonder why I can't quite get it out of my head...

14

I have woken up in darkness not unlike the darkness I fell asleep in but, after glancing at my phone, I know that it's 10 a.m., so it's definitely morning.

I dare to roll over in bed, but Millsy isn't there. He must have closed the curtains when he got up, to give me some privacy in the daylight.

I'm facing the bedroom door now, that's how I notice it slowly opening, a small amount of light creeping in a little bit at a time. For a moment I just stare at it. It might be morning now, but I'm still in semi-darkness, still here in this room all alone, in this house, in the middle of nowhere, with no idea where anyone is...

I listen carefully for signs of life in the house. That's when I hear the strangest noise... heavy breathing, perhaps? Coming from my side of the bed now. No, not heavy breathing, sniffing, it's...

I flip over quickly and glance down at the floor.

'Oh my God! Hello!'

I jump out of bed and crouch down on the floor to give the

gorgeous little white Scottie dog all the love and attention the little cutie deserves.

A few seconds later Millsy comes running in.

'Dougie, there you are,' he says. He flicks the light on. 'Sorry, Cara, did he wake you?'

'No, no, I was already awake,' I tell him.

Dougie licks my neck, trying to advance his kisses towards my face.

'Come on, Dougie, give her some space,' Millsy insists.

As he makes a move towards Dougie, Dougie runs out of the room.

'Anyway, good morning,' he says. 'Sleep well?'

'I did,' I reply.

'Were you having bad dreams?' he asks.

'No, I... Oh, my dream has just come back to me a bit – you were in it,' I tell him.

'Do you remember what was happening?'

'I don't,' I reply. 'I just kind of remember you being there...'

'Huh. Because you were really writhing around at one point. I thought something awful must be happening...'

'Oh...' I feel myself blush. 'Nope, that's it. I don't remember at all.'

And I really hope I never do. Given what was on my mind before I fell asleep, he was either killing me or... or... God, I feel as if I'm blushing even harder, if that's even possible.

'Anyway, the adults are going out for a walk. Would you rather just chill out here? Have some food, take in the view – or you could try out the fancy bath.'

'That would be great,' I reply. 'I'll just shove some clothes on quickly so I can meet your gran before they set off.'

'OK, sure,' he says. 'I'll leave you to it, see you out there.'

As soon as Millsy is gone I feel my cheeks start to cool down. I shove some clothes on, brush my hair, and pop into the bathroom to wash my face and brush my teeth.

I walk along the little corridor into the living room where Millsy's dad, Rod, his stepmum, Mhairi, and his gran, Iona, are sitting. I need to keep reminding myself of their names, so that I don't forget.

'Good morning,' Rod says. 'Sleep well?'

'Oh, amazingly, thank you,' I reply.

I can see that the three of them are all dressed and ready to head out for their walk.

'This is my gran, Iona,' Millsy tells me. 'Gran, this is Cara.'

'Hello, hen,' Iona says. She pulls herself up from her chair and heads over to give me a hug.

'Happy birthday,' I tell her brightly.

'Oh, thank you,' she replies.

Iona looks great for her age. She's small and skinny and moves around easily. It's great that she's still so active. I suppose people usually think of old ladies as the type who just want to sit in their chair and knit but it's just not true.

'We're going to go for a walk,' she says. 'Nothing too far, but Millsy says you're going to have some breakfast.'

'Yes,' I reply. 'We'll have a proper chat when you get back.'

As the three of them filter out, it occurs to me that she calls Millsy, well, Millsy. Not Joe, as the rest of the family does.

'Oh, Millsy, remember about Dougie,' Iona says, popping her head back in the room.

'Will do,' he calls after her. 'See you soon.'

'Does Dougie not like walks?' I ask Millsy, once it's just me, him and the dog.

'Well, he's getting a bit older now. Sometimes, when you walk him, he sits down and refuses to move. Gran was reminding me not to let him out in the back garden without his lead, because he sometimes forgets that he can't swim and jumps into the loch.'

It suddenly occurs to me that I'm standing in the middle of the living room surrounded by windows, but I haven't looked outside yet.

Sure enough, at the bottom of the back garden, through the trees, I can see the loch shining under the sunshine.

'Oh, wow,' I say.

'We could have something to eat, put Dougie's lead on and then take a stroll down the garden, if you like. You won't believe how far you can see.'

'I'd love that,' I reply.

'OK, well, how about you go upstairs and have a bath, get ready, and while you're doing that, I'll make us some... pancakes?'

I bite my lip.

'God, you say all the right things,' I tell him.

He just laughs.

'Bathroom is at the top of the stairs, there are clean towels on the side, I checked.'

I don't need much persuading. I grab the bag with my toiletries in, along with my clean clothes, and head upstairs.

I had heard that the bathroom was nice – but I had no idea just how nice it was.

At the back of the room, with beautiful granite tiles and cream candles dotted everywhere, there's a large free-standing copper bath. I've never seen anything like it in real life. Well, the only baths I've ever been in have been made of some kind of plastic, and they're usually squashed against a wall with a shower above them. This is like something out of a hotel I probably couldn't afford to stay in.

I use the delicious-smelling products to run myself a deep bath before gently lowering myself in and lying back. Oh, God, this is the life. I think I could stay here all day – I could even sleep in here, save me having to share a bed with Millsy again. Who am I kidding though? It wasn't so bad sharing a bed with him, and now he's making me breakfast. There is a lot to be said for platonic relationships with men. I'm almost certain I could happily marry him and live like this forever. Although I suppose that's easy to say now, but God knows what I'd be dreaming about if I signed myself up for a sexless marriage.

Anyway, that's a thought for another time. All I need to think about now is absolutely nothing. I just need to relax, enjoy my bath, and then go and eat my breakfast. Oh, and then we're walking down the garden to see the loch. What an amazing morning I'm having so far, and it's only going to get better from here. It could almost make me want to rush my bath but, for now, I'm going to make the most of how relaxed I feel. And I can't think of a single thing that could ruin this moment for me.

15

I feel the bubbles gently tickling the sides of my face as I relax in the bath with everything but my face under the water. With only my mouth, nose and eyes above the surface, the smooth warm water caresses almost every inch of me and it's glorious. I had no idea deep baths could be so relaxing. Well, I didn't have a bath in my old flat, and even in the one at my parents' house I always had my head, boobs, knees or a combination of them poking out of the water. I would almost have to let my different body parts take it in turns to be under the water, but not here, not in this amazing bath.

There's something so peaceful about having your ears underwater. It's the way the water fills them, blocking out the sound from the room, sort of like when you pick up a seashell and raise it to your ear to 'hear the sea'.

My state of ultimate relaxation is disturbed when I notice a faint sound. Is that... is that a ringing in my ears? Do I have tinnitus? Is that even what tinnitus sounds like? Like a sort of strange alarm sound.

I sit up quickly and realise that the noise isn't in my head (or my ears), it's in the house. It sounds like a smoke alarm.

I spring from the water, giving my body the fastest once-over with a towel before throwing on my clothes and my trainers, which I'd thankfully brought up with me. I dash down the stairs with a level of athleticism I didn't know I had in me and, for some reason I don't run out of the front door, I run to the kitchen, where the alarm is coming from, where I left Millsy.

I breathe a sigh of relief when I realise that he's absolutely fine. He's just wafting a tea towel under the smoke alarm. The room is a little smoky but there are no signs of a fire. With the large patio door open in the living room the smell will hopefully drift outside, and the fresh air coming in will clear out the smell of smoke before people get back.

'What happened?' I shout over the alarm.

'Huh?' he calls back.

'What happened?' I shout again, raising my voice even louder. The alarm cuts off halfway through my sentence.

'I accidentally set the pan on fire,' he says, a little more casually than I would have expected.

'Well, I did figure it would have been an accident,' I reply. 'You OK? Where's the pan?'

'I ran outside with it,' he tells me. 'Don't worry, I put it out.'

'Maybe we should check,' I suggest. 'Imagine if you destroyed your gran's garden – imagine if it spread to the house.'

'OK, yeah,' he says. 'Let's go.'

Sure enough, on the patio outside the large sliding door, there is a frying pan with rather black-looking contents inside it. It smells a little smoky but the fire is definitely out.

'Phew,' he says. 'Crisis averted.'

'Thank God,' I say. 'I feel like things always go wrong around us. It's like we're jinxed.'

Millsy just laughs.

I glance down the garden, towards the loch, tilting my head to try and get a better look through the trees, as though that's going to help. Where we're standing right now the trees hide the view.

'Want to go look?' Millsy suggests. 'There's a jetty down there. You can walk out onto it, see up and down the loch. It's an incredible view.'

'I'd love to,' I reply.

At the bottom of the garden, at the edge of the water, there is a wooden boathouse and a small jetty. I walk down the hill, making sure to keep my balance as I head for the jetty to take in the view – we want absolutely no more accidents.

From here I can see far and wide across the loch. The water is so flat and so clear, it's acting like a mirror, reflecting an exact copy of the view. It's almost creepy, like an optical illusion, or something... It's just mesmerising.

'Wow,' I blurt. I feel as if I'm saying that a lot here. 'It's just so... *what is that?*'

In the centre of the loch there's a small island. Too small to have anything on it, apart from plant life, but there's something else on there...

'Is that...?' I narrow my eyes to get a better look. 'Is that Dougie?'

'Fuck,' Millsy blurts. 'Fuck, fuck, fuck. He must have got out when I ran out with the pan. Fuck.'

'OK, wait, let's not panic,' I start. 'He swam out there, right, so he must be able to swim back? Did your gran say he couldn't swim?'

'He... he sort of forgets that he can't swim, tries to swim, swims a bit, then gets stuck.'

'At least he's safe on the island,' I reply. 'Maybe he can swim back? If he sees us waiting for him?'

'Maybe,' Millsy replies, running a hand through his hair as he puffs air from his cheeks. 'Dougie. Come here, Dougie. Good boy, you can do it.'

Dougie approaches the edge of the island, looks down at the water, and retreats a few steps. There is no way he's going to swim back.

'Even if I swam out to him, it's no use, there's no way I can swim back holding onto him,' Millsy says as he anxiously shifts his weight between his feet. He doesn't take his eyes off Dougie for a second.

'Is it deep?' I ask curiously.

'I'm pretty sure my gran once told me it was nearing 150 feet deep, at its deepest point, so...'

'OK. Erm...' God, that is deep, isn't it? 'So... did you say there was a boat?'

Millsy finally takes his eyes off Dougie and darts towards the boathouse.

'Dammit, it's locked,' he says, tugging on the side-door padlock.

Feeling pretty confident that Dougie will not get back in the water, I hurry over to Millsy, to see if I can help.

I watch as he walks a lap of the wooden boathouse, checking each piece of wood to see if he can loosen it, explaining as he does so that the main door for the boat opens from the inside. The boathouse is in good nick though; there's no way he's getting through the walls. Not without an axe, but I don't think I'll suggest that just yet.

'Shit, there's no way to get in,' Millsy says. 'Seriously, Cara, my gran loves that dog, and I love my gran. We need to save him before she gets back.'

Perhaps I should suggest finding an axe...

'Is there no other way in?' I ask.

'Well... yeah, actually, there's water inside. I could jump in the loch and swim under the door, open it from the inside.'

'Can't you just kick the door in?' I ask. 'I really don't think jumping in the loch and swimming under the door is a great idea.'

'The way the hinges go, if I kick the door in, I'll destroy it.'

'I'm really not sure this is a good idea, Millsy,' I say nervously.

'I honestly think this is our only shot at doing it without anyone finding out,' he replies.

'Can we not just search the house for a key?'

'There's no key,' he tells me. 'Just a padlock. OK, I'm just going to do it, no more messing around, OK?'

'Millsy, wait,' I say quickly. I stop him just in time.

'What?'

'What kind of padlock is it?' I ask.

'Cara, seriously? Is now really the time to nerd-out over padlocks?'

Millsy rolls his eyes.

'I'm *not* nerding-out,' I insist, making my way towards the boathouse door. I crouch down and examine the padlock. 'Ah, see, it's a number padlock...'

'What, you think my gran is going to have an obvious combo and we can guess it? Life isn't an escape game,' he tells me with a bit of a chuckle. He seems too anxious for a full-blown mocking laugh.

'Well, there is that,' I reply. 'But I can absolutely crack these.'

'Crack them?'

'Yeah, like, open them without the code,' I tell him. 'When I worked in the escape rooms, before I designed them, all the time we would have people accidentally resetting locks to new combinations, or staff members doing it, ruining the flow of people's games and, well, at some point, everyone just learns how to do it.'

'Really? How?'

I'm not sure he believes me.

'OK, watch closely,' I tell him. 'For next time you're here, without me, and you don't have anyone to save your arse.'

'Fair,' he replies. 'Go on.'

'So you pull down on the lock, away from the shackle, and hold it there. Then you slowly move the number dials, one at a time, until you find the one that is hardest to move.'

I explain the process as I'm doing it, not only to try and get Dougie back over here before Iona gets back, but because I worry that, if I'm not quick, Millsy will just dive into the loch.

'Then you move the dial and, when you're on the right number, you'll hear a louder click. And you just do that three times and then, with the fourth one... there are only nine numbers so... voila!'

The padlock pops open in my hand.

'Cara, Cara, Cara, you big nerd, thank you,' Millsy tells me.

He kisses me on the cheek, which makes my cheeks flush. I quickly turn to look out towards Dougie so Millsy can't see my face.

I shrug casually. I always hoped my lock-picking skills would come in useful for something real. Maybe working in an escape room wasn't a totally stupid job after all. Oh, and I suppose it landed me the real job I have now, which is probably a far better benefit, right? Still, it felt cool (in the most uncool way) to pop that lock open.

Millsy goes through the side door, opening up the main door from inside the boathouse before hopping into the wooden row boat.

'Come with me?' he asks. 'You could hold Dougie while I row, make sure he doesn't jump out?'

'Of course,' I reply, although I'm a little uneasy about crossing the water – water that is potentially 150 feet deep – in the tiny wooden boat. Still, I hop in, because Millsy needs my help.

As we slowly make our way across to poor little Dougie the view completely opens up to us. I can see so far, in so many directions, and so many different things too. The loch, the castle across the water, and there are trees for days!

Millsy gets us safely to the island. I grab Dougie, who is very soggy and kind of smelly, and we head straight back to the jetty. With Dougie safe in my arms, and the two of us standing back on dry land, Millsy carefully returns the boat to the boathouse and locks the door, clicking the padlock shut before shuffling the numbers to lock it again.

'I probably should have looked at the combination,' he says with a laugh. 'Memorised it in case I—'

Millsy takes one step too far backwards, wobbling back and forth for a couple of seconds, holding out his arms to regain his balance, flapping them as if it might just save him, but it's no good. He topples over with nowhere to land but the loch below him. It's only shallow water, by the jetty, and I know he can swim. Still, I'm pretty sure he didn't want to do that.

'Shit,' he calls out as he falls down. Despite him falling back into the water, every inch of him getting absolutely soaked, he calls this out in such a casual way. Sort of like you would if your pen rolled off your desk or something else equally low stakes.

He scrambles to his feet, the weight of the water in his clothes making him walk funny as he climbs to the shore.

Millsy stands next to me. He's soaking wet.

'Shit,' he says softly. He blows air through his lips to blast off the water running down his face.

I can't help but laugh.

'Don't worry, I was about to dry my hair – you can use my hairdryer,' I tell him.

'It's a good job I didn't have my phone in my pocket,' he says as we make our way back to the house.

Once the three of us are safely back inside Millsy throws on some dry clothes and washes the evidence of burnt pancakes from the pan while I blow-dry Dougie's coat. With everything that belongs here restored to its normal state, it's just me and Millsy who look wrong, both with wet hair.

'Cara, seriously, thank you so much, you've saved the day again,' he tells me.

'It was nothing,' I insist.

'No, it wasn't nothing, it was seriously cool. Come here.'

Millsy wraps his arms around me and squeezes me tightly; right as Rod, Mhairi and Iona walk through the door.

'Hello,' Rod says brightly. 'Are you two...?'

He stops what he's saying the second he claps eyes on us before rejigging what he was going to say.

'Are you two wet?' he asks.

'I had a bath,' I tell him honestly. Well, it's true, so it should sound true, right?

'You both had a bath?' he asks.

'Yeah,' Millsy replies quickly.

Rod's eyebrows shoot up.

'Oh, no, not together,' I quickly insist.

'Group baths, an obnoxious car...' a voice chimes in. 'Very on-brand, Joe.'

Shit! The last person through the door is Jay, Millsy's dreamy stepbrother. I thought he wasn't coming. Double shit, he thinks I've been taking baths with Millsy!

'We had separate baths, didn't we?' I insist.

'Oh, absolutely. Cara hogged it, actually. I only had time for a quick dip.'

'Is that really what the kids are calling it these days?' Iona asks with a cheeky laugh as she hangs up her coat.

Damn, she's such a cool older person. I can't help but giggle.

'So, how are you?' Jay asks me.

'Oh, I'm—'

'We're pretty busy, right now, actually,' Millsy informs him. 'Come on, Cara, we've got that thing to do.'

'Catch you later, I guess,' I call out to Jay as Millsy leads me off to our bedroom. I can't imagine that is a good look either, not if I want people to believe we really are just friends.

'Yeah, see you later,' he calls after me.

'Little bit rude, Millsy,' I tell him once we're alone. 'And what are we busy with right now?'

'He's a little bit *something*,' he replies. I imagine a swear word replacing the word something. I never make my wittiest remarks when I'm annoyed either.

'Anyway, I'm taking you into Pitlochry, to a café, to buy you lunch, seeing as though I, you know, set your breakfast fire. Oh, and to say thank you, for saving the day.'

'That's very sweet of you,' I tell him. 'Thank you. I'm excited to see the drive to town in the daylight.'

'It's amazing,' he tells me. 'Plus, now Jay is here, I just want to get out. Absolute trip-ruiner.'

I nod. Funny he should say that because, as far as I'm concerned, this trip just got a whole lot better now Jay has turned up.

16

Last night, when we were driving along the road to Millsy's gran's house, if I knew then what I know now, I'm not sure I would have found it such a relaxing and enjoyable ride.

When Millsy told me that the road ran alongside the loch, he wasn't kidding. In some places the loch is only a few feet away from the road. Far too close for comfort given the fact I learned today about the depth of the loch. Even with Millsy's reassurances that he knows the road well, I think I'm going to be insisting that we only drive along the road in the daylight from now on.

Pitlochry is a seriously cute place. It's very touristy but in a way that isn't in your face. The main part of town is on, or just off, the main street. There are a few pubs, a lot of shops selling shortbread, tartan and Irn-Bru-flavoured things, and then there are the cafés. There were so many to choose from but Millsy recommended a place called Ella's. He must come here a lot when he visits Pitlochry because the ladies working there all recognised him. Then again, wherever Millsy goes, women pay attention to him.

We looked over the menu and naturally I was drawn to the dessert items. I ordered a cup of tea as I ummed and ahhed over what to eat. Turns out, if you're an indecisive eater, with a willing friend, you can order a dessert platter that features mini versions of each sweet treat: brownies, blondies, millionaire's shortbread, chocolate crispies. The only possible downside is the impossibly romantic presentation of this heart-shaped platter. I do wonder how many girls Millsy has brought for one of these over the years but I honestly don't care because I would sit down at that table and eat heart-shaped chocolate, with rose petals scattered around the table, with absolutely anyone just to eat it again. Not right now though. Right now, after putting away too much food, we're walking it off.

The scenery in Pitlochry isn't limited to lochs and trees. Millsy took me to see Pitlochry Dam, which you can actually walk across and peep inside. At the other side there is a fish ladder – apparently the fish use it to travel upstream, up the River Tummel, but I can't for the life of me figure out how just by looking at it, and I didn't see any fish using it, hard as I tried.

So now we're just strolling along the edge of the river, chatting about anything and everything, taking the long route to the Co-op where Millsy wants to stop for supplies for tonight's gathering. It's weird but, if you'd told me a few weeks ago that I would be doing this now, I would have imagined it all feeling really awkward and forced. Somehow it just feels right.

'So, what do you think of the house?' he asks me.

'It's gorgeous. Absolutely stunning,' I reply.

'Yeah, Loch Tummel certainly puts the Leeds Liverpool Canal to shame,' he says with a laugh. 'Could you live somewhere like this?'

'You know what? I don't think I could. I think it's too isolated for me. Isolated can be good but I work from home so... I'm imagining something like *The Shining* right now.'

'The book or the movie?' Millsy asks curiously.

'That's a very good question,' I reply, excited that the conversation has gone in a direction that taps into something I feel passionate about. 'The movie, one hundred per cent. I'm not worried about the place being haunted – it wouldn't need to be. It's the descent into madness that terrifies me. I do like the book, but I love the way the movie is a little more ambiguous. Is it haunted? Is he mad? And, oh my God, that maze. What I'd give for a go in that maze. Just, you know, preferably without the added pressure of my psycho dad chasing me with an axe. That would make one hell of an escape game though...'

Millsy laughs.

'I like that,' he says. 'My usual... the type of people I usually hang out with don't want to chat about movies.'

'Do you want to star in movies?' I ask curiously.

Millsy often talks about his past theatre roles, but never about what he's doing now. I doubt his theatre gigs made him enough money for him to live off for the rest of his life.

'I've had... bits in movies,' he tells me kind of vaguely. 'But yes, I want to do more. My agent is currently working on some things. Watch this space.'

I decide not to delve deeper. I get the feeling he's telling me as much as he wants to.

When we get to the supermarket Millsy leads me straight to the booze.

'I know my dad has food covered but I thought I'd get some extra drinks, make sure there's something you like.'

'What does your gran like to drink? Perhaps I could take her some to go with her chocolates?' I suggest.

I didn't know what to buy Iona for her birthday, having never met her, and I wanted it to be something I knew for sure that she would like, so Millsy helpfully steered me in the direction of her favourite sweet treat.

'You know, not a very grandma drink, but she likes rum. My dad loves it too. Do you drink rum?'

'I used to love it but, well, let's just say there was a night out where I drank too much. I can't stand the stuff now.'

'That sounds like an interesting story,' Millsy says. He claps his hands together excitedly, ready to listen.

'Erm, it's not, actually,' I confess. 'I just drank too much of it on a rare work night out and it made me feel so sick that I went right off it. I can't stress enough how boring my life is – or at least it was until I started hanging around with you. I get into scrapes now – I never used to get into scrapes!'

'We're having fun though, right?'

'We absolutely are,' I reply.

'Well, that's all that matters,' Millsy says. 'I wonder what sort of trouble we can get ourselves into tonight.'

He waggles his eyebrows playfully.

'I have no idea,' I say with a laugh. 'But I'll bet there's something.'

There's always something these days.

17

Iona's birthday dinner was an informal affair, with a buffet spread out across the large table, so that everyone could help themselves. Food ranged from classics, like cocktail sausages and cheese and pineapple on sticks, to local foods. The food Millsy hyped up the most beforehand was the 'square sausage sandwiches', which, for some reason, when I thought of them I imagined sort of rectangular sausages, rather than the slices of sausage loaf I was ultimately presented with. They were delicious though, in local bread, with ketchup. It was all really casual with the option to sit at the dining table or on the sofas. Now, all suitably stuffed, we're all gathered around the table.

After we give Iona her presents we're going to move to the party room, where various relatives will be joining us. I asked Millsy who but, I suppose because they're only his step-relatives that he never really sees, he doesn't think he can confidently tell me who is who. I told him to pay attention when people introduce themselves to me, so that he can learn their names. He suggested I could just learn names for both of us but it's not as if I'm going to be here next year to remind him, is it? Not unless I can somehow get Jay to fall head over heels in love with me. Not going to be easy when, despite my best efforts to insist nothing is going on, I'm sharing a bed with his brother.

Iona was really happy with her chocolates and the bottle of rum I picked up in town. Millsy definitely steered me in the right direction.

We're currently sitting around the table still, waiting for Jay to return with his present. Apparently it's in his car.

'Notice how he says, "It's in the Range", rather than, "It's in the car",' Millsy whispers to me. 'And for someone so preoccupied with the environment, that's not a very environmentally friendly car, is it?'

'No, not like a convertible Mercedes,' I reply through a smirk.

'Erm, that's a hire car,' he reminds me. 'And I only chose a convertible so you could make the most of the views while I was driving. The Mercedes was all they had left.'

'Only teasing,' I tell him with a friendly squeeze of his arm.

Millsy is easily the most confident person I have ever met. He's so outgoing, so sure of himself, so content with who he is... apart from when Jay is around. There's something about Jay that gets to him, bringing out his insecurities, and I can tell that he's trying to keep a lid on *something*. I suppose it must be difficult, having a stepbrother like Jay, when he appears to be the perfect man. That must be hard to compete with. I mean, take it from someone whose brother is a much better feminist than she is, you can't help but measure yourself against your siblings. He may only be his stepbrother but that only seems to make their rivalry stronger.

After a few minutes, Jay is back with a very large, beautifully wrapped present. I'd say it's about up to my chest in height. It's sitting on a little wooden board with wheels, to help him move it around. The present is wrapped in shiny gold paper with a large red ribbon tied around it.

'Here we go, Gran,' he announces.

Iona jumps up excitedly.

'Oh, Jay, you shouldn't have,' she insists, still with no idea what is inside.

'It's nothing you don't deserve,' he replies. 'Go on, open it.'

Iona gleefully tears away the wrapping paper to reveal a new armchair.

'It's an electric recliner,' Jay tells her. 'To replace your old one.'

'Oh, Jay... Oh... Thank you,' Iona gushes. 'So thoughtful, thank you.'

'Go on, then, try it out,' Rod insists, jumping up to help Jay put it into place.

'Oh, yes, lovely,' Iona says as she makes herself comfortable in the cream leather chair.

'These are the buttons to recline it,' Jay says as he presses one.

Everyone coos impressed sounds – everyone apart from Millsy, of course. I don't think he'd let himself be impressed by anything Jay did. It does seem like a really thoughtful present though; Iona's old chair was looking pretty tired.

'Joe, why don't you bring your present over to Gran, so she can stay in her chair?' Jay suggests.

'OK,' Millsy replies through lightly gritted teeth.

I watch as he pulls a gift bag from under the table. It seems so small, compared to a chair, but I'm sure he's got her something awesome.

Millsy hands Iona the bag, leaning forward to kiss her on the cheek.

'Happy birthday, Gran,' he says.

'Aww, thank you, darling,' she replies. 'Let's see what's in here, shall we?'

Millsy sits back down next to me. There's a confident smile on his face. Whatever he's got Iona, he thinks it's going to kick the chair's arse.

As Iona carefully lifts the present out of the bag I narrow my eyes. Is that...?

'Is that a *Walking Dead* box set?' Jay blurts in disbelief.

'It is,' Millsy says.

'What?' Mhairi says, rushing over to inspect it. 'Let me see.'

'Did you think that was an appropriate present for an elderly lady?' his dad asks him.

'It isn't at all – look at this box,' Mhairi says with a look of disgust.

'It's not even the first season,' Jay points out with a chuckle. 'Did you just grab something you already owned?'

'Oh, Joe, thank you,' Iona says, snatching the boxes back from her daughter.

'It's the two most recent seasons,' Millsy tells her.

'Oh, you can't imagine what it's been like, after that season finale, wondering what happens next. I don't like that Negan *at all*.'

'Wait, you watch this?' Mhairi asks. 'My mum watches a zombie TV show?'

'I certainly do,' Iona insists. 'I love it. Joe and I message each other about it.'

'As soon as they get your high-speed broadband sorted, I'll get you set up so you can stream it, so you can keep up to date,' Millsy tells her.

'Oh, Joe, thank you so much,' she says, getting up to give him a hug and a kiss. 'I'd been so looking forward to everyone coming to visit. Now I can't wait for everyone to go so I can watch these in peace.'

Millsy laughs as he hugs her. Everyone else looks surprised.

I'm surprised myself. Iona just keeps getting cooler and cooler. It's lovely, how well Millsy knows her. His present to her is easily her favourite; she can't hide it.

Jay looks a little deflated.

'And, of course, I can sit in my chair to watch it,' Iona assures Jay. 'Such lovely boys, thank you.'

'I'm not sure you should be watching that, Mum. What if it scares you?' Mhairi fusses.

'Don't be so daft,' Iona says with a roll of her eyes. 'Zombies aren't real and, even if they are, I'm in the safest place. Hardly any people around here. I could row out to one of the islands in the loch – I'd be fine. Stop worrying.'

I can't help but laugh. Iona is brilliant. It's easy to see why Millsy loves her.

'Enough about zombies,' Rob says. 'The other guests will be here soon. Let's move to the party room, shall we?'

'Yeah, let's,' Jay agrees.

I feel a little bit sorry for him; he seems a little put out by Millsy's gift. Well, imagine spending so much money on something, only to be upstaged by DVDs. Both are incredibly thoughtful gifts though and I'm sure she'll make good use of them.

'How cool is it that your gran watches *The Walking Dead*?' I say to Millsy as we head downstairs.

'Yeah, she's awesome,' he replies. 'She watched *Breaking Bad*, *Game of Thrones* – the works. This lot treat her like a bit of an old dear sometimes but she's so cool.'

My gran might seem young for her age but there is no way on earth you would be able to convince her to watch all the stabbing and shagging that goes on in *Game of Thrones*. Not in a million years. She's a *Downton Abbey* and a cup of tea kind of lady.

Once we're in the downstairs room Rod is straight over to the

TV. He puts on a music channel that is showing music videos under the title of Golden Oldies. Knowing how cool Iona is, I'm surprised she doesn't prefer a little Kendrick Lamar.

I don't feel weird or on edge around Millsy's family at all. I certainly feel more relaxed than I do around my auntie Mary. With the exception of the friction between Millsy and Jay, everyone is so nice and friendly, which makes a refreshing change.

As the room starts to fill with other family members and friends I notice Jay hanging around by the pool table. He's rolling the white ball across the table with his hand, bouncing it off the cushion, catching it before doing it again. With Millsy busy being fussed over by a couple of older ladies, I head over to chat to Jay.

Jay looks good in a pair of black skinny jeans and a white shirt. His hair and beard are neat as ever. I don't think I've ever seen him with a hair out of place. In contrast, Millsy, who really does spend a lot of time and money on his appearance, often loses control of his longish curly locks. I do love Millsy's hair though. It's wild and unpredictable, just like him, but it can be briefly tamed for formal events.

'It's a gorgeous chair,' I tell him.

'Oh, thanks,' he says. 'Not quite a zombie apocalypse but I thought it was nice. Speaking of which, I see you've lost your man to the aunties.'

I glance over at Millsy. He has an auntie either side of him. One is stroking his stubbly beard while the other is feeling his biceps. Now it's Jay who seems a little insecure. Honestly, if these two just decided to get on with each other, and stop competing against one another, they would find it so much easier to spend time together.

'If it's any consolation, I'm almost certain the only reason they're not fussing around you like this is the old blood-relation thing holding them back,' I point out. 'And Millsy isn't my man, we're just friends.'

'So, you're just his friendly neighbourhood plus one?' Jay asks as he narrows his eyes.

'That's exactly what I am,' I confirm.

'You know, my mum always makes sure I get the four-poster bed,' he tells me. 'But because you're here with Joe I've been relegated to the sofa.'

'Well, look on the bright side – if they'd given me the sofa, then you would be in with Millsy.'

'There is that,' he says with a smile. 'Perhaps we need a reshuffle of who is sleeping where.'

I feel my throat tighten. I'm not sure if what he just said made me nervous or if this is my body trying to stop me from saying the wrong thing. Thankfully, Jay changes the subject.

'Do you play pool?' he asks me.

'Do I play pool?' I repeat back to him. I think people usually take one look at me and rightly assume I'm terrible at all sports so I'm a little taken aback by his question. 'I don't. Well, I've never tried, so...'

'How about I teach you?' he suggests.

'What, right now?'

'Yeah, why not?' he says. 'It's not that hard.'

'I'm more of a puzzles and video games kind of girl,' I confess.

'Well, it's not all that different once you know how to hold the cue,' he explains. 'It's all about working out which shot to take, how best to take it, which move to make next. I think you'll be great at it.'

'OK, cool,' I say, trying not to sound too excited, but actually sounding the exact opposite. 'Let's do it.'

Jay places the balls inside the triangle before positioning them in the right place on the table. Then he grabs a couple of cues and the little cubes of chalky stuff you see the pros using. He hands me one of each.

'Do like I do,' he says as he rubs the tip of the cue. 'See, we already look professional.'

I'm not even sure how necessary this is but I feel as if I look professional. I can't help but smile.

'OK, are you ready to break?' he asks.

'Are you kidding me? Breaking things is what I'm best at,' I joke.

Jay smiles.

'OK, the first important thing to learn – because if we're doing this, we're doing it right,' he starts. 'Before you break you need to make sure your cue is chalked and that the rack is frozen – meaning all the balls in the triangle are touching. I've done this for you but if you're going to go pro, you need to know this, got it?'

'Oh, I got it,' I say with a playful salute.

'The cue ball is in place. I'm sure you've seen enough pool on TV and in films to have a guess at how to stand so, get yourself in position, then I'll tell you what to do.'

Christ, is it hot in here, or is it me?

I have a crack at how you're supposed to stand to break before looking to Jay for feedback. I'm sort of bent over the table with the cue rested on my left hand in front of me.

'Not bad actually,' he says. 'But just...'

Jay stands close behind me.

'Spread your legs a little wider,' he suggests. 'So, for a normal shot you want to be like this, for a break, you want to straighten up a little, so you can generate more power.'

As I attempt to straighten up a little I gently press my body against Jay behind me. He doesn't even flinch.

It suddenly occurs to me that I'd forgotten about everyone else in the room. I glance over to where I last saw Millsy but he isn't there. I only have to look around the room for a second to spot him, sitting in an armchair, glaring over at us. Suddenly being bent over a table by his stepbrother feels awkward.

'You want to keep your grip loose and slowly draw back the cue,' Jay continues. 'Then drive forward with both your hand and hips simultaneously.'

As Jay tells me how to do this he guides me with his body behind mine, practically thrusting me into the table. Who knew pool could be so sexy?

'Wahey, you did it,' he says. 'That's a really good break.'

'Yeah? Thanks,' I reply, glancing over to see if Millsy is still giving me evils. He isn't there though.

'How about we play?' I hear his voice all of a sudden. 'Now you've finished me-too-ing Cara.'

'Oh, no, it's fine,' I insist. 'He was just showing me how to play.'

'Great, you can be the umpire for our game,' Millsy tells me.

'She could be the *referee*,' Jay corrects him. 'But I'm not playing you, I'd thrash you.'

'Come on, you're not scared, are you?' Millsy goads him.

'Joe, you know I've played in tournaments. It wouldn't be fair,' Jay reasons.

'Chicken,' Millsy says under his breath.

'Why don't you play Cara?' Jay suggests. 'I can advise her. It would be a good way for her to learn.'

'I'd like that,' I say with an encouraging smile.

If I can get Millsy and Jay playing together, but not exactly competing with each other, then maybe we can all find some common ground and try to get along. Even if we just make a tiny bit of progress, I'll feel as if I've done something positive.

'He's just worried I'll kick his arse,' Millsy tells me. 'He's scared I'm going to make him look bad in front of you.'

'Erm, no, I'm not,' Jay insists. 'You're the one who needs to worry about getting your arse kicked. It's how you make all your money, isn't it?'

I snap my neck in Millsy's direction so quickly I feel dizzy.

'Oh, nice one, big mouth,' Millsy snaps at him.

'What does that even mean?' I ask.

'Hasn't he told you? He's Tom Hardy's bottom,' Jay explains. 'Or Freddie Bianchi's or Henry Cavill's – that type.'

I mean, I thought I knew what being someone's bottom meant, but I'm pretty sure I must be wrong in this instance.

'I'm a body double in movies,' Millsy tells me.

'What, like you do stunts?'

'No, I'm literally people's body parts. So if someone has to get naked, I fill in for them.'

'Oh, no way,' I reply. 'That's actually really cool. Why do you keep it a secret?'

'Well, people usually ask to see my arse, either in person, or ask to know what movies they can see it in,' he replies.

'I would be interested to know,' one of the aunties chimes in. I didn't even realise she was listening.

If I feel anything about Millsy being a body double – other than being impressed – I'm just sad that he felt as if he couldn't tell me.

'Right, are we playing or not?' Millsy asks Jay. 'I'm even more motivated to beat you now.'

'OK, fine, you asked for it,' Jay replies as he resets the table.

Oh, wonderful. A nice, friendly game of pool between stepbrothers. What could possibly go wrong?

18

Earlier today I thought that narrowly avoiding drowning Millsy's gran's dog was as bad as things could get, but I've been through so much since then. I'm older and wiser now. I didn't think it was possible but somehow someone else's birthday has aged me.

Don't ever make the mistake of thinking that things can only get better because, I promise you, they can always get worse, and they usually will.

I'm tempted to say it's hard to work out exactly where things went wrong but I'm pretty sure that, in addition to the series of events where things kept getting worse, something went wrong between Millsy and Jay long before I came into the picture. I can't help but wonder what though, because there is no way this is just your run-of-the-mill sibling rivalry. They were both grown men who weren't living under their parent's roof when their families merged, so it isn't as if anyone's nose was put out; there must be more to it.

So Millsy and Jay were playing pool and, despite the table being in the centre of the room – the heart of the party – it was as if someone had drawn a circle around the table and extracted the party atmosphere from inside it.

Things were tense. It was like being in a bar in the Wild West, watching a stand-off between two cowboys, and I should have known that there was no way they were both coming out of this showdown unscathed.

It's hard to say what happened. Well, actually, it's easy to say what happened: Millsy gave Jay a black eye – but it's hard to say how, exactly.

As far as I could tell they seemed to be quite evenly matched, which only seemed to be frustrating them even more, but then Millsy wanted to use a cue rest, and for some reason Jay didn't want him to, and then rowing over it turned into fighting over it, both with a hand on the cue rest, refusing to let go. At first to 'win' the argument the goal was to refuse to let go but then, when they both realised that 'winning' the argument might be down to being the bigger man and letting go, there could only be one person to let go first. So Millsy let go, Jay wasn't expecting him to, and he essentially hit himself in the face with cue rest. But it was Millsy's fault, as far as Jay was concerned – as far as everyone was concerned – so Millsy was banished to his bedroom. What kind of friend/plus one would I be if I didn't go with him?

So we sat in our room for a while, chatting, playing cards on the bed. I asked Millsy if he wanted to talk about Jay, but he didn't. Instead we talked about his career as a body double, which is a job I've never really thought about, but one that sounds so interesting. More than anything though I was just relieved to know that he makes money legally, meaning I can keep renting a room from him and not be in danger. Well, any more danger than I seem to be creating for myself lately.

It's been a fun few hours but now Millsy is flat out asleep in bed – spooning Dougie, which is pretty cute – and, with the noise of the party having fizzled out a while ago, now feels like the perfect time for me to go and get that cup of tea I've been craving all night, now I know that everyone is tucked up in a bed and probably fast asleep.

I creep out of the bedroom, careful not to wake Millsy or Dougie, and tiptoe along the corridor towards the living room.

'Oh, sorry,' I blurt the second I clap eyes on Jay in the dimly lit room.

He's lying back on the sofa with a duvet over him. When he said he was sleeping on the sofa I assumed he meant something like a sofa bed in a spare room, not the actual living-room sofa. At least I know that I didn't wake him up. He's currently holding a bag of frozen peas on his face.

'Don't worry about it,' he says. 'You OK?'

'Yeah, just fancied a cup of tea,' I tell him. 'Fancy one?'

'That would be lovely, thanks.'

'Milk and sugar?'

'Just milk, please,' he replies with a half-smile. It seems as if maybe it hurts him to move his face.

'OK, back in a sec.'

By the time I get back to the living room with the cups of tea, Jay has sat up straight, leaving me room to sit down next to him.

I place the cups down on the table and take a seat next to him.

'How's the face?' I ask.

'Sore,' he replies, wincing as he removes his bag of frozen peas.

'Is that helping?'

'Not really but I'm hoping it will keep the swelling and the bruising to a minimum. I've got a presentation at work in two days. I really don't want to do it looking like I've been in a bar fight.'

'I bet,' I reply. 'And I don't suppose the truth sounds great either, does it?'

'Not even a bit,' he says with a laugh.

His cheek is bright red, which is probably from the frozen peas, but you can see a real shiner blossoming. There's no way he's going to be doing this presentation without a black eye – or a tonne of concealer.

'Can I ask you a question?' I start cautiously.

'Sure,' he replies.

As he leans forward to grab his tea I realise that, under the duvet on his lap, he's only wearing a vest and boxers. Well, I suppose I'm technically in his bed right now. I swear, this wasn't what I had planned when I decided to pop to the kitchen, although it does seem suspicious that I turned up in my pyjamas. Then again, if I were making a move on him, I definitely wouldn't have turned up in these absolutely not sexy plaid PJs.

'What's the deal with you and Millsy?' I jump to the chase. 'Because, I don't know, things between the two of you are pretty intense, way worse than your regular sibling rivalry. I just wondered why.'

'Hasn't he told you anything?' Jay asks. He seems surprised.

'He hasn't...'

'Of course, he hasn't,' he says with an eye roll. 'Things didn't used to be so bad between us – we weren't exactly one another's cup of tea, but we got along OK. Things were ticking along just fine until one day when, well, Millsy being Millsy...'

Whatever Jay is trying to say, I feel as if he's struggling to get it out.

'What, did he do something?' I prompt. God, I'm gripped now.

'Yeah, he... he slept with my girlfriend.'

'What?'

'Yep. So, as you can imagine, it's quite hard for me to be

around him. I try my best but, I don't know, I guess the bad blood just isn't going to go away any time soon.'

'My God, that's horrible. Was it not some kind of misunderstanding?'

'I don't think so. It was a girl I was seeing, maybe he thought we weren't that serious or...' He sighs. 'I don't know. I'm sure you know what he's like by now.'

People keep hinting – or straight up telling me – about Millsy's reputation as a 'love 'em and leave 'em' type but, honestly, if I hadn't heard it from other people, I wouldn't know that to be the case. I mean, I could believe it. He's good-looking, charming, women flock to him. I just feel as if he's been so good to me, for nothing in return, he's never tried it on with me – all I can do is take him at face value. But obviously, if he did sleep with Jay's girlfriend, that's awful and I'm not surprised they don't get on. I'm going to put it to the back of my mind, unless Millsy tells me himself, but even then, he doesn't seem like that sort of person now – and it's not like we're romantically involved, is it? I don't need to worry about him breaking my heart.

'Do you think the two of you can figure it out?' I ask.

Jay seems so easy to talk to. He's so mature and level-headed. I don't find it difficult, talking about the big stuff with him.

'Maybe one day,' he replies. 'Not tonight though.'

'He's asleep anyway,' I point out with a smile.

'You not tired?'

'Not really,' I reply. 'I don't suppose the caffeine will help either.'

'You wanna hang out for a bit?' Jay suggests. 'It will be nice to have a chat, get to know each other, just the two of us.'

'Yeah, definitely,' I reply brightly.

I pull my legs up underneath myself and grab my tea, making myself comfortable.

'So, what do you want to talk about?' I ask.

'Everything,' he replies with a smile.

19

'Good morning, Cara,' Millsy says as he gently rocks me by the shoulder.

'Morning,' I reply. I can tell it's light in the room, even with my eyes closed, so I keep them tightly shut.

'Sleep well?' he asks softly.

'Mmm, great, thanks,' I reply. 'You?'

'Yeah, not bad,' he says.

I furrow my brow, my eyes still closed. Something isn't right, I don't know what it is... Millsy's voice sounds weird.

I open my eyes to see Millsy sitting in front of me. That's when I realise I'm still in the living room, on the sofa with a duvet over me. Millsy is sitting on the coffee table, up and dressed, staring at me.

'Erm...'

I sit up straight as I try to work out what happened. Shit, I must have fallen asleep on the sofa while I was chatting with Jay. Double shit, Jay is still asleep next to me.

'You slept with my brother then, huh?'

'Yeah, well, I mean... I slept *next to* your brother, by accident,' I insist, keeping my voice as low as possible.

Jay is lying in what I'd imagine is his usual place, flat on his back across three seats, whereas I am next to him on the chaise longue at the end. It's a pretty big sofa but it still looks odd. I must have just dropped off – and I must have fallen asleep before Jay because he's covered me up with his duvet. God, I hope I didn't make any embarrassing noises or sleep with my mouth open.

'Interesting,' Millsy says. 'Very interesting.'

'What?'

'Oh, nothing,' he says as he pulls himself to his feet. 'At least I found you before anyone else did. Might not look ideal, if they spot you here...'

'Oh, totally,' I agree. 'I'll go get dressed.'

I carefully peel back the covers and stand up in a way that doesn't wake Jay up.

'This is almost like a walk of shame,' Millsy says as I tiptoe towards the bedroom.

'It's nothing like a walk of shame,' I insist firmly. I'm so embarrassed though.

As I hurry on clothes and try to cover my red cheeks with foundation I wonder why Millsy thinks it's so interesting that I 'slept with his brother'... Oh, God, you don't think he thinks this is some kind of revenge thing, do you? If Millsy did sleep with Jay's girlfriend, does he think Jay might sleep with me to level the playing field? Would Jay try to sleep with me just to even the score? I'm sure he wouldn't. People don't do things like that in real life, do they? Especially not someone like Jay, who seems as if his head is well and truly screwed on.

By the time I get back out into the living room Jay is awake. Millsy must still be in the kitchen.

'Good morning,' he says with a smile.

'Morning,' I reply. 'Sorry, did I fall asleep on you last night?'

'Oh, don't worry about it,' he says with a casual bat of his hand. 'I tried to wake you but you were flat out so I just covered you up.'

'Oh, God, was I embarrassing?'

'No, you were fine,' he says. 'You're pretty cute when you're sleeping.'

I feel my cheeks starting to flush again so I quickly change the subject.

'You off home today?' I ask.

'Yeah. You?'

'After breakfast, I think. In fact, I'd better go give Millsy a hand with it. He said something about wanting to make breakfast for everyone to try and make amends for last night.'

I don't mention that the main reason I want to help him cook is because he literally started a fire yesterday.

'Tell him I'll take something cold to put on my bruised face,' he jokes before wiggling his jaw, testing how much he can move his facial muscles without being in agony.

'I absolutely won't tell him that,' I reply with a smile. 'Anyway, see you soon.'

'Yeah. You'll be at Rod's surprise party, right?' he asks in hushed tones.

'Yeah, I'm sure I will be,' I reply.

'We can hang out more then,' he says.

He gives me that Prince Charming smile of his as I head for the kitchen.

I find Millsy fussing around by the kettle, preparing cups of tea and coffee.

'I figured you'd want tea,' he says.

'Yes, thanks,' I reply. I can only wait for a second or two before I bring up the elephant in the room. 'Millsy, you know nothing happened last night, right? I'm sure it goes without saying but I'm saying it anyway. I went to make a cup of tea, I got chatting to Jay, I fell asleep. I probably really embarrassed myself.'

'Cara, it's fine,' he says. 'You're right, it does go without saying. Don't worry about it. But if I can just say one thing... be careful with Jay, OK? He isn't what he seems. Everyone thinks he's so perfect but I see right through him.'

'Morning, campers,' Rod says as he joins us in the kitchen. 'Assaulted anyone today?'

'Not yet, but the day is young,' Millsy jokes. 'It was definitely an accident – it could have been either of us who got hit in the face. Better it's the one who doesn't need his looks to make his living.'

'You get by just fine without your face,' his dad reminds him.

'I'm making breakfast to say sorry for the accidental altercation. What can I get you?'

'You can get me an apron. I'll help you,' Rod replies. 'The only thing you'll make is a mess.'

As Rod roots around in the cupboard below the sink, Millsy and I exchange a knowing glance. He doesn't know the half of it.

'Hmm, does this frying pan smell a bit funny to you?' he asks as he emerges from the cupboard with it. 'It smells really smoky.'

Being on fire will do that to you.

20

What springs to mind when you think of hen parties? A gaggle of rowdy women with L-plates, cocktails, and penis-shaped everything from headbands to drinking straws? Dancing around handbags, going to the toilet in groups of no less than six, groping a male stripper in a police uniform? Something like that? That's what I think of – it's what pop culture has taught me to think of when I imagine hen parties. I've never actually been on one before today.

Well, I say before today, but I'm not actually on one today either. I should have been tipped off that this wasn't a real hen party when I realised that my mum, gran, auntie, et cetera were all invited. Flora was never going to give my grandma Stephanie a shot of tequila in a nob-shaped glass, was she?

Shortly after I arrived I had a bunch of realisations at once. First of all I realised that this wasn't going to be your typical hen party. Second of all I realised that we weren't even going out for drinks, we were going to a crafting café. And my third and final realisation was that, not only is this hen party not really hen party-ish, this isn't even Flora's real hen party – she had her real hen party weeks ago and I wasn't invited. This is just her fake hen party for her older relatives.

I suppose when I politely bowed out of my bridesmaid duties I got myself disinvited from the real hen party too.

So here we are at Tarts & Crafts, a craft café in the cute little town of Horsforth, about to take part in God knows what, but whatever it is I feel completely inappropriately dressed for it in my new black and white body-con dress. Lucky for me they provide aprons for everyone to wear. Unlucky for me it's an impossibly ugly pink apron with excessive frills – no one had better take any pictures.

'Hello, I'm Julie, I'll be your activity co-ordinator today,' a short woman with a loud voice announces to our group. 'What we're going to be doing today is... painting a portrait of the gorgeous bride!'

Oh, God.

'So, Flora, if you would like to take a seat over here, and if everyone else would like to sit at an easel,' she continues.

I link my arm with Stephanie, my grandma, as we walk towards our seats together.

'I'm sitting with you,' I tell her.

'I haven't painted in years,' my gran says. 'Perhaps not since school – my gosh, that's seventy years ago.'

'Well, I am hopeless at anything like this,' I tell her. 'At least we can be terrible together.'

It might seem strange that I'm so impossibly terrible at art, given the creative nature of my job, but I really am hopeless. My job involves drawing blueprints – very neat, technically room schematics. I'll illustrate where things go but I won't ever have to actually draw them, and I'll bet a padlock is way easier to draw than my cousin Flora.

Flora excitedly takes her seat in the middle of the room. Obviously she knew this was what we were doing today, so she's dolled herself up accordingly. She's wearing a long, floaty floral dress, a full face of make-up and her hair looks so perfect I'll bet she's been to a salon for a blow-dry. Flora perches on her stool and crosses her legs before placing her hands on her knees.

'I'm ready,' she announces.

So there's me, my mum, my gran, my auntie, as well as Flora's nanna and auntie from her dad's side, all gathered around her, ready to immortalise her in paint (although I'm sure the best I could do is accidentally cover her in it).

'Your mum tells me you have a boyfriend,' my gran leans over to say.

'He's not my boyfriend,' I insist. 'We're just friends.'

'She said you were living with him...'

'Yeah but, again, we're just friends. I'm paying to live with him.'

'It is very fast to move in with someone,' my gran points out. 'But I'd only known your granddad for six months before we got married so... I suppose when you know you've met the one, you just know.'

I nod thoughtfully.

'But you're just friends,' she practically reminds me with a smile.

'Yep,' I reply, smiling back – why do I feel as if she knows something I don't? 'You can meet him at the wedding.'

'I really think we need to meet him before the wedding,' my mum chimes in from the other side of me.

I didn't realise she was listening and it makes me jump.

'You can meet him at the wedding,' I tell her.

'I think we need to meet him *before*,' she says again.

'The wedding is a matter of weeks away – can't you just wait?'

My mum leans in close, looks around to make sure everyone

else is too busy with their painting to pay attention, and lowers her voice.

'Auntie Mary says I need to check him out,' she whispers to me. 'Don't make that face.'

I didn't realise I was making a face.

'She just wants to make sure he's OK,' she continues. 'She doesn't want strangers at the wedding.'

'I don't want ex-boyfriends at the wedding but you can't always get what you want, can you?'

'Oh, you know what she's like,' my mum says with a bat of her hand. 'But, well, we would really like to meet him. You're like a whole new woman and your father and I just really want to see the man responsible for the new you.'

'I'm still me,' I insist. 'But I'll ask him if he's free any time soon. That OK?'

'Thanks, darling,' she says with a smile. When she catches sight of my painting her face falls. 'Why have you drawn her in a big, poofy dress? And with a veil? Aren't we supposed to be drawing her now?'

'I *am* drawing her now,' I say. 'That's not a veil, that's her hair, and that's not a big, poofy dress, it just keeps getting bigger every time I try to make it even.'

'Thank goodness you don't need to be able to paint to make a living,' she says with a reassuring squeeze of my arm. She's teasing me. 'And you'll always have your looks.'

'I barely have my looks now, but I definitely won't always have them,' I reply with a laugh. 'But thanks.'

I glance at my handiwork. Yeah, it's not great. I'm trying my best though, what more can I do? The problem I'm having – and it's the same problem I have when I'm doing my eye make-up – is that I just can't seem to get things even, and the harder I try, the bigger things get. When I'm winging my eyeliner I'll start with one perfectly neat little flick on my left eye – I'm absolutely amazing at my own left eye – but then, when I try to do my right, it's thicker or longer so I go back to the left to add more. I'll do this until I wind up looking like Amy Winehouse. A similar thing has happened with my portrait of Flora; to try and make her even, I've kept adding bits until she looks like Mr Blobby, or Mrs Blobby, at least – you can definitely tell she's wearing a dress.

I finished my portrait long before everyone else so now I'm just waiting for them to catch up. I've caught a sneaky peek at my mum's and my gran's and they're not winning any awards any time soon, but they're way better than mine. Even if they're not good, they're flattering.

I thought this was going to be so bad I actually arranged a get-out strategy with Millsy. Basically, if it were all to get too much, all I would need to do would be to text him a frog emoji and he would call me up pretending to be work with some kind of emergency, giving me an excuse to rush off. We decided on the frog because we couldn't think of any possible reason why we would ever need to use it. So far though, as little as I'm enjoying myself, I haven't actually needed to use it.

Eventually, when everyone is done, Julie wanders back in and tells us that we all need to turn our canvasses around, so that they're forming a semicircle around Flora. She's going to pick the best one and whoever painted it is going to get a prize. Woo.

'Oh my Gosh! They're all so...' Flora's voice trails off. 'What is that? Whose is that one?'

I hazard a guess she's talking about mine and step out from behind it.

'What?' Auntie Mary asks, hurrying out to join her daughter. 'Oh, Cara, come on, that's so offensively bad. You can't have done it that bad by accident. Look how fat you made her!'

'I'm sorry,' I say. I try to sound sincere but obviously I didn't make her fat on purpose – why on earth would I do that? 'I did try my best.'

'Did you?' Flora replies. Wow, she actually sounds a bit upset. 'At least you made my legs skinny.'

'I think that's actually supposed to be the stool legs,' Julie ever so helpfully points out.

'I am really sorry,' I say. I am. I didn't do it on purpose, but I am truly sorry if she's finding it upsetting. 'I'm just not very good at this stuff.'

'Flora's nanna has cataracts and even hers looks better than yours,' Auntie Mary points out angrily.

To be honest, I'm sure I could have been Pablo frigging Picasso and they still would have told me that my painting sucked. Then again, with the way her face is so wonky, it wouldn't look out of place next to a Picasso.

There's only one thing for it. I need to send a frog SOS.

I take a sneaky step behind my canvas before removing my phone and smashing out a quick and stealthy frog emoji to Millsy. I click my phone off silent mode and return it to my apron pocket. In a matter of seconds my phone is ringing. Good old Millsy.

'I'm so sorry, I have to take this, it's work,' I insist. 'Hello?'

'Hey,' Millsy says. 'Things are bad, huh?'

'Oh my gosh, what happened?' I ask theatrically.

'Oh, solid acting, Cara.' Millsy chuckles down the phone. 'Maybe dial it down a notch. No one cares about their job that much.'

'A child locked in a cupboard?' I shriek. 'And you can't find the bolt cutters?'

Suddenly everyone in the room is listening to my conversation.

'Wow,' is all he says.

'Yes, of course, I'll be there right away,' I continue.

'You want to meet me in town?' he asks. 'I'm popping out in a bit anyway.'

'Yes, I will see you there,' I reply. 'I'll sort it, don't panic. Bye.'

I re-announce my fake emergency at work to the room, even though I know they were listening, make my excuses and leave. I am only outside a couple of seconds before my mum joins me.

'Let me give you a lift to work,' she says when she catches me up.

'Oh no, Mum, don't leave the party,' I insist, not stopping, edging in the direction of the train station. 'I'm going to get the train.'

'Well, let me give you a lift to the station then.'

Why do I feel as if she's on to me? Her tone and expression are giving nothing away but that in itself speaks volumes. I think she knows I'm just trying to get out of here.

'Honestly, Mum, it's fine.'

'You're not going to work, are you?' she asks, finally showing a knowing smile.

It's never worth trying to keep anything from your mum, is it? This is why it didn't seem worth pretending that Millsy and I were a couple – she would have seen straight through an act like that.

'OK, no, I just needed to get out of there,' I admit.

'I'm proud of you for sticking it out as long as you did,' she tells me. 'It's no fun, is it?'

'I just feel like they're both so mad about the bridesmaid thing, I'm not going to be able to do anything right.'

'I know, love,' she says. 'You know your auntie just likes to moan. Let me give you a lift to the station.'

'OK, thank you. It is actually quite far from where we are, isn't it?'

My mum nods.

'So are you going to meet this Joe?'

'Yes. We really are just friends, Mum.'

'Just make sure you're happy,' she says.

She's right, my auntie has always been a moaner, she's just especially moany because of the wedding. Once the wedding is over everyone will forget about the time I didn't want to be a bridesmaid in a dress that didn't fit me. Until then I just need to clock as little face time with my auntie and Flora as possible. And, sure, I'd rather not endure an entire wedding with my ex-boyfriend sitting at the same table as me, but at least I'll have Millsy there with me. It's going to be weird when our plus-one pact is over and I have to go back to being truly single, turning up to events alone, having no one to laugh in the corner with.

I feel really lucky to have him on my side now though. I just need to make the most of having his undivided attention. I'm even looking forward to seeing him now – well, everything is more fun with Millsy around.

21

When Millsy said he was popping into town I assumed it would be to do something very Millsy-esque. You know, something fun like shopping or drinking. What I have wound up doing instead is sitting on a sofa outside a fitting room in some stuffy menswear shop that specialises in suits.

We're here so that Millsy can be fitted for his suit, for Ruby's wedding – he is her best man after all. Well, apparently we're not calling him a best man, we're calling him a bridesmale.

When we arrived Millsy instructed me to sit on the leather sofa where patient friends and family members are supposed to wait while their loved ones try things on. Millsy assured me that it wouldn't take long, he just needed to make sure his suit still fitted OK, and to pick out a shirt.

I've been sitting out here for a little while now and to be honest, as boring as it is, at least it's nice and cool, and no one is expecting me to paint anyone, so that's great.

'I can't believe you painted her fat,' he calls from behind the curtain.

I've just told Millsy the full story and he finds it hilarious.

'Not on purpose,' I say for the millionth time. 'She wasn't even that fat. Just… I don't know, lumpy?'

'Did they let you keep it?'

'I think Flora was keeping them but I'm sure she's had mine destroyed already.'

'I'd love it for my office, if you can get your hands on it,' he says and, while I can't see his expression behind the curtain, I'm absolutely certain he's just kidding.

'I'll see what I can do,' I reply with a laugh.

'Oh, I do have some good news for you,' he says. 'Ruby is completely happy for you to come to the wedding. She's sold on you being a real adult.'

'I am a real adult,' I insist.

The man fitting Millsy's suit emerges from behind the curtain with a garment bag. I jump out of my skin. So much for being a real adult.

'Almost done,' he assures me. 'We just need to decide on a shirt.'

'OK, thanks,' I reply.

'I do actually need your help picking a shirt,' Millsy calls out. 'Might see if you'll come and have a look at them.'

'Yeah, no worries,' I reply casually. Whatever makes this go faster. Whenever I've read or watched men in fiction complaining while their significant other shops I've always thought it couldn't possibly be a fair representation but sitting here, waiting for Millsy to try stuff on, I am bored out of my mind.

I pull back the curtain and step inside the fitting room, only to find myself standing behind Millsy, who isn't wearing anything apart from a tight-fitting pair of boxers and a bemused smile on his face. Because this is a fitting room there are mirrors at a variety of angles, so there's no hiding anything and no pretending I didn't see anything.

So far while I've been living with Millsy, and sharing a room with him when we were in Scotland, I have managed to get by without seeing him undressed and now here I am, standing in a fitting room with him, unable to move off the spot.

'I didn't mean right away, but you're here now,' he says with an amused chuckle. 'Have a seat.'

As he nods towards the stool next to him I feel the flush of embarrassment commandeer my cheeks. No amount of air con can cool down my face right now. I feel as if I've fallen asleep in the midday sun for a couple of hours.

'I'll come back,' I say.

'Don't be daft,' he insists. 'I need your help with these shirts anyway.'

I sit down as instructed but wherever I look there are mirrors reflecting a different angle of almost naked Millsy at me.

I knew that he was a buff guy from his clothed physique, but now that I've seen him without clothes on I can see what a seemingly perfect figure he has. It's no wonder he makes so much money as a body double; I'll bet he has a better body than most of the actors he stands in for. I cast my mind back to that time I watched that terrible *Edge of Eden* movie. You know the one, a sort of *Fifty Shades of Grey* type flick about an S&M-loving lawyer who has a steamy affair with the woman he's defending on a murder charge. The leading man, Freddie Bianchi, had his arse out constantly in that movie. I wonder if that was Millsy... Could you even recognise an arse? I doubt it.

'Cara Brooks, are you looking at my bum?' Millsy asks.

I'm even more embarrassed now, if that's possible. Millsy, who clearly thinks this is hilarious, is grinning like an idiot.

'No, of course not,' I reply. 'I was just thinking about your job and, who knows, I've probably seen you in movies before.'

'Looking for distinguishing features?' he asks with a wink. 'I've actually got a little birthmark on my left cheek, but they usually cover it with make-up or edit it out in post. We can't have everyone knowing I butt-double for a few people.'

'I suppose not,' I say. I'm looking down at my shoes now.

'OK, how about this one?' Millsy asks before flexing pretty much every muscle he has. He points his arms down in front of his body to tense his pecs and I honestly don't think I've ever seen anyone so sexy in real life. It's always been really obvious to me that Millsy is an undeniably good-looking guy but now that I'm in here with him, at close quarters, watching him in his pants, flexing his muscles...

Once he's in position Millsy starts making his pec muscles dance, bouncing them up and down as he hums a tune that seems so familiar to me.

'Oh my gosh, it's that iconic scene, from that romcom movie, oh, what's it called?' I babble, excited to recognise what he's doing, and for his silly dance to dispel an otherwise tense moment. I know I've seen this scene in a movie before. How weirdly cool is it that it's my friend whose muscles play the muscles in the film?

Right on cue the man fitting Millsy's suit joins us. Millsy freezes as soon as he notices. I'm frozen. Even the man is just staring at us.

'Some shirts,' he says after a few seconds. 'I'll leave you to it.'

'Oh my God,' I blurt when we're alone again.

'Do you think he wants an autograph?' Millsy jokes.

'Just, put your trousers on,' I tell him as I grab them from next to me and throw them at him.

'Are you worried I'm going to get you in trouble?' he jokes.

'Something like that,' I reply.

I decide that it's probably best that I step outside until Millsy has clothes on. Not just so I can cool down, but so I can try and forget what I saw. I can still see Millsy's abs whenever I blink. If I can just forget then things won't be awkward, but that's the problem when you see the man behind the curtain – your eyes are opened and you can't go back to how things were before.

22

The more that I think about it, the more pointless school reunions seem these days. I'm sure you could make a case for them, once upon a time, but not any more, not in the age of social media.

Before, a five-, ten- or twenty-year school reunion would be the only way to see people you hadn't seen in years, to find out what they had been up to and what they turned out like. The thing is, everyone I wanted to keep in touch with I have on Facebook (plus a few I would have rather not kept in touch with), so I don't just have a general sense of how well they're doing, I know exactly how they're doing – I know details I really don't need to know.

Take my old friend Becky, for example. We were best friends at school but when we grew up, we grew in different directions. I thought we were going to be friends forever. Our other female friends all got boyfriends and we would joke about them, because their boyfriends were their entire world. We'd refer to them as the Boyfriend Club. As the Boyfriend Club all slowly dropped out of sixth form our group got smaller and smaller – well, who cares about A levels when all you want to do is start a family? – and it was all fine until Becky caught the bug too. She was married before I'd sat my A2 exams. And so the Boyfriend Club became the Baby Club, and our lives just became too different for me to be included. They all wanted to be mummy-ish and talk mummy things and I guess at some point they decided that I wouldn't be able to fully participate and that was it, I was out of the clique. I'm surprised they kept me in the group chat for as long as they did.

They are, however, all still friends with me on Facebook, and they're all quite vocal – Becky especially. I know everything about Becky. I know everything about her kids. Everything from their first words to their rashes to the backlash at school when she put a Frube in her kid's lunchbox. I can tell you where she's been on every single holiday she's been on over the past decade (it's *always* Florida – mostly because she's Disney crazy), I know her job (full-time mum these days, and she's had five kids, so it really is a full-time job). So, when I am inevitably standing in front of Becky, and we start catching up, what do we even have to talk about? What is there that I don't know? I know exactly how it's going to go: we'll make polite conversation until she eventually asks me if there's any sign of a husband or a baby in my future, because that's what Becky deems a success, so she thinks everyone else should too. I don't think there's anything wrong with her, for wanting a family of her own more than anything else in life, if she's happy that's great, but when people project those desires onto me it makes me feel really uncomfortable.

Of course I'd like to get married and have kids but it isn't the be-all and end-all for me. I don't think I'm a failure because I don't have them yet. At this stage in my life they're just concepts. I wouldn't want to marry someone, to have kids with just anyone. Still, it doesn't feel great when you're standing with a bunch of people who think you haven't amounted to anything. I don't think that about myself, obviously. If my life had played out differently I wouldn't be living in the city, doing my dream job. I suppose there's a lot to be said for being chubby and shy at school – I couldn't get a boyfriend so I threw myself into my exams, then uni, then my career. As proud as I am, I can still see that inevitable 'no baby though?' look of pity that will be in Becky's eyes.

So this is actually our fifteen-year reunion, even though it's technically only been fourteen years, but for various logistical reasons the team organising it decided it would be better for everyone if it were to take place a year earlier. I'm not entirely sure I want to be here at all, but I was worried it might look worse if I didn't show, as if I had something to hide. At least I have Millsy with me – well, I will when he gets here. He had an appointment to get new headshots taken, although I do wonder if they're headshots, knowing his usual line of work now. Infuriatingly, since the suit fitting last week, I'm sort of looking at Millsy differently. Before he was just Millsy but now when I look at him I see an attractive man and it makes me nervous. I suddenly feel a little self-conscious and like I want to impress him. I want him to see me as a woman, rather than the charity case he adopted to give a life makeover when he was bored.

I don't know if it was to impress Millsy or my old school friends, but I made appointments with Luca and Dani, the hairstylist and make-up artist who gave me my initial makeover, to make me look the best I possibly could this evening. So my face (or at least the layer of make-up covering it) looks flawless and my long red hair is looking all big and bouncy and impossibly glossy.

Luca asked me if Millsy had tried to sleep with me yet. I said no, laughing off his question, and I wouldn't ever want to ruin our friendship with what sounds like one of his trademark brief encounters, but I still keep wondering what's so wrong with me that he hasn't even given it a go. If he'll allegedly sleep with anyone – even his stepbrother's girlfriend – then I guess he really does just see me as completely unsexy. I don't even think my perfectly highlighted cheeks, my sleek hair, my nude lace pencil dress or the sky-high heels I'm wearing will change that. It bugs me a little – I suppose because it makes me think something must be really wrong with me.

I don't really want to walk in on my own so I'm currently standing in the corridor – because, of course, we're having it in the school hall – looking at the photos on the display. There aren't any I haven't seen before, they're all in the yearbook we were given on the last day of year eleven, but I haven't looked at them in a long time. We all look so young and yet, somehow, when I look at the sixteen-year-olds of today they look like babies – unless they've learned to contour from a YouTuber, in which case they look older than I do now.

'Spotted yourself?' a man asks as he sidles up alongside me. He's tall – really tall, like 6' 5". I only remember one person from my year who was that tall.

'Sean?' I say. 'Sean Sharples?'

'You remember me?' he says.

'Of course I do – who else could touch the ceiling with their head?' I joke.

'I'm sorry,' he starts. 'I don't remember you... I'd definitely remember you. Are you in the right place?'

I turn to face him, flashing him my name badge.

'Oh my God, Cara Brooks? No! You look so different.'

Sean Sharples is one of my former classmates who I don't have on Facebook. He doesn't look much different though, just older. I didn't think I had changed much since I was at school but I suppose my recent makeover is quite the departure from my old look.

'Ah, it's just a bit of dye,' I reply a little awkwardly.

'And you've lost weight since school,' he points out. 'You look incredible.'

'Thanks,' I reply. 'What do you do?'

I change the subject from me as quickly as possible. I've never been very good at taking compliments.

'I cut people up,' he tells me very matter of factly.

I just stare at him for a moment.

'You think that's bad,' he continues. 'I've got a friend who gives people drugs – sometimes he gives them to kids.'

'Erm...'

'I'm a surgeon,' he says with a laugh.

'And a comedian,' I point out.

'What do you do? Are you a model?'

I just laugh.

'I design escape rooms,' I tell him.

'Wow, really? That's so cool. I don't remember you being this cool at school.'

'I wasn't,' I reply. 'And I don't suppose you ever spoke to me...'

'Well, more fool me,' he says. 'You're absolutely stunning.'

I can't really hide my bemused smile. I wasn't expecting him to be so nice to me. I guess maybe he's just grown up.

'Listen, I'm going to pop to the toilets but can I meet you in the main hall after? We can chat more?'

'OK, sure,' I reply.

'I'd love to finally get to know you, after years of being absolutely, completely blind.'

As Sean says this to me he caresses my bare back with his hand, after somehow working his arm around me.

'See you very soon,' he tells me.

I watch with widened eyes as Sean disappears down the corridor. Wow, was he just hitting on me? After two literal minutes of conversation? What a sleaze.

I decide to head into the main hall, rather than stand here on my own, waiting for Sean to come back and get handsy with me again. I'll feel better when Millsy gets here. No one is going to mess with me with that Greek-god-looking geezer on my arm. Only I know that he's so scared of damaging his face that he would avoid confrontation at all cost. He might even use me as a shield.

I head into the hall and I'm surprised to say it doesn't look all that different. It must still be doubling up as a gym because there are tennis courts painted on the floor and some of the bunting is fixed to climbing frames that fold open from the walls. The room is nicely decorated though, with bunting, balloons and fairy lights, all of which bring it to life a little. I can still tell it's the same old cold hall I hated as a kid though. I feel as if any minute now I'm going to have to fake period cramps to get out of doing a bleep test.

I decide I'll get a drink, wandering over to the pop-up bar in the canteen, which opens up into the hall.

'Jason, is that you?' I ask the man behind the bar.

I recognise him. It's Jason Berry – they made us sit next to each other in maths for years because our names were next to each other alphabetically and we were always in the same set. He was quite weird though; no one really liked him. I built up a sort of tolerable rapport with him to make maths lessons easier but he really was an odd lad. He had this pencil case that was made from a rabbit – or at least he told us that it was, and that's weird however you look at it. He used to give himself dragon tattoos with a combination of gel pens and Tipp-Ex – no sign of them now, real or fake.

He looks at my badge.

'Cara? I wouldn't have recognised you!' he says. I definitely recognise him. He still has a shaved head and a hoop earring in one ear. On a school kid it seemed like a really weird look, but it styles out a little better on an adult.

There's a brief glimmer of a smile on his face but then it drops. 'You were invited, then?'

'I was... weren't you?'

'Nope. I work for a catering company in Leeds. When the agency said they had a pop-up bar job in my hometown I was quick to take it, to have a look inside my old school, see if things had changed. Then I turned up and it was my *own* school reunion that I *wasn't* invited to. So nothing has changed at all really, has it?'

'I'm sure it wasn't on purpose,' I attempt to reassure him although, now that I think about it, I'm sure I'd heard a rumour that he'd accidentally overdosed and died a few years ago. Obviously he hasn't because he's standing here.

'I live in Leeds too,' I tell him, attempting to change the subject.

'Oh, really?'

'Yeah, I work there so...' Oh, God, what if he thinks this is me trying to strike up some kind of social relationship? I need to change the subject as quickly as possible.

'So, what do you do?' I ask.

Jason slowly looks down at the bar and then back up to me.

Oh, God, right, of course. He's working now.

'I'm just gonna... yeah...'

I take one of the pre-poured glasses of Prosecco from in front of him and wander off. There's something about the look in his eye that makes me feel as though, if I say the wrong thing just one more time, he's going to turn me into a pencil case.

I circulate around the room, looking for someone I recognise or feel brave enough to talk to. Eventually I find my old clique. Becky, Christina, Joanne and Kelsey. The Mum Club. None of us were especially cool at school but, somehow, Joanne has wound up marrying the most popular boy in our class, Luke Lockwood, who was on track to play for Leeds United. Well, I guess he must have wandered off that track at some point, because he has a dad bod instead of a footballer's physique. Kelsey has her husband here with her, but Becky and Christina are alone. I imagine their significant others are at home, looking after the kids. Well, they do have seven between them.

'Oh my God, Cara, hello,' Becky says as she forcefully pulls me close for a hug. 'We haven't seen you in forever. I suppose, now you live in the big city, you don't want to come all this way to see the likes of us.'

I bite my tongue. I am twenty minutes away on a train and I visit home at least once a fortnight, but what's the point in getting into it?

'Hello,' I say. 'Hello, everyone.'

'You look so different,' Christina points out. 'What did you do to your hair?'

She asks this in a similar way you talk to a child with bubblegum stuck in their locks.

'I dyed it,' I tell her with a nod and a vacant expression. I would have thought that was obvious. I suppose I'm still salty about being kicked out of the group chat.

'How are you all doing?' I ask.

'Well, I'm pregnant again,' Christina tells me.

'Us too,' Kelsey chimes in. I assume by 'us' she means her and her husband. I must have missed a biology lesson at some point.

'Which one were you?' Luke asks me.

I can tell by his question that he hasn't changed at all. He still seems like the same bully he used to be.

'She looked nothing like she looks now,' Becky tells him. 'She had that purple backpack with the stars on it that everyone used to make fun of.'

'Oh, Space Nerd,' Luke says. 'Hello, how are you?'

'Oh, I'm fantastic,' I reply.

You dare to be a teenager with a backpack with constellation patterns on it and suddenly you're a space nerd.

'How are you?' I ask him. 'Still playing football?'

'Nah, not really. My kid plays though. Under sixes.'

'My little Sonny plays for the same team,' Becky says.

Becky takes my left hand and examines it.

'Oh, Cara, no husband? No kids, then?'

'Still no kids,' I confirm. Why does it make me feel so crappy to say that? Why would I want a kid right now? I'm not in a position to have one and I know it. What am I going to do, get knocked up so my old friends get off my back? No way. They just have this way of making me feel uncomfortable about something I am completely comfortable with.

'She's working on the husband bit,' a voice says from behind me as a pair of arms wrap around my waist.

I am so relieved that it's Millsy's voice.

'Hello,' I say. I'm so pleased to see him.

'Hello, gorgeous,' he replies, kissing me on the cheek.

'Oh... is this your boyfriend?' Christina asks. She looks surprised, as if perhaps she doesn't think someone like me could pull someone as hot as Millsy.

'This is Joe,' I tell them.

I have spent weeks telling Millsy that the last thing I wanted to do was pretend that we were a couple and I regret that so much now. I wish I could tell them he is my boyfriend, just for tonight, to get a break from their pitying looks.

'Yep, I'm her boyfriend,' Millsy says. 'Lovely to finally meet you all. I've heard a lot about you.'

'You two are a couple?' Christina checks.

'Yeah.' Millsy squeezes me tightly. 'No kids just yet though. I'm in the movie business so we jet around a lot. You know how it is. We don't want tying down just yet. Not until we've made our first million, right? So maybe next year.'

I don't think any of them know what to say. Their jaws are on the floor.

How is it that, just like that, Millsy knew to start pretending to be my boyfriend? I really stressed how much I didn't want him to, and he's been doing as I asked, and yet he was somehow, without even seeing my face, so in tune with what's going on and what I want.

'Prosecco?'

We all look towards the server next to us. It's Jason, holding a tray of glasses. When he realises who he's looking at his face falls.

'Hey, look who it is, it's Elmer Fudd,' Luke jokes.

You genuinely can't do anything at school and get away with it – not even once. That (maybe) dead rabbit is going to haunt Jason for the rest of his life.

'Prosecco,' he says again, this time with less warmth.

'Let's just go over here,' Millsy says, dragging me away from the crowd. He waits until we're alone. 'What the hell was that?'

'Jason? He went to school with us. He's here working, he wasn't even invited. He was our year's weirdo.'

'Did you go to a circus school? I saw the freakishly tall bloke too.'

'Oh my God, that's Sean! I had a chat with him when I got here and the creep actually felt me up a bit. I'm going to spend the rest of the night hiding from him.'

'Make sure you do,' Millsy warns me. 'He's married.'

'What?'

'He's married. One hundred per cent.'

'How can you even know that?' I ask. Obviously the plan was already to stay the hell away from him but I'm curious how Millsy knows.

'I passed him on the way in, frantically tugging at his finger. It made me laugh when I realised he was removing his wedding ring,' he replies as he glances around the room nosily. 'Now it sounds like he was doing it for your benefit.'

'Oh, that creepy bastard,' I reply. 'I don't suppose I noticed if he had a ring on. I didn't have much reason to look, you know? One minute we're talking, then he's got his hand... Millsy?'

I can tell that Millsy isn't listening to a word I'm saying. In fact, he's staring at something. I follow his gaze to a server who is clearing glasses from a table. She has fiery long red hair, not unlike my own latest dye job. I watch her for a second as she wipes down a table.

'Do you know her?' I ask him.

'She's my ex,' he replies.

Oh, shit. Jason did say it was a catering company from the city. It doesn't surprise me at all that Millsy's ex was probably working at a pop-up bar in town when they met. It does kind of surprise me that he has an actual ex.

'You have an ex?' I blurt, although I probably should have kept that thought to myself.

'What? Do you think I'm a monk?'

'Everyone says you are the opposite of a monk,' I point out. 'I just... I don't know, you don't seem like the kind of person who would get freaked out like this if he ran into an ex.'

'Well, I absolutely am,' he tells me quietly, his eyes still firmly fixed on her. 'I almost didn't recognise her. Do you mind if I go?'

'Oh, I'll come with you,' I tell him. 'I've been offended quite enough for one evening. My ego is suitably in check.'

'Thanks,' he says.

As we make our way towards the hall exit we happen upon Sean. He notices me. 'Oh, hello again, Cara. Is this your—?'

'Yep,' Millsy says. 'So, you know, back off, save it for your wife.'

Sean, despite being very tall, is very skinny. Even I could have a good go at taking him down. Sean knows this and instantly goes on the defensive.

'What? No! I didn't... I didn't... I didn't,' he stutters. 'I'm married. I would never d-do that.'

'Why did you take your wedding ring off, then?' I ask him, nodding towards his hand.

'It... fell off,' he says. 'It fell off and it rolled and it fell down one of the gaps in the floor. You know, the store gym equipment under the trapdoor? It rolled down there.'

'So your ring is underneath the floor right now?' I ask in disbelief.

'Yes!'

'So... you're just going to leave it there?' I continue.

'Yes, well, no, the trapdoor is locked so I'm just waiting for the caretaker to come with the key and he's going to get it out for me.'

Sean, as hard as he is trying, is gasping like a fish that just flung itself out of its tank. He's coming up with these excuses on the fly but they're terrible. Horrifying to think that a surgeon could be so useless under pressure.

'So you're just waiting?' Millsy asks.

'Yes.'

'Until the caretaker gets here to get your ring out for you?'

'Yes!'

'OK, then,' Millsy says. 'We'll wait with you.'

'What?'

'Yeah,' he continues. 'We'll keep you company until he gets here.'

Sean starts to sweat. We've got him now. There's no way he's getting out of this one.

It's only four awkwardly silent minutes before Sean starts theatrically patting his pockets. Eventually he locates and pulls out his phone.

'Oh, no, I have to go,' he says. 'It's the hospital. I've been called in to perform emergency surgery.'

'Really?' Millsy says, clearly not believing a word of it.

'Really,' he replies. 'Some kind of freak accident at the fair.'

'The fair?' I say.

'The fair,' he replies. 'I'd better go.'

'But your ring,' Millsy calls after him.

Sean doesn't reply. He gets out of here as fast as his legs will carry him.

'I have to say, you really did go to school with some wonderful people,' Millsy points out sarcastically. 'Honestly, just the absolute best.'

'Hmm,' I say. 'It's interesting, isn't it? It's like school never actually ended. You've still got the cliques, the weirdos, the bullies, the couples, everyone being obsessed with who is sleeping with whom.'

'And these are supposedly adults,' Millsy says.

'Adults are just kids who have kids,' I tell him. 'That's it. Anyway, let's get out of here.'

As we walk along the corridor towards the entrance I feel a feeling I haven't felt in years – that rush to get out of school as fast as possible.

'Leaving already? Is everything OK?' the man on the door says.

I don't recognise him as someone I went to school with; he must just be working the event.

'Yes, all fine,' I say. 'It's just our bedtime.'

'That's a relief,' he says. 'We had another couple rush out just a few moments ago. Apparently one of their relatives had got hurt in some kind of accident at the fair.'

Millsy and I stare at each other for a second. Well, would you listen to that? I still don't buy Sean's story about his ring rolling off though. But while I might not know for sure what happened, there is one thing I am certain of: I am never going to a school reunion again.

23

'Are you sure you want to do this?' I ask Millsy.

'I'm sure,' he replies.

'But... this is a big deal, right? This is what proper couples do.'

'You seem more nervous than I am.' He laughs. 'You must have done this before?'

'Of course, I have,' I insist. 'With my ex – the one who is coming to stay.'

Millsy and I are about to take the next step in our relationship – he's going to meet my parents.

'My family love my ex,' I remind him. 'Especially my mum. So you're just going to be this hot new man walking in, ruining things.'

'You think your mum will think I'm hot, huh?' he replies with a wink. 'God, I'm kidding. You should see the look on your face. Seriously, Cara, it's going to be fine. And anyway, we're here now.'

I glance down the path towards my parents' front door.

'I have told them we're just friends,' I say for maybe the millionth time. 'I guess they just want to see who I'm bringing to Flora's wedding, that's all.'

'Cara, take a deep breath,' Millsy instructs, holding me by the shoulders. 'It's going to be fine.'

'OK, let's get it over with, then,' I say.

My mum, who called me this morning and insisted it was time for me to bring Millsy to meet her and my dad – well, it is only a couple of weeks until Flora's big day – said that she would be making dinner for 6 p.m., and that she would love it if we could be there.

It's two minutes to six and the second we walk through the door the smell of dinner drifts towards me, tempting me deeper inside the house. I love my mum's cooking so much, there's no way I could turn back now.

'Hello?' I call out.

'In the dining room,' my mum calls back.

'Here we go,' I tell Millsy. 'This way.'

Inside the dining room my mum, dad and brother are all sitting at the table, ready to eat. There are two places set out for us. It's as if they're suspended in time, just frozen here, waiting for us to arrive so they can spring to life.

'Hey, everyone, this is Joe,' I tell them. 'Joe, this is my mum, Annie, my dad, Ted, and my brother, Oliver.'

'Hello,' he says. 'Thanks for having me over.'

'No problem at all,' my mum insists. 'We're just so pleased to be meeting you finally. We've heard so much about you.'

'All good, I hope,' he says with a smile as he takes his seat at the table.

'Oh, yes, Cara sings your praises,' my mum tells him.

Millsy shoots me a teasing glance.

'Cara says you're the best man at your best friend's wedding next week,' my mum says as she serves our food.

'I am,' he replies. 'My friend Ruby. We've been friends since we were babies.'

'Ruby?' my dad chimes in. 'That's not a fella's name.'

'No, she's a she,' Millsy says. 'I was going to be a bridesmaid but the dress didn't fit.'

I shoot him a glance.

'Whoops,' he says. 'That was just supposed to be a joke-joke, not a joke about your predicament, Cara.'

'I think it's cool that your friend has a best man instead of bridesmaids,' Oliver says. I should have known he would approve. 'The more people who break convention and decide on their own rules, the happier we'll be as a society.'

'Don't worry,' my dad tells Millsy. 'He does this a lot.'

'Oh, yeah, Cara said you were doing a PhD,' Millsy says. 'Do you know what you want to do after that?'

'I pretty much just want to get straight into teaching,' Oliver says. 'What do you do?'

'I'm an actor,' Millsy replies.

'Not much money in that, is there?' my dad asks. 'Unless you're in big Hollywood films?'

'Have we seen you in anything?' my mum asks.

'I make a pretty good living actually,' Millsy tells them. 'You could have seen me in something, but you wouldn't know. I'm a sort of stand-in for other actors. So when the actor isn't on set, I'll fill in for them.'

'Like the back of your head and stuff?' Oliver asks.

'Yeah,' Millsy says. 'Stuff like that.'

'We didn't think you were successful when Cara said you were an actor,' my dad says. I cringe.

'I get that a lot,' Millsy jokes.

His friendly, jokey attitude seems to be making him a hit with my family.

'Football your sport?' my dad asks. Now that Millsy has

impressed him with his job he's clearly trying to bro-down with him. It's kind of cute.

'Nah,' Millsy says. 'Rugby league.'

'Really?' my dad says. 'Who's your team?'

'Leeds Lions,' Millsy tells him.

'And, not only does Millsy know the team, but he used to be Leo the Lion, the mascot,' I chime in. I'd forgotten that my dad is way into rugby league and I'm weirdly proud of Millsy.

'I have so many questions,' my dad starts.

'So you'll be going to two weddings only a week apart,' my mum points out, interrupting my dad. 'You both will.'

'Yeah, I guess we will,' I reply. 'Hmm, I wonder which one will be the most fun?'

My sarcasm goes either unnoticed or ignored.

'You can get ideas for your own wedding,' my mum ever so helpfully – and hopefully playfully – points out.

'The only thing I learn from weddings is what I don't want to do,' I tell her. 'I don't really want a ceremony, I don't want bridesmaids, definitely don't want flowers.'

'Yeah, I've never seen the attraction with flowers either,' Millsy says.

'I used to love them but then one day I realised that with every beautiful bunch of flowers came their inevitable death. The process of removing the dead ones and cleaning the vase was really starting to get me down. I'm strictly a plants girl now.'

'You're going to carry a plant at your wedding?' my mum asks in disbelief. 'Like, in a pot?'

'I'm not saying that.' I laugh. 'Just that I think cutting flowers, that are only going to die, is kind of a waste.'

'Here's what you do,' Millsy starts, laying down his cutlery so he can really get into it. 'You carry one of those hanging plants, wrapped around one of those hoops brides have flowers on –

Ruby is having one. Except, you know how you're always complaining that women's clothes don't have enough pockets? You have a wedding dress made with pockets, and one pocket is for the soil and the roots for the plant.'

'Yes!' I reply with enthusiasm. 'And that way you can keep the plant – you can keep it for as long as you can keep it alive.'

'For as long as you keep the relationship alive,' Millsy adds.

I realise my mum is just staring at us.

'So you two are having this at your wedding, are you?'

'Our separate weddings,' I remind her.

'Obviously,' she says. 'Because you're just friends.'

I pull a face at her.

'Anyway, at least I'm invited to Ruby's hen party,' I tell my mum. 'Not like Flora's. How was the rest of it?'

'Oh, it was fine,' she says. 'Only what you'd expect.'

'Cara told me her painting didn't go down well,' Millsy says. 'I wish I could have seen it.'

'We've got it upstairs,' Oliver says excitedly. 'Shall I get it?'

'Yes!' Millsy says eagerly.

'OK, I'll get it now,' Oliver replies, springing from his seat with an energy I didn't know he had.

'Mum, you kept it?'

'Someone had to take it,' she tells me. 'Flora took all the other ones home.'

'Maybe I'll put mine on my wall,' I say.

'You'll have to fight Oliver for it,' my mum says. 'He loves it. He says it defies a toxic culture or something, I don't know.'

I nudge Millsy.

'I'm a feminist icon,' I tell him.

'Oh, for sure,' he replies playfully. 'I'm just wondering who will play you in the movie.'

'I refuse to have anyone but you play me,' I joke.

I catch my mum just staring and smiling at us again.

'Can I get you some more food, Joe?' she asks, spotting his clean plate.

'Yes, please,' he says. 'Nicest chicken I've ever had. What is that sauce?'

'Really?' my mum replies. 'Thank you. It's gooseberry sauce.'

'It's incredible,' he tells her before turning to me. 'Can you make this?'

'I can't,' I admit. 'I want to learn.'

'If you do then you can make it for us,' he says. 'Otherwise I'm going to have to keep coming here, begging your mum to make it for me.'

'Oh, any time,' she insists. 'You come here for dinner whenever you like.'

'You don't even have to bring Cara,' my dad jokes.

It's nice, seeing my family get on so well with Millsy. I think, knowing how much everyone loved Lloyd, I would always worry that, when the time came, it would be hard for my family to accept someone new. And while Millsy might not actually be my boyfriend, it's still reassuring to see them welcome another person in so easily.

Yes, I think we can safely say that Joe Mills is a big hit with the Brooks family. I just need to hope that my auntie and my cousin feel the same. They're the hardest ones to impress, after all.

24

If only relationships were as easy as my friendship with Millsy. I'm aware that this plus-one pact has to come to an end some time but in the meantime life is just such a breeze. It's like having a boyfriend, who gets on really well with your family, and you get on really well with his family, and there's no sex to complicate things. No need to worry about money stuff or future plans. The last thing on your mind is whether or not your partner might be cheating on you. This really is the simplest relationship I've ever been involved in.

It's quite nice, having someone else's family stuff to go to. Well, you can relax at other people's family events in a way that you can't do at your own, can't you? You don't need to worry about your relatives being embarrassing, and it's genuinely hilarious when other people's relatives are embarrassing. You're always the guest, on other families' turf, so you don't need to worry about doing jobs. You just get to enjoy yourself.

Today I'm at Millsy's dad, Rod's, surprise party. It's his sixtieth birthday so they've thrown a party for him at the golf club where he usually plays. It's Sunday evening now but, when we surprised him earlier this afternoon, he turned up here thinking he was playing a round of golf, so he's actually dressed in his golf clothes. He fits right in though, because it's a golf-themed party, so we're all wearing dorky golf attire.

I'm wearing a pink polo shirt and a short white skirt. I think the skirt might be more of a tennis thing but I like it. Millsy is wearing a pair of chinos and a baby-blue Ralph Lauren polo shirt.

I've noticed Jay around. He's gone all out. He's wearing the trousers, the polo shirt, the cap – he's even wearing the glove. I haven't spoken to him yet. At first it was just because Millsy and I were talking to various family members, but for the last hour or so Jay has been sitting at a table chatting with a twenty-something woman who I don't recognise at all. She's gorgeous, with long brown hair that doesn't look as if it's glued in like mine is. Not that mine looks glued in, I just know that it is. Hers definitely looks real though.

I've been watching him for a while, casually glancing over at him, trying to work out what's going on between the two of them. I don't know if maybe, just maybe, I might feel a tiny bit jealous.

'Right, I'm going to go and get the cake set up,' Millsy tells me. 'Back in a minute.'

After our cake for Fran's baby shower went down so well (we'll just forget about all that business with the balloon, shall we?) we offered to arrange Rod's cake too. What we have is something truly spectacular. There is a place in North Yorkshire, on the coast somewhere, where they make bespoke cakes, and they'll have a go at anything you could possibly imagine, if they think it's possible. So we have a cake man (that looks like Rod), brandishing a golf club, ready to strike the ball. His club is actually the sparkler that you light, when it's time to sing 'Happy Birthday'. I can't wait to see it in action.

Millsy has only been gone for a few seconds when I see Jay

standing up too. I wonder if he's going to help him, as unlikely as that seems. It becomes quickly apparent that he's walking towards me so I try to pretend I wasn't looking in his direction at all.

'Hey, Cara,' he says. 'Mind if I sit for a minute?'

'Oh, hi,' I say, as though I've just noticed him. Not subtle at all. 'Of course not, take a seat. Millsy has just gone to sort the birthday cake out.'

'That's why I've popped over now,' he tells me. 'He's been with you the whole time – we haven't had chance to chat.'

'You've been quite busy yourself,' I point out. I immediately wish I hadn't because it sounds as if I care.

'Just chatting with Amy,' he says. 'You know Amy?'

'I don't,' I reply. Now I'm trying so hard not to care I've gone too far the other way.

'My cousin Amy,' he says. 'Didn't you meet her at the baby shower?'

God, and Millsy told me he was the one who is terrible with names and faces. I suppose it's the little pangs of jealousy clouding my judgement, fogging my memory.

'Oh, right, of course,' I say.

'I'd better make it quick,' he says, leaning in a little closer. 'Because I don't think Millsy will be too happy to see us fraternising.'

'OK.'

'When are we going to go on a proper date?' he asks me.

I'm a little taken aback. I think that's the last thing I was expecting him to say.

'Us?'

'No, that lady golfer behind you. *Yes*, you.'

I laugh.

'Whenever you like,' I reply. Suddenly, now I know that he's into me, it feels easy to be a little more casual.

'Are you free on Friday evening?' he asks.

'Oh, it's Ruby's hen party on Friday, sorry.'

'Thursday? I could come to Leeds – we could go for dinner?'

'That would be great,' I tell him.

'OK, well, I don't want to upset Joe but...' Jay reaches into his pocket and removes a small piece of paper, '...text me and we'll make proper plans.'

'OK, sure,' I reply. 'Looking forward to it.'

'Me too,' he replies. 'I've had you stuck on my mind since Scotland.'

I just smile at him.

As the lights dim and Millsy emerges with a cake, we all get ready to sing Happy Birthday to Rod. Jay sneaks off as quickly as he snuck over. The only difference now is that we have a date planned. An actual date. Not a pact date, not a pity date. A date-date.

I wonder whether or not I should tell Millsy about it, but I worry it might upset him. If he hates Jay as much as he acts like he does, then he isn't going to want him dating his friend, and he definitely isn't going to want him dating his roommate, because that would mean Jay coming over to the flat. I know, I'm getting ahead of myself. Perhaps it's best if, for now, I don't tell Millsy that I'm going on a date with Jay. I should just go and have dinner with him, see how I feel, see where it goes. And if it goes well, which I really hope it does, then we'll cross that bridge when we come to it.

25

I like to think of myself as a good person. I might not be a very good artist, and I'm certainly not winning any Cousin of the Year awards any time soon, but I've never cheated on anyone. I don't think I could if I wanted to. It's just one of those things that I find absolutely abhorrent. If you want to be with someone else so badly then there's obviously something wrong with your relationship and you should leave the person you're with. You can't have your cake and eat it, you can't test the waters, there's no room for overlap. You get to be with one person at a time – that's just the way it is when you're in a monogamous relationship.

But, while I've never cheated on anyone before, I have to say that what I'm doing here tonight certainly feels as if it's in the same family as cheating. A distant cousin, at least, probably not winning any Cousin of the Year awards either.

I decided it was probably for the best that I didn't tell Millsy I was going on a date with his stepbrother. I felt awful, keeping it from him, telling him that I was going out with a friend, but it just felt for the best. And he didn't suspect a thing – but why am I thinking things like that? I'm not having an affair. I'm just not telling Millsy about my love life in real time. I, for some strange reason, actively avoid knowing the ins and outs of his love life too. I was aware of times he would go out but I would never ask where.

While it does feel wrong sitting here having dinner with Jay, behind Millsy's back, it also feels so right. We've had an amazing dinner, in a gorgeous Italian restaurant, we've chatted without worrying who was listening or how it might look, and now we're tucking into our desserts. The conversation just flows so easily between us, and Jay seems so undramatic, which I like. He's looking pretty good in his shirt and chinos too.

We're in Vici, the best Italian restaurant in Leeds. It's such a romantic place, dimly lit, with little twinkling fairy lights dotted around the room, and sweet Italian music gently drifting from the speakers. I had the most incredible roasted vegetable pizza for dinner and now I'm tucking into their signature Italian dough-nuts. Little balls of yummy wonder dipped in a cream that I could happily eat until I died.

'This really has been the most amazing date – even better than I had hoped,' Jay says after polishing off the last of his cheesecake. 'It's gone so well that I think we might need to mention the M-word.'

'Marriage already?' I joke. 'It hasn't gone *that* well.'

'Very funny,' he replies. 'But I'm talking about your M-word.'

I'm tempted to make another joke but I keep a lid on my relentless sense of humour.

'I have to tell Millsy,' I say seriously. 'If it hadn't gone well then maybe we could have just forgotten about it, but I'm just having such a wonderful time.'

Jay reaches across the candlelit table and takes my hand in his. He caresses it gently as he talks.

'Me too,' he replies. 'And if you think you need to tell him then you have to do what you have to do but, if it were me, I wouldn't tell him yet. He'll only try to poison you against me.'

'He's my best friend,' I reply. 'I trust him more than anyone. He's done so much for me – he always has my back. Why wouldn't I just be honest with him?'

Jay looks a little frustrated.

'Because he doesn't live in the real world,' he replies. 'Everything he's ever had has come so easy to him. I have to work myself stupid every day, exhausting myself, dealing with animals, getting covered in mud and God knows what else. I earn my money the hard way. Not Millsy though, oh no, instead of working for his money he just flashes his genitals at a camera for a few minutes and cashes a big cheque for it.'

I feel as if I might have just accidentally tapped into the Jay Millsy warned me about, that's been lurking inside him somewhere. Millsy did tell me that he wasn't the perfect man he seemed and, as I'm figuring all of this out, it seems as if Jay has noticed his halo slipping too.

'I just mean that he'll overreact. He won't take it like a normal person. He won't be happy for us,' he backtracks.

'I think he'll be happy for me if I'm happy,' I tell him. There's a snippiness to my voice that I hadn't intended. It's just coming out naturally as I defend my friend. 'I don't really know what I'd do without him now. I don't want to risk losing him.'

'You don't want to risk losing him for me?' Jay asks, starting to sound a little pissed off. 'Tell me, I'm dying to know, what the hell is it that you women see in him? The muscles? The money? The man's a joke, you can't tell me it's his personality.'

Jay stares at me expectantly, waiting for an answer. For a moment I just stare at him. The intense glare of his eyes. The tightness in his jaw making my own ache just by looking at it.

Wow, I can't believe it. Everything Millsy told me about him was absolutely right. Jay really is a dick. Why has it taken me so long to see that?

If I felt bad about being here before, I feel even worse now. I am a horrible, shitty, disloyal friend. And after everything Millsy has done for me, I'm going on dates with his stepbrother behind his back? Things have been great between us. Really great. Why would I risk ruining it?

I'll finish my dessert, because I'm not stupid, but I'll make my excuses and leave after that. I don't want to spend another minute with Jay. Suddenly all I want to do is get home to my friend.

It just goes to show that even the least complicated relationship in the world can be complicated when you try to factor in any kind of romantic relationship – even if it is with someone else.

I just need to be completely honest with Millsy and hope that he still wants me to go to Ruby's wedding with him, and that he still wants to go to Flora's wedding with me, but most importantly of all that he forgives me. More than anything, I just really hope he forgives me.

26

Millsy and Ruby might have stopped hanging out all the time since she got together with Nick, but that's not to say Millsy isn't still totally on the same page as her.

As Ruby's bridesmale – or male of honour, which seems to be the term being thrown around this evening – Millsy was solely in charge of organising her hen party, and, my God, has he delivered with something amazing.

I didn't get in too late last night. Millsy was nowhere to be seen so I figured he'd gone out to see some of his friends and get drunk, even though he doesn't do that as often as he used to. I suppose he has been pretty busy with all of our joint activities. Millsy might be used to having lots going on but I'm finding it exhausting. Between my events and his, we're pretty much doing at least one thing every week at the moment, and even when it is just one thing, there are usually a few things that make it up. Like, it's not just a birthday party, there's all the prep. Buy an outfit, buy a present, arrange the cake. And all the while trying to work from home too. There's always that worry, when you work from home, that you'll get distracted or purposefully procrastinate – or think of something way more fun than working that you can do with your flatmate and do that instead.

When I woke up earlier today I walked into the living room to find out that Millsy had made me breakfast. Pancakes – the ready-made ones that you pop in the microwave, I noticed, lest we have another fire – and fruit. I was already feeling pretty guilty about being out with Jay last night and not telling him, but then when I saw the lovely breakfast he'd made I didn't think I could feel worse. And then I found out that Millsy wasn't actually still out when I got in last night, he hadn't been out at all, he was *asleep*, *in bed*, making sure he was well rested for tonight.

The Millsy I first met didn't care about being well rested. He certainly didn't get early nights. Perhaps I'm having a positive influence on his life too.

After we had breakfast Millsy went straight out to make preparations for this evening – insisting on keeping the plan from me, so that I could appreciate the surprise too – which means I've been alone in the flat all day today. I had time to work, and plenty of time to get ready for tonight, but I mostly spent my day thinking about what I had done. I still can't believe I was so sucked in by Jay's act. I'm supposed to be observant. I guess I just saw what I wanted to see.

If I allowed myself any time to think about anything else, other than kicking myself over Jay, it was to wonder what Millsy had planned for tonight. I expected quite a lot from him – he never does things by halves – but he's really impressed me tonight. I never would have guessed what he was planning but it's perfect.

Back in the day, when Millsy and Ruby were both younger, freer and singler, they would spend all of their time going out in the city. Visiting every bar, trying out new restaurants, going to clubs. At one point (Millsy tells me 2014 is when they peaked) they were the toast of Leeds, apparently. So that was their thing, but then Ruby met 'sensible boring Dr Nick' (as Millsy calls him), and they stopped going out all the time until eventually it became a once-in-a-blue-moon kind of thing. So, to give Ruby the send-off she deserved, Millsy planned one last bar hop around Leeds – the ultimate bar hop.

We started the night in Thin Aire, which is where my friend-ship with Millsy started too, but I felt far less nervous walking in there this time, with my fake-haired head held high. There was a table waiting for us on the terrace, already decked out with silver balloons and bottles of champagne on ice. The waiters poured our drinks and Millsy raised a toast to his friend, and while his words were encouraging about Ruby starting the next chapter of her life, I could tell that he was sad to close the book on the friendship they enjoyed together as singles. I don't think anyone else noticed though, only me, but my heart felt heavy as I watched him.

So not only have we spent the evening visiting various bars, but we've been transported from point to point on an actual tour bus – a real one. A big sleeper bus like the ones rock stars travel around in. The idea was for us to be able to hop around different venues in Leeds all night, essentially taking our hotel around with us. So, at any point, if you just wanted to sit down or use the loo, or even if you wanted to bow out early and go to bed, the bus would be there waiting for you, ready for you to make yourself feel at home wherever you were.

After visiting many bars, and drinking many drinks, I'm really starting to feel tipsy. It's 2 a.m. now so we've graduated from bars to clubs. We're currently in Saturn, a nightclub largely frequented by students, but I think everyone is drunk enough to fit right in.

There's me, Millsy, Ruby, her cousin Gemma, and then there's Erica and Lizzy, who Millsy tells me are her new couple friends –

they're not a couple together, they both have husbands, so the six of them all hang around together and do couple stuff. I imagine Millsy not being invited to take part in couple stuff with his friend is like me not being invited to do baby stuff with mine. I totally get how infuriating it is.

Everyone, apart from me and Millsy, is on the dance floor. Instead of busting moves we're popping the cork on yet another bottle of fizz, tucked away in a dark, private corner of the club that Millsy reserved just for the occasion.

'I'm having such a good time,' I shout to him over the music.

'I can tell,' he replies. 'You look so happy.'

'I am happy,' I shout back. 'So much stuff just feels so right. When I got ready earlier, and I was doing my hair and make-up, I actually felt like I was looking at myself, for the first time since my makeover, even in this tiny black sparkly dress. This is me now and I love it.'

With great alcohol consumption comes great self-confidence.

'You look amazing,' he shouts. 'And this new self-confidence is only making you seem sexier.'

I'm starting to realise how unstable self-confidence can be. You can think you have it, question it, find more – you can maybe, just maybe, even have a little too much of it at times. It's such a fluid state that changes day to day. On the one hand, I feel so much more confident now that I stand out more, but with that comes a vulnerability. Sometimes I feel more myself, other times I feel like a fraud. But when I'm around Millsy I just feel so at peace with who I am. I feel as if he sees me, not what I'm wearing. He's always seen me. And whether I'm a lonely jilted blonde in the corner of a bar or a wild redhead dancing on a table to The Weeknd in a club (honestly, you should have seen me earlier!), it doesn't matter; Millsy has always looked at me in the same way.

We've been sitting pretty close together so that we can talk, practically screaming into each other's ears at point-blank range so that we can hear what the other is saying.

I move back a little, to look into Millsy's eyes. He's so sweet and I feel so guilty. The Jay stuff has been weighing so heavy on me all day. As soon as I start enjoying myself it pops back into my head and I feel so terrible.

'We need to talk,' I tell him.

'About what?' he asks.

'About... about...'

I swear someone just turned the music up.

'Can we go someplace quieter?' I ask.

'Sure,' he replies.

We leave Saturn and walk down the road a little to where the massive tour bus is parked. Everyone knows the drill. We can just come back here at any point. It's great, like a mobile chair, toilet and bed, with no need to queue and no taxi required either.

The bus driver opens the door to let us on. Millsy gives him a large tip and asks him if he'd like to wander to the twenty-four-hour café across the road to grab a decent hot cup of coffee. He's more than happy to do so.

'We've got the bus to ourselves,' Millsy says. 'I thought it might be weird chatting with the driver here.'

'Yeah, definitely,' I reply with a nervous giggle.

We walk up the stairs and along past the sleeping bunks, towards the back of the bus where there is a sort of living room. A U-shaped sofa wraps around the walls, surrounded by large windows that you can see out of, but no one can see in.

'I'll get us a drink,' Millsy says.

I'm sure we've had enough but it might make this conversation go a little more smoothly.

I watch Millsy as he grabs a bottle of Prosecco from the fridge.

'Ruby's favourite,' he says as he pours it. 'I'm more of a champagne man myself... who's actually more of a beer man, but it's Ruby's night, right?'

I laugh.

He's such a sweetheart, doing all this for his friend, giving her a proper send-off into married life. Millsy looks great tonight too. He's wearing blue trousers and one of his tight-fitting white shirts, which I'm not sure are actually supposed to be tight-fitting, I think they just look that way as they stretch over his muscles. He's got two buttons undone, just as he had the night I met him, which only adds to the strange sense of déjà vu I keep experiencing.

'So what's up?' he says sitting down next to me, pushing a drink into my hand. 'You seem kind of freaked out.'

'I fucked up,' I blurt. 'I haven't been totally honest with you and it's killing me.'

Millsy takes my hand in his.

'Hey, Cara, come on, it's me,' he says. 'You know you can tell me anything.'

'I went on a date with Jay,' I blurt. 'Last night. I went for dinner with him. I didn't want to tell you because I knew you hated him and figured that, if it was a bad date, I could just forget about it. But I thought it was going to be good, because he seemed so great, but you were right, he's a dick. He's an absolute dick. I should have listened to you. But nothing happened, I swear, nothing at all.'

I am drunk and I am babbling. I'm not even sure how much sense that made.

'Are you finished?' Millsy asks me.

'Yes,' I say weakly. I can't read him. I don't know if he's mad or upset or what.

'I'm sorry you had a bad date,' he says. 'I should have done more to warn you off him, but you're a grown woman. I wanted you to make your own mind up about people.'

Oh, God, he feels sorry for me. Now I feel even worse.

'I'm clearly a shit judge of character,' I say. 'I was with my ex for ages before I realised how possessive and jealous he was getting.'

'That's exactly why you need to figure people out on your own though,' Millsy says.

'Wait, why aren't you mad at me?' I can't help but ask. It's not that I want him to be, I'm just confused.

'Am I crazy about you lying to me? Of course not. Have I told bigger lies in the past? Absolutely.'

'I know but—'

'Cara, just forget about it,' Millsy insists. 'I'm glad you're OK.'

'I don't ever want to see Jay again.'

It feels important to get that out there just in case it doesn't go without saying.

'Well, that makes two of us,' he replies with a laugh. 'No such luck for me. What did he say to upset you so much?'

'Oh, a bunch of stuff,' I reply.

'He was talking shit about me, wasn't he?'

I don't want to hurt Millsy's feelings by telling him what Jay thinks of him.

'In Scotland, he told me about some cheating stuff,' I say. 'And I guess everything stems from that.'

'Wait, he told you about that?'

'Yeah,' I reply. 'Is it true?'

'You still went out with him, knowing that? That doesn't sound like you *at all*.'

'Are we even talking about the same thing?' I ask.

Why would any of that stop me from going out with Jay?

'What are you referring to?' Millsy says.

'Jay told me that you slept with his girlfriend,' I say. 'He said that he was seeing someone and you slept with her.'

'Unbelievable,' Millsy says. He actually looks really annoyed now. 'That's what he told you? That I slept with his girlfriend? No, no. He slept with the girl I was seeing. Remember the waitress, from the reunion? That's Jane. She wasn't my girlfriend, but I was dating her, and it felt like things were starting to go somewhere, and then she met Jay. He didn't even want to steal her, he just wanted to sleep with her. But he took her from me, so easily, and I knew he would try to do the same with you.'

'OK, if you had told me that this was why you hated him, it would have made a lot more sense,' I say. 'I can't even imagine what that must have been like.'

'It was a while ago now,' he says. 'The wounds are getting smaller, but they open up sometimes. But, if he's telling people that it was the other way around... I should confront him.'

I'm not sure if he's looking for his phone or if, in his drunken state, he thinks paying Jay a visit right now is a good idea, but I'm not taking any chances.

'You absolutely shouldn't,' I insist. 'He lives miles away, you're very drunk, your biggest fear is being hit in the face, you have a wedding tomorrow, remember.'

Millsy is already on his feet so I push him back down onto the sofa and sit myself down on top of him. I'm facing him, sitting on his lap, holding his wrists with my hands. It feels as if I've got him restrained but I'm sure that he's more than strong enough to put me to one side and storm out of here.

'Do you know why I'm not mad at you?' Millsy says, suddenly a lot calmer.

'Why?' I ask.

'Because Jay took Jane from me so easily and there was nothing I could have done. And, I suppose, he tried to take you away from me too, but you've seen through him. I didn't have to stop you – you binned him off on your own.'

'As funny as it sounds, I would never let a boy come between us,' I tell him with a smile. 'Especially not a disgusting liar like Jay.'

'I'm just so glad I didn't lose you to him,' Millsy says sincerely. 'You're too important to me.'

'Come on, Millsy, we'll be friends forever. After everything we've been through this summer. We've nearly ruined every event we've been to. I don't doubt for a second that we we'll ruin the weddings,' I joke. At least I hope I'm joking.

'Well, there is no one I'd rather ruin weddings with than you,' he tells me.

'You too,' I reply. 'It's going to be so weird when I have to start going to these things alone again.'

'Unless...'

'Well, yeah, unless we keep up the pact forever, but I'd like to think at least one of us will find love at some point,' I say with a laugh, but then I notice Millsy isn't amused. He looks so serious, and he rarely ever looks serious. 'I don't know why you're frowning, because you stand more of a chance than I do.'

'You're not getting this at all, are you?' he says.

'Getting what?' I reply, pretty much proving him right.

'This,' he says.

I'm already sitting on top of him but Millsy finds a way to pull my body closer before reaching up and pulling my lips towards his. We kiss for a few seconds before he lets me go. It's as if he's testing the waters, seeing how I respond, trying to work out if I'm into it.

It isn't just a kiss though, it's something else, because feelings bubble up inside me that I have been trying to keep hidden under the surface. I want Millsy to kiss me again. I think I've wanted him to kiss me for a while. I don't think I've ever felt a kiss like it.

He stares at me expectantly, waiting for me to say something. He actually looks pretty nervous.

I don't even know what to say. I just know that I want to kiss him again.

I grab his face and pull it towards mine. Our first kiss was gentle but this one is something else entirely. There's something wild about it, something so desperate. I close my eyes tightly shut, hardly able to believe this is actually happening. I know I've had a lot to drink, but I'm not hallucinating this, am I? It seems too good to be true.

Whether I'm imagining this or not, I'm making the most of it. Before I know what I'm doing I'm unbuttoning Millsy's shirt. Yes, me, making the first unbuttoning move. This isn't like me at all. I'm not confident like this, not with men. There's just something about Millsy that is making this so easy, that's making me feel as if I can do anything I want.

He follows my lead, gently running a hand up my back before dragging it back down, the zip of my dress between his fingers. I let go of him for a second, only to allow my dress to slip off. Millsy unhooks my bra with a level of skill I didn't realise any man possessed. I remove his shirt before tangling myself up in his arms again. Amid all of this, we barely part lips for more than a second.

Is this what we've been building towards, all of these weeks? Thinking that things were totally platonic, all the while harbouring these feelings for one another? I have absolutely no idea, but this feels right. It feels so, so impossibly right that it's hard to even consider what comes next. Right now I'm just enjoying the moment and we'll deal with tomorrow when we get there – not that I'm in any rush for tonight to be over.

27

My hangover taps me awake, right between my eyes, with an ice pick.

The headache is the first thing I notice. Then it's the pain in my back. Finally the heavy feeling across my body, but that isn't from drinking too much or getting up to all sorts in a tour-bus bunk all night, it's Millsy's arm. He's behind me, spooning me, in this sleeping bunk that is absolutely only intended for one person. It would be nice if I weren't so freaked out because I, you know, *had sex with my best friend.*

I'm too scared to move, too scared to wake him up, too scared to face the reality of what I've done. Don't get me wrong, I wanted to do it, but just because I wanted to doesn't mean that I should have. He isn't just my best friend, he's my landlord. More than that, though, he's Millsy. He's a good-time kind of guy; he doesn't want a girlfriend. He hooks up with people and then he's done with them, right? That's what everyone keeps saying.

I can't be like that though. I'm boring and monogamous. This is why I'm so annoyed that Lloyd is going to be at Flora's wedding because, once things are over between me and someone I have slept with, I am too awkward to ever make eye contact with them again. I only want to sleep with people I have strong feelings for – I don't want hook-ups with my friends – and that's the problem. Somehow I have only just realised it, but I also feel as if I might have known all along: I have strong feelings for Millsy. I spent so long telling myself again and again that we were just friends, trying not to worry about why he didn't fancy me when he'll supposedly chase anything in a skirt, that I was kidding myself, pushing to the back of my mind that my feelings for him were only getting stronger by the day.

And now here we are. The last thing I expected, when we came up with our plus-one pact, was for either of us to get hurt, and yet here I am, sabotaging the best friendship I've ever had and the coolest flat I've ever lived in, for what? A quick night of passion? Well, OK, it wasn't exactly quick, and the fact that I was so emboldened by a combination of alcohol, and Millsy's unique way of making me feel amazing about myself, gave me this level of self-confidence that I've never experienced in the bedroom (or in the tour-bus bunk, in our case) that just made it the absolute best. It was just sex though, and just sex just isn't worth it.

I can hear someone snoring. It's a sort of gentle, almost feminine snore, if there is such a thing. That must mean that other people are asleep on the bus too. It's only 6 a.m. We all agreed to set our alarms for 8.30 a.m. so that we could start getting ready for the wedding, which is today. I feel as if people hardly ever have their hen parties/stag dos the night before their wedding any more. I know that I wouldn't do it; it feels like flying too close to the sun. You don't have to be a genius to figure out how many things could potentially go wrong by having wild parties the night before the big day. Anyone who has ever seen one of the *Hangover* movies could advise you against it. But Millsy said that it was what Ruby wanted. One last crazy night out like the good old days to see her into married life with a bang.

I try to gently wiggle free from Millsy's embrace but as soon as I start getting anywhere he squeezes me tighter in his sleep. Brilliant, just brilliant, I'm going to have to wake him up if I want to get out of here, and I want to get out of here so badly right now. I know that it's Ruby's wedding day, and that I said that I would be there, and I will, but right now I just want to get out of here.

'Millsy,' I whisper, tapping him on the arm that's wrapped around me. 'Millsy.'

I wiggle my body to try and wake him.

'Oh, morning,' he says sleepily. 'You OK?'

'Yeah, yeah, I'm good,' I say casually – although I don't sound casual at all. 'I just, I need to go.'

'What? Is everything OK?'

He takes back his arm and lifts himself up onto his elbows. Poor guy, he isn't even awake yet. He's looking at me through one eye because he's still half asleep.

'Oh, yeah, it's fine, it's just... one of my hair extensions has come loose – it's hanging off. It's hurting a little, pulling on my hair, and I'll need it sorting in time for the wedding, so I'm going to go now.'

'Shit, I didn't do that, did I?'

'No, no,' I quickly insist. 'Luca said this could happen. It just needs fixing back in place.'

I feel terrible lying to him, but I don't know what else to say.

'I can come with you,' he says. 'Just let me find my clothes.'

'Oh, no, it's fine,' I reply. 'You know how long they took to put in the first time. It's going to take more than a quick brush to fix this mess. You need to be here for all the wedding morning stuff with Ruby.'

'I'll see you at the wedding, then?' he says.

'Yeah, see you there,' I tell him.

I notice him lean towards me – to hug me, I think – but I pretend not to notice. I don't look to see how he reacts, trying so desperately hard to style all of this out as cool and casual, even though I am neither of those things right now.

I quickly and quietly locate my clothes, hurry them on and then make my way to the front of the bus. I find the driver sitting in the downstairs living area, drinking a coffee and reading a newspaper.

'Morning,' he says. 'Good night?'

'Great,' I reply. 'Just delicate today. Think I overdid it last night.'

I massage my temples, as though it's going to do anything to chill my hangover, but it's my only option until I find some painkillers.

'Getting off?' he asks.

'What?'

'Are you wanting to go?'

'Oh, yes, please,' I say. God knows what I thought he meant.

The driver lets me off the bus. It's so bright outside – the summer sun is beaming already – causing me to shield my eyes while they adjust to the light. It takes me a few seconds to figure out where I am.

It turns out we're in a car park just off The Headrow. Leeds isn't a massive city but the walk from The Headrow to the docks, where Millsy's flat is, is about twenty minutes. Twenty-five if I stop to grab a takeaway coffee along the way, which might go some of the way to calming down the demon playing the drums in my head right now.

Walking through the city at this time in the morning, practically wading through all the mess everyone left last night, offers a unique glimpse into city life. During the day such a gorgeous stretch, usually overflowing with people, alive with chatter, buskers, magicians – even the preachers with megaphones telling the world how we're all going to die – give it character. Right now the street is the deadest I have ever seen it. The only noise I can hear is from the road sweeper, making his way up and down a road that is covered with empty bottles, litter from takeaways, a whole host of bodily fluids. It's unbelievable how much carnage people leave in their wake after a night out. I can even see some drips of blood on the floor next to a discarded, seemingly untouched kebab. I'll bet that's a story. I suppose we take for granted the people who are up at the crack of dawn to get rid of all traces of Friday night, so that by the time we're all ready to kick off our Saturday, the streets are clean.

There's something really satisfying about watching the road sweeper. The machine itself drives along so slowly but the brushes move so fast they look blurry – unless that's just my eyes. I like the way it ploughs through the mess, leaving a perfect trail of clean behind it, as if the mess never happened. That's what I need right now: a road sweeper to just plough into me. Not to take me out, things aren't that bad, just to clean up the mess I seem to have made for myself. I guess I was right when I was making my excuses to Millsy earlier. It's definitely going to take more than a quick brush to clean up this mess.

28

You don't have to travel too far outside Leeds to find Kirkstall Abbey, a ruined Cistercian monastery. Sitting in a park on the edge of the River Aire, the abbey ruins stand tall. You can spot the highest-standing part peeking out above the trees from a distance – I always look out for it from the train, on the other side of the river, when I travel to and from visiting my parents.

It may be ruined but it is one of the most complete examples of a Cistercian abbey in Britain. So much of the structure is still standing, and it's situated in so much greenery, it's a must-visit if you're in the area. It's used for all kinds of public events – fairs, outdoor concerts, outdoor cinemas. Today it was used for Ruby and Nick's wedding ceremony. Yes, she's got married in the abbey ruins, and it was romantic and yet so dark and gothic.

I met Millsy there. We were supposed to travel there together but my fake hair emergency lasted for 'longer than expected'. I knew that I was going to have to see him eventually, if I still planned on going to the wedding with him – well, I wasn't going to back out last minute, was I? – but I still just wanted to leave things as long as possible, hoping my brain would find some peace somewhere and things wouldn't be awkward. Obviously, with him being part of the wedding, we didn't get to chat for long before it was time for me to take my seat with the rest of the guests, but that's exactly what I wanted. No time to ourselves means no time to have serious conversations.

'Did you get your hair sorted OK?' he asked me. 'It's looking great.'

'I did, thanks,' I replied, a little stiffer than I intended. Look, I'm sorry, but I'm not exactly fighting the fellas off with a stick, am I? I don't know how to play these games.

'You look amazing, honestly,' he continued. 'You've really made this new look your own. I don't even think we should call it a new look any more, I think it's just you.'

I awkwardly attempted to smile, nod and – for some completely bizarre reason – salute Millsy in response to this lovely compliment, which baffled him even more than it did me. I was so relieved when we were interrupted by Ruby's mum, to say the ceremony was starting, and after that it was straight on to the photos before an open-top bus dropped us at the hotel where the reception was taking place.

Flash forward to now and we're at the ultra-modern Mode hotel sitting at tables underneath a marquee in the large grounds that surround it. Tables have been set up around their bizarre feature fountain made up of fish spraying water from their mouths. One thing I hadn't really considered was that, with Millsy being the bridesmale/male of honour, he would be sitting at the top table with Ruby and her family. This means that I, as Millsy's plus one, have been seated at a table with Rod and Mhairi. I am so, so thankful that Jay wasn't ever invited. To be honest, not sitting with Millsy is suiting me just fine today, I'm doing everything I can think of to avoid him. The only time I can feel even close to relaxed is when everyone is forced to sit in their seats, either when we were eating before or now, while the speeches are going on.

Ruby's dad is currently giving his speech. It's so sweet and moving. I do wonder, if I got married, what my dad would say about me.

'Anyway,' he continues, 'I don't think I could ask for a better man than Nick to take care of my little girl, so, if you'll join me in making a toast...'

His best man was one-half of one of his and Ruby's couple friends and his speech confirmed what Millsy had predicted: that Nick's stag do would be incredibly tame. Apparently they went to the cinema, to the pub and then home to bed. I like that though; I think that's the way it should be. I hear so many horror stories about men on stag dos.

With Millsy being the male of honour, Ruby has asked him to make a speech too. I know that he's been working on it for a while, but I have no idea what it says. I've noticed that he doesn't like to run things by people, he prefers to surprise them.

As the microphone is handed to Millsy I notice that he is the only person who starts their speech without a nervous wobble in their voice or a crumpled-up piece of paper in their shaky hand. I suppose, because he's an actor, learning his speech is no different from learning lines, and delivering it is basically just performing.

He looks incredible in his suit, but I already knew that, after getting a sneak peek when he tried it on. Somehow it looks even better today though. I suppose it's because he's got his hair neatly slicked back, and the biggest smile on his face, that just makes him look so good.

'Good afternoon, ladies and gentlemen,' Millsy starts. 'I'm Joe, although I'm sure most of you know me as "Millsy". I'm actually Ruby's chief bridesmaid – her only bridesmaid, in fact. Basically just because she couldn't get any of the other girls to like her during high school. It's fine though, neither could I.'

Everyone in the room laughs. Everyone apart from Nick's best man, who looks a little bit irritated that Millsy also gets to make a best-man-style speech, and so far it's seeming as though his is going to be way funnier.

'But really though,' Millsy continues as soon as the chuckles have died down, 'Ruby actually had trouble finding someone to give a speech about her today. Naturally she asked her funniest friend first – they said no. She asked her most charming friend – they said no. She asked her best-looking friend – they said no. Eventually Ruby called me up and asked me to do it... and I figured, after already turning her down three times, I should probably say yes.'

Laughter again. You can tell that he's a performer; he's got the room eating out of his hand, even with his naff best-man jokes.

'You're supposed to tell jokes like these when you do these speeches, aren't you? Well, I'm sorry to disappoint you but that's the last one. Instead of taking the mick out of my friends, I want to talk about how they got together. So, I don't know how much you know about the history of Ruby and Nick – I don't know how much is public knowledge – but I do know all's well that ends well, so I'm sure they won't mind me telling you. They actually lived together as flatmates, before they were a couple, and they absolutely hated each other. I mean, it made perfect sense to me. They were polar opposites. Nick was this sensible doctor, tidy, quiet, spending his evening learning how to turn lentils into mince for his vegan girlfriend who, I think it's safe to say, we all hated deep down. Ruby was this wild child. Messy, always late for work, always drunk or hungover. They had nothing in common – barely a kind word to say to each other – and yet here we are. If there's one thing I've learned from their story, it's that we're all taught that we need to find the perfect person for us, someone we have everything in common with, someone who is exactly like us. But, Ruby, Nick, you've proven that that just isn't true. Real love is wherever you find it, wherever you make it. I think if we can all remember that – that it's OK to love people even if they don't fit the mould of the person we think we're supposed to be with – then we're all going to be a lot happier, and we're going to have a lot more love in our lives, so, if you'd like to join me in toasting the happy couple, for the last time, I promise, then you can stop trying to conserve your Prosecco and knock it back, like I can tell you're all dying to do… To Ruby and Nick.'

'Ruby and Nick,' everyone echoes.

I sip my drink along with everyone else but there's something on my mind. Millsy's speech… If we were to take what he just said and apply it to our relationship… is he saying that real love is made of something more than shared interests? Is that how he defines relationships, and why he sees me as just a friend, and why he has done all this time until, what, he was drunk enough to sleep with me and I basically threw myself at him. His speech, which has somehow touched the hearts of everyone else, feels more like a poke in the eye to me.

Now that the speeches are over, people are leaving the confines of their tables, gathering at the seats out in the sunshine, hanging around the bar, lingering around the dance floor, waiting for the music. It's only now, after hours of hardly speaking to each other, that Millsy has time to sit and chat to me.

'Weddings are exhausting,' he says, plonking himself down next to me. 'Remind me to never do all of this when I get married.'

My initial reaction is to think that this is him making a marked effort to talk about his own wedding in a way that points out that I won't be there, but I'm feeling so anxious after his speech that it could just be me, making things into something bigger than they are.

'You OK?' he asks. 'You seem quiet.'

'I'm fine,' I insist. 'Just tired.'

'Me too,' he says with a smile. 'Hey, can you keep a secret?'

'Sure,' I reply.

'This is Ruby's day, so I'm not going to tell anyone else, but I've been called for an audition. I got the call this morning just after you left. My agent has been working on something for a while... There's this part, in one of those big comic-book superhero movies – a villain, who they think I'll be perfect for. My agent thinks the gig is basically mine and, get this, just in case you're thinking what I was thinking, because I did wonder if they only wanted me for my arse, but you're not even going to see my arse – I'm not even going to have an arse. The character is some alien thing, it's all mocap.'

'Millsy, that's amazing,' I tell him. 'That's so cool. I'm so happy for you.'

'Thanks,' he says with a cute smile, flashing me his dimples. 'The only downside – that is not even remotely a downside – is that I have to fly to LA tomorrow.'

'So soon?'

'Yes. And I was wondering if you might want to come with me, keep me company, have some fun while we're over there...'

As Millsy says this he smiles and strokes my hand, and I don't know if it's because he seems so sure I'll sleep with him again, or if it's just because I want to, but I quickly snatch it away.

His smile drops from his face, his dimples vanishing as quickly as his mood shifts.

'We'll be back in time for Flora's wedding,' he quickly adds. 'And I know your ex is arriving at your mum and dad's a few days before. I thought you'd be happy to get away.'

'I think perhaps you should go on your own,' I tell him rather blankly. I'm trying to keep my words as empty as possible, because I really don't want to get into this now, but that in itself causes alarm bells for Millsy.

'Erm, OK,' he replies. 'Is this about last night?'

I don't say anything.

'It's not a big deal,' he starts, but I don't let him finish. It's not up to him to decide what is and isn't a big deal.

'Of course it's a big deal,' I reply. 'It might just be sex to you, but I'm not cut out for stuff like this.'

'Cara, come on,' he says, trying to take my hand again, but I won't let him. 'This is the last thing I wanted.'

I get that this sort of thing is much easier for him than it is for me, but, as it turns out, I can't just have sex with people. It would be great if I could, but I can't. The only thing last night did for me was allow me to realise that I want to be more than friends with Millsy, and if I go to LA with him, if I have sex with him again, I will fall in love with him. I know where this road is taking me but, by the time I get there, I'm almost certain he'll be somewhere else. Sex might be no big deal to him, but to me it isn't just a bit of fun between two adults, it's the confirmation that I'm falling for him. If I don't hit the brakes, I'm going to get hurt.

'Last night was clearly a mistake,' I tell him, my voice crackling a little. 'We both know it was.'

'Is that really what you think?' he asks.

I find myself getting lost in Millsy's big brown puppy-dog eyes. It hurts me to be so blunt with him, but I've got to.

'It's true, right? You're always saying how you don't like complicated.'

'I don't, but—'

Oh, God, why is this so hard? And why do I feel as if I'm making it worse? I'm trying to kill my romantic feelings to save our friendship but, in doing do, I'm just making things even more awkward. I need to stop. To try and figure things out. I definitely don't need to be making a scene at someone's wedding.

'I'm going to go,' I say.

'Cara...'

'Can we just, can we have a bit of space? You go to LA, don't worry about me, nail your audition and then we'll talk when you get back?'

'Is that really what you want?' he asks.

'It really is,' I tell him. 'I just can't believe what a mess we've made. I wish it hadn't happened.'

'OK,' he says. 'OK, sure. It doesn't need to be messy, if you don't want it to be. I'll be back in a few days.'

'I think I might go stay with my mum and dad, at least until after Flora's wedding. I'm sure there will be lots of stuff going on, so...'

The words leave my lips before I've really thought about how they sound. I just want us to take a breather to figure out what is going on. That's not going to happen if we're around each other, having sex again, which, even in all this stress, I still kind of can't stop thinking about, because last night... oh my God.

I'm just trying to do the mature, sensible thing. To protect myself. To not get hurt. If there is one thing I've realised since Lloyd and I broke up it's that I spent way too long thinking that things were going to get better, that Lloyd might be my happy ever after. And ever since I've given every date the benefit of the doubt, given them the chance to be the right person for me, and they've all, always, been so, so wrong for me. Being hopeful is one thing, but perhaps what I need more than anything is less hope and more rational consideration. It would be great to assume I'd found my Prince Charming in Millsy but what if that didn't last either, and came at the cost of the best friendship I've ever had?

Millsy nods thoughtfully as he takes the hint.

'OK, see you around,' he says as he jumps to his feet. On that note, he walks off.

I feel terrible but I'm just doing what I think is best. There's no way he wants to be in a relationship with me, not a real one, but my genie is out of the bottle now, so to speak. I can't pretend I don't have feelings for him. I can't watch him flirting with people at weddings. I can't bump into his exes with him. I can't hear all the little jokes people make about how many girls he's been with. It's just too hard.

I gather my things and head for the door, booking my taxi as I go. I know that I should say goodbye to people but I can't bear the thought of having to explain why I'm leaving early. More than anything I feel as if I'm going to burst into tears at any second and I really don't want anyone to see me cry. I can't believe what a mess I've made of all this. It's all because of sex. Stupid, stupid sex. I was right before, when I said that all the best relationships were sexless. I couldn't just be happy being friends with Millsy, I had to reach for more. And, in doing so, I've probably ruined everything.

29

When I moved out of my parents' house it wasn't because I hated living with them. I was working in Leeds, commuting every day, and it just felt like the right time to grow up and go out into the world on my own.

There were things that I missed about home. Not just the obvious things, like how much cheaper it was, and how much easier life was when I had my parents to ask for lifts. I'm talking about things like my mum's cooking. Having someone to watch *The Great British Bake Off* with over cups of tea – and cake, obviously, because the biggest mistake you can make is to watch that show without something sweet to tuck into. I missed my dad's cheesy dad jokes and having my brother around to play co-op video games with. So, after monumentally blowing things with Millsy, I decided the best thing to do was to move back in with my mum and dad, not only to give myself a little time to figure out what to do next, but to enjoy all those little bits of home I've missed since moving out.

What I hadn't realised, though, is that it's impossible to move back home because once you move out you forget all of the things that annoyed you about living at home. You only remember the good.

When I lived on my own I didn't have to answer to my parents. There was no one asking me where I was going, no one knocking on my bedroom door on a morning to tell me I'm sleeping in. I didn't have to ask my mum if she'd been in my room and taken all my knickers to wash. No explaining what a Mooncup is to my dad when he goes looking for mints in my handbag instead of my mum's. You know, stuff like that.

And, of course, the yucky icing on the worst cake I've ever eaten is that Lloyd, my ex-boyfriend, is turning up today. He's staying with my parents for a couple of days in the run-up to Flora's wedding, which, yep, he's still invited to. I really, really hoped that this was all just hot air, to teach me a lesson for not dieting into a bridesmaid dress, but, nope, it's still happening. I haven't told anyone that Millsy probably isn't coming to Flora's wedding now. Mostly because I don't want to admit that I've managed to fuck things up – after all, he was only going with me in the first place so that I could save face. If I tell people he isn't coming I'll lose face, I guess. I can't afford to get into negative face right now. Maybe I'll just tell people that he's ill on the day.

Another thing I hadn't realised about Lloyd's arrival was that my mum had been banking on letting him stay in my room. Yep, my childhood room, which is a weird place to imagine your ex-boyfriend hanging out, but it's also kind of funny because they wouldn't let him in there when we were together.

But, you know, he's a guest, as my mum keeps reminding me. I'm genuinely being demoted to the sofa for the four nights he's staying here. As far as my mum is concerned I'm just here in the run-up to the wedding, to be on hand to help if anyone needs/trusts me, to spend time with family members who are visiting for the occasion. She doesn't know that I don't want to go home to my own bed. I certainly hope she doesn't think that I'm here because I want to be close to Lloyd.

It will be fine though. At least I'm sleeping on the sofa in the conservatory, so I'll have my own space.

'Lloyd should be here any second,' my mum says. 'Ted, Ted, get that vacuum back out. You've missed a bit of Shake n' Vac.'

My dad waits until my mum has dashed upstairs for something before rubbing the offending powder into the carpet with his foot. He gives me a wink.

'That'll do,' he says.

My mum has us all lined up at the bottom of the stairs like the von Trapp kids, in anticipation of Lloyd's arrival. The good news is that she has me, my dad and my brother here. I honestly believe that she doesn't see Lloyd as an extension of me any more, and I don't think she wants me to get back with him. She just sees him as someone who she's known for a long time, but also as a house guest. We always treat house guests with the utmost respect.

A knock at the door has my mum rushing downstairs, giving the already over-dusted bannister one final sweep with her sleeve.

'Lloyd, hello,' she says as she opens the door. 'So lovely to see you, after all this time.'

I brace myself for the blast from the past that I know has been coming for months and yet I still don't feel quite prepared for it, but as Lloyd walks through the door it isn't like seeing a ghost, it's like looking at a whole new person.

'Lloyd?' I squeak. It sounds more like a question than a greeting. I can't quite believe it's him.

'Hey, Cara,' he says in his Somerset accent – so he still sounds like himself at least.

'You look so different,' I blurt.

'So do you,' he reminds me.

Oh, yeah, so I do. The last time Lloyd saw me my hair was shorter, blonde, and I was probably dressed as if I were going to a smart-casual funeral. The last time I saw Lloyd he was skinny, with a floppy fringe that wouldn't have looked out of place on Justin Bieber back when he was still wholesome. He isn't so skinny any more though, he's put on some weight, but it's clearly muscle, not fat, and he's rocking a buzz cut. He used to look kind of wimpy – now he looks like someone you'd see in an advert trying to get young people to join the army.

'It's lovely to see you,' my mum says. 'Come in, let's get you a cup of tea.'

'You too, Annie,' he says as he kisses my mum on both cheeks. 'I prefer to drink black coffee these days.'

'Well, let's get you a black coffee, then,' she says. 'Shall we sit in the kitchen?'

'Let's do it,' he says enthusiastically.

My parents and Lloyd disappear into the kitchen, my mum and Lloyd chatting away like old friends.

Oliver and I just stand in the hall.

'I thought he was supposed to be obsessed with you,' Oliver says.

'I know,' I reply.

'He barely looked at you,' Oliver points out.

I noticed that, obviously. Not only did Lloyd not seem like his usual clingy self, he seemed completely indifferent towards me. I thought the only reason he was coming to Flora and Tommy's wedding was to try and get back with me, and that the reason I hadn't heard from him in all this time was because the last time we spoke was when we broke up and he exploded with rage at me – I figured he was probably too upset to talk to me. Have I really just not heard from him because he's over me? Is he really just here because he feels as warmly towards my family as they do towards him?

'Reckon I can go back to my room?' Oliver asks.

'Yeah, definitely,' I reply.

'Oh, can I get Millsy's number?' he asks.

'What?'

'Can you give me Millsy's number, please? We said we were going to play FIFA one evening but we forgot to swap PSN names.'

'Oh, OK. Sure. I'll send it now.'

Speaking of men feeling indifferent towards me, I haven't heard a peep out of Millsy since Ruby's wedding so that's that, I guess. Perhaps I should spend a little of this free time I've got at the moment looking for somewhere new to live. It really was tremendously stupid of me to give up my flat to move in with him. I don't think he would throw me out, but I can't bear the idea of living with him now that things are so messy. Oh, what I would give to have my small, impossibly noisy flat by the bus station back.

With Oliver heading back up to his bedroom I decide to go to the kitchen. Now that Lloyd is here, and he's seemingly indifferent about my existence, I'm fascinated by him. I broke up with him for being overly possessive and incredibly jealous and here he is, just chilling. I can't get my head around it.

When I arrive in the kitchen there's no one there. The only sign of life is the kettle boiling, so they must have been in here.

'Hello, love,' my mum says as she comes in from the back garden.

'Hello,' I say cautiously. 'Where's Lloyd?'

'He's outside chopping wood with your dad,' she says very matter of factly.

'Lloyd is chopping wood?'

'Yes.'

'Like... with an axe?'

'No, with a butter knife. Yes, with an axe, Cara,' my mum jokes.

'Why?' I blurt in disbelief.

'We thought it might be nice to sit around the fire pit tonight,' my mum says. 'You're welcome to join us, obviously.'

'Yes, obviously I'm allowed to join *my* parents in *my* family home in anything,' I say, moody teenager style, as I head towards the sink to look out of the window above it.

Sure enough, my dad is lining up pieces of wood for Lloyd to chop in half. He swings down with the axe, hacking each piece clean in two. He stops for a moment to wipe his brow with the back of his hand. As he looks over towards the house I panic that he can see me watching him so I duck down.

'Isn't he handsome now?' my mum says.

'Erm... I don't know about "handsome now",' I reply. 'He's certainly a lot more rugged.'

'Not your type, then?' my mum says.

'No, is he yours?' I ask, only half serious.

'Your dad is my type,' she says. 'Lloyd is like a son to me, you know that. Joe, on the other hand...'

I notice that she's getting ready to take the drinks out to the manly wood-chopping men.

'Yeah, he's a babe, everyone thinks so,' I reply quickly. 'Can I carry the drinks out?'

'Erm, sure,' my mum says, placing the two cups of coffee down on the worktop for me to pick back up.

'Are you sure you don't fancy him still?' my mum asks.

'I'm just intrigued by him,' I admit. 'He seems so different.'

'Go have a chat with him,' my mum suggests. 'We've been

talking a little, when we've been planning his trip, and he seems a lot more chilled out than he used to be.'

'Coffee's up, boys,' I say as I walk outside.

'Oh, thanks, love,' my dad says.

'I thought you were more of a milky tea man,' I point out.

'Lloyd recommended the black coffee,' he replies before leaning in close and lowering his voice. 'Did your mum put three sugars in it?'

'Yes,' I whisper back through a smile.

I turn my attention to Lloyd right as he whips off his T-shirt, like something out of a Diet Coke advert.

'I don't think I've ever seen you use a tool,' I joke to him. He just smiles at me.

'I do lots of stuff now that I probably wouldn't have done when we were together,' he replies.

I rock my head from side to side thoughtfully.

'I don't think I ever stopped you chopping wood,' I say.

Lloyd gets back to his chopping.

'So, have you been well?' I ask.

'Yes, thanks,' he replies. 'Doing great, eating cleaner, working out more. Are you well?'

'Yeah, I'm great, thanks,' I reply. 'Still working in the same place, living in Leeds.'

I can tell he doesn't seem at all interested in anything I have to say.

'Anyway, I'll get back inside,' I say. 'Leave you men to being manly.'

I wander back inside and chat with my mum about wedding logistics while I watch my dad and Lloyd being blokes in the back garden. My dad always used to say that Lloyd wasn't a very manly man; I guess he's changed.

I wonder why Lloyd doesn't want to talk to me. I was honestly terrified he was going to try and get back with me, but this is so much worse. I feel so awkward. I feel as if I need to overcompensate by being nice to him but it's like talking to a brick wall.

At this rate, I am going to be alone at Flora's wedding. Millsy won't be there, Lloyd won't be talking to me – I'm sure I'll still be persona non grata, probably for a while after the wedding too...

How hard do you think it will be to find a date for the wedding, last minute? I could try and find one on a dating app, maybe? Perhaps I could sit in a bar, pretend I've been stood up and hope that another Millsy type takes pity on me and comes to my rescue? Maybe I should just post an advert on a job-search website looking for someone willing to take on the role as my plus one, for the experience. Hmm, maybe that last one sounds a bit too much like something out of a bad romantic comedy.

Well, with only a couple of days to go, I'd say I've probably run out of time. I'm just going to have to suck it up and go alone and, if all else fails, at least I know how to sneak out of a wedding now.

30

I've never really given much thought to karma.

Sure, I believe that we should treat people in the same way we would like them to treat us, but that's more of a transactional agreement. Karma is a little bit more like: do good things and good things will come to you, right?

Well, whether I believe in karma or not, I figured it wouldn't hurt me to try and get a little of the good stuff coming my way, and, even if it isn't real, at least I'll be buying myself a favour with my cousin.

Flora's friend Emmie, who was supposed to be putting together her party favour bags, has had to abandon her wedding duties to fly to Florida to visit her sick grandma. Naturally Flora is really upset. Not because Emmie's grandma is ill, although I can see why you might think that. No, Flora is upset because this means that there is no one to put together her party favours.

So, knowing how mad everyone is at me, I saw this as my chance to try and turn things around, and do you know what? It's worked. Flora and Auntie Mary are so relieved that I've agreed to do it that they actually had smiles for me when they dropped the stuff off for me to use. Flora even gave me a hug! And there was no mention of my hideous portrait of Flora, so I'm hoping that saving the day, the day before the wedding, makes us even.

It isn't easy being a hero though. Oh, no. I'm currently sitting at the dining table at my mum and dad's house surrounded by boxes of different bits and pieces. I take an item from each box, place them inside the little silver bags, tie the little silver bags with blue ribbon, and then I place the correct number of bags in the vases that are going to be placed in the centre of each table, but each table has a different number of people sitting at it, and the kids' bags have different contents, so this is honestly a fucking nightmare of a military operation that I really don't feel qualified for, but I said I'd do it, and everyone is happy with me for doing it, so I need to force myself to get on with it.

I just need to look at it as if I'm in an escape room. It's all numbers and puzzles and figuring out the right patterns. This is like a day out for me. In fact, with all the boxes in this room right now, just trying to climb over them to go to the bathroom would be like an escape room all of its own.

'Hello,' Lloyd says, sticking his head around the door.

'Hi,' I reply.

He still isn't really talking to me, other than in a general friendly acquaintance kind of way. I can't get my head around it.

'So you've landed party favour duties, huh?'

'I offered,' I tell him. 'Flora seemed a bit frazzled and I wanted to lighten the load.'

Lloyd moves boxes so that he can get into the room, so that he can sit down at the table next to me.

'See, that's not what I heard,' he starts. 'I heard you were trying to sabotage this wedding.'

I look at him and realise he's laughing.

'My mum told you about the bridesmaid stuff, then,' I say with a knowing nod.

'She did,' he says. 'Absolutely ridiculous. They should have just had the dress altered.'

'Thank you, rational person,' I say.

'And Oliver showed me the portrait you painted of Flora,' he adds. 'Just... awful.'

'Well, this seems to have eased me back into their good books, and in a way that I can hopefully sustain throughout tomorrow, so no one can be salty about the bridesmaid business. It's the best I can hope for.'

'Well, can I help?' he asks. 'If it's for the sake of the wedding, and for keeping the peace...'

'Oh, are you sure you don't mind?' I ask.

'Of course I don't mind,' he replies. 'It will give us a chance to catch up.'

See, this seems more like the Lloyd I know, but the Lloyd I dated while he lived locally, not the possessive, jealous, immature boy who I tried to have a long-distance relationship with.

'You seem good,' I point out. 'You seem really healthy and happy.'

'I am,' he replies. 'I'll admit, I didn't take our break-up all that well, but I'm better for it now. I've actually been doing a bit of app dating recently.'

'Oh, God, me too,' I reply. 'I actually gave up on it recently. The men on there are just all absolute nightmares. Are the women any better?'

'I've been catfished a couple of times. It's usually just photos with bodies cropped out or old photos taken when people were ten years younger. You know me though, I'm not superficial.'

'Still, lies aren't a great foundation to build a relationship on,' I say.

'That's true,' he replies. 'Probably why things fizzle out. Your mum says you're living with someone?'

'Millsy, yes,' I reply. 'He's just a friend.'

'He's your date for the wedding.'

'He is,' I reply. 'Although he's in LA for work at the moment. I'm worried he's not going to make it back in time.'

I'm pretty sure he's back already, he said he was only going for a few days, but this could be my reason for him not turning up.

'That would be a shame,' Lloyd says. 'I'd really like to meet him.'

'You would?'

'Of course,' he says. 'Everyone seems to really like him – you seem to really like him.'

I must not say anything for a good few seconds because Lloyd senses something is up.

'Cara, is everything OK?' he asks.

'Oh, yeah, it's fine.'

'Do you like him as more than a friend?' he asks curiously.

God, I feel as if he's rooting around inside my brain, not the cardboard box he's pulling little bags of sugared almonds out of.

I nod.

'So, what, does he not feel the same?' he asks.

I shrug.

'I'm not sure he feels as strongly as I do,' I say. It feels so weird, to be confiding in my ex about other men – especially an ex like Lloyd, who had jealousy issues.

'Well, more fool him then, because look at you. You're an amazing lady, Cara Brooks, and you look even better now than you used to. If he doesn't realise that, forget about him, OK?'

'Thanks,' I say with a smile. 'It's nice to be able to talk to you about these things.'

'It's nice to be here for you,' he says. 'I've done a lot of growing up since we broke up, and I'm sorry that I drove you to end things. I take full responsibility.'

'It's just nice to be on nice terms,' I reply.

Lloyd and I both reach for the scissors at the same time, our hands bumping clumsily over the table.

'Oh, you go first,' I say.

'No, after you,' he insists.

'Thanks.'

It really is nice to be civil with one another; it's going to make tomorrow go much easier, that's for sure. I still haven't heard from Millsy so I'm pretty sure he isn't coming. Thankfully I have an excuse in place now.

At least it isn't going to be like being trapped in a nightmare with my crazy ex and my angry relatives any more. It's almost as if things have completely reset. Shame really, I was starting to like the new me.

31

You know that bit during a wedding ceremony where the person marrying the happy couple asks if anyone knows any reason why this man and woman shouldn't be married? And you know how no one else says anything, unless it's in the movies, and it's usually some grand gesture so that true love can take its course, or it's some naff relative making a joke – something absolutely no one would do in real life?

Everything was going perfectly fine with Flora and Tommy's ceremony. I was just sitting in my seat, in my gorgeous purple dress – not standing at the front of the room in a dress I couldn't fit my boobs in – when the official asked that question, and we all heard the door at the back of the room being flung open.

Naturally everyone gasped and turned around to see who was turning up to object, storming in just in time.

'Oh, shi...' Millsy blurted as he barged in. He stopped himself just in time to not fully commit to swearing, but somehow it felt as if the damage was done.

I couldn't help but snigger to myself. If I were Tommy, I'd be shitting myself if someone as gorgeous as Millsy burst through the doors, looking dapper in a suit, at my wedding, right at the moment when it was time for people to speak now or forever hold their peace.

'Sorry I'm late,' he told the room. 'Please, go on.'

He sat down on the first available chair, sinking low into his seat.

He looked so amazing in a black suit with a pinky-purple tie. He also looked really bloody embarrassed.

'Who is that?' Flora asked Tommy. He shrugged.

When the ceremony was over I turned around to see that Millsy had disappeared. I wondered if perhaps he might have changed his mind about coming, but as soon as we were all manoeuvred into the room where the reception is taking place, we bumped into each other.

Millsy and I haven't actually spoken since Ruby's wedding, so I can't say he didn't take my request for space seriously, but with that in mind I definitely didn't think he would turn up today. I hoped he would. I've been hoping all week. But the more time passed, the bigger the space between us felt. Suddenly he seemed too far away for me to reach out to.

And now here we are, face to face, both of us waiting for the other person to say something.

'Hi,' Millsy eventually says with a smile.

'Hi,' I reply, feeling my own cheeks pull into a smile. I'm not only pleased he turned up to the wedding, I'm just genuinely pleased to see him.

'How are—?'

'Are you—?'

We both speak at the same time, talking over each other, both stopping at the same time to let the other speak.

'You OK?' he asks me.

I nod.

'You?'

'Yeah, you know,' he replies. And I absolutely do. I've really missed him this past week.

'Ladies and gentlemen, if everyone could take their seats,' my auntie's voice splutters out through the speakers, complete with feedback. 'The seating plan is on the wall by the entrance.'

'That woman shouldn't have access to a microphone,' I say to Millsy, right as Lloyd rocks up alongside us.

In today's episode of *You Could Not Make This Shit Up*, I have found myself standing in between Lloyd and Millsy, the two of them looking each other up and down. Not only that, but the seating plan says I'll be sitting between them at the table too.

That's where I am now, waiting for my main course, after nearly an hour of polite conversation between everyone on the table.

In an interesting twist of events, my mum, who is usually Lloyd's biggest fan, is mostly chatting with Millsy. My dad is too, chatting about rugby league with him. With Lloyd clearly feeling a bit pushed out I've done my best to keep chatting with him. Millsy and I are yet to chat one-on-one.

Our main-course plates are placed down in front of us. I haven't really eaten much today so I'm absolutely starving. I've been so looking forward to this steak but, when it arrives, I'm disappointed to see it covered in mushrooms.

'Ergh, mushrooms,' I blurt. 'Why do people ruin food with mushrooms?'

'They barely taste of anything,' Millsy points out.

'You can't say anything,' I tell him. 'I know you're not going to eat those parsnips.'

'They're just so...' Millsy pulls a face and chews the air. He doesn't look happy. 'You know what I mean?'

'You want my mushrooms?' I ask. 'And I'll eat your parsnips?'

'You've got yourself a deal,' he replies. 'That's the best thing about you, Cara. I get so many bonus mushrooms when we eat together.'

'She has far greater qualities than that,' Lloyd insists.

I frown at him, puzzled. Why is he butting in?

'I was just joking, buddy, stand down,' Millsy says.

'Would you like my parsnips too, Cara?' Lloyd asks.

'Oh, it's OK, you like them, don't you?' I say. 'I've got plenty with these ones, thanks.'

'He'll be offering you his jacket to walk on next,' Millsy says under his breath.

'Anyway, how was LA?' I ask him, changing the subject.

'It was really good,' he replies. 'I wish you could have come with me. The audition went well – in fact, it sounds like a sure thing.'

'Aw, that's great,' I tell him. 'You really deserve it.'

'Thanks,' he says. 'I had one of the casting people completely charmed. You probably helped me in a way. She was talking about how she was going to a gender-reveal party later that day and, I hope you don't mind, I told her about our drama.'

'What drama?' my mum asks curiously.

'Oh, God, don't tell my mum.' I laugh. 'She'll ban me from all family parties.'

'Oh, go on, tell me,' she insists. 'You'll tell me, won't you, Joe?'

'Come on, let me tell your mum,' he says. 'She'll find it hilarious.'

'She doesn't want you to,' Lloyd says angrily.

Everyone just stares at him.

'Erm, it's OK,' I tell him, before turning back to Millsy. 'Go on, tell them.'

'OK, so, we were at my sister Fran's gender-reveal party, and it was our job to bring the cake. So we get this awesome cake and we set it down on the table and leave it there to join the party. Later, when we went back to get it, I guess Cara was a bit distracted and she just opened the first box she saw. It was the gender-reveal box and before we knew what was happening, with no time to stop it, we saw the blue balloon fly off towards the sky.'

'Oh my God, no,' my mum says, absolutely captivated. 'What did you do?'

'Well, we managed to find a balloon in Millsy's parents' kitchen drawer,' I reply.

'My stepmum keeps them for emergencies,' Millsy adds. 'I'd always wondered what kind of emergency required a balloon.'

'Except the only balloons she had were... white,' I continue, pausing for dramatic effect.

'What did you do?' Oliver asks, suddenly interested in what we're talking about.

'I blew one up, I grabbed a blue pen, I wrote "It's a boy" on it, and I put it back in the box.'

'Did people find out?' my mum asks.

'No one knows it was us,' he says. 'I think my sister wrote a letter of complaint to the company she got it from.'

'That's terribly unethical,' Lloyd says.

'Well, what would you have done?' Millsy asks him. 'I didn't want Cara getting in trouble or feeling bad. We've always got each other's backs. When I nearly killed my grandma's dog it was Cara who was there to help me. Did you know she can pick padlocks?'

'I did,' my mum says, unamused. 'And yet she still can't fold hospital corners when she's making a bed.'

'I don't even know what they are,' I confess with a laugh.

'Go on, then, lad, tell us how you nearly killed this dog,' my dad insists.

Now that we're talking about us, Millsy and I are getting on just fine. Just as things were before the sex-cident. It's nice. I'm just not sure I can keep this up forever.

Millsy tells him the story in that charming, animated way he talks. He's always been amazing at commanding an audience. For a while I just watch him. It's crazy, how much I've missed him. But do I miss him so much that I would be willing to settle for being just friends? I don't know if I could handle that.

We get through dinner, we survive sitting through the speeches, and then it's time for the bride and groom to enjoy their first dance. Flora and Tommy take to the floor and slow-dance to Elton John's 'Your Song'. I thought Flora might have been the type to take dance classes, to do something fancy, but they're just happily dancing together in the most normal way. I like that. Sometimes it doesn't matter how things look, it only matters how they feel.

By the time everyone else is joining them on the dance floor I get this heavy feeling in my heart.

'Fancy a dance?' Millsy asks. He asks so casually, as if it's no skin off his nose if I say yes or I say no.

'Erm,' Lloyd starts, but I don't let him finish.

'I'd love to,' I reply.

Millsy takes me by the hand and leads me to the dance floor. He finds us a space and wraps his arms around my waist. I hook my arms around his neck, exhaling deeply, relaxing into his embrace.

'Another fantastic dress,' he tells me.

'Thanks,' I reply. 'It's one of the ones you talked me into buying.'

'I know,' he says. 'I have excellent taste.'

Millsy steers me in a particular direction, so I can look back at our table.

'Your ex is glaring daggers into me,' he says.

'He doesn't look happy at all, does he?' I reply. 'I think that might be my fault. I told him some stuff about us. We've been talking, it's been nice. He seems really mature now.'

'You're not thinking of getting back with him, are you?' Millsy asks, moving away from me just a little so that he can look into my eyes.

'Come on, Millsy. You don't care,' I remind him.

'Of course, I care,' he replies. 'Why would you think I don't care?'

'I really don't want to get into this here,' I say.

'I know, but we need to talk about this at some point. If not now, then when? Don't think I haven't noticed how much stuff you took to your mum and dad's while I was away.'

'I'm not doing this here, on the dance floor, at my cousin's wedding,' I tell him. 'Come on, let's step out.'

I grab Millsy by the hand and lead him out of the reception room, to the quiet sitting area outside where the toilets are.

'Erm, what's going on?' I hear Lloyd call after us.

'It's fine, Lloyd, just give us a minute,' I say.

'Are the two of you sneaking off together? You tell me that he doesn't feel the same way about you as you feel about him and then, what, because he dances with you, you're sneaking off to the toilets with him?' Lloyd asks accusingly, as though he has any right.

'Holy shit,' Millsy says. 'He's even more intense than you said he was.'

'Wow,' is about all I can say. 'I just... wow.'

'Well, what else are you going to be doing?' Lloyd asks.

'Talking,' I say to him very clearly and very slowly. 'You haven't changed at all, have you? Practically negging me the day you got here, swooping in to help me yesterday, being really terrifyingly intense right now.'

'Why do you always push me away?' Lloyd asks. 'I'm the perfect person for you. We didn't have a problem with us, it was the distance that was a problem – but I'm here now, and I still love you. And I think you might still love me. This guy is just your rebound. I know you.'

'You don't know me at all,' I say. 'If you knew me you'd know how uncomfortable you're making me.'

'I know that *The Shining* is your favourite book. I know that you love any cocktail with rum in it. I know that gerbera daisies make you smile – remember how I always used to bring you bunches? You loved them,' Lloyd says.

Millsy sniggers.

'What?' Lloyd asks him.

'Mate, you don't know her at all,' he tells him.

'And you do, huh?'

'I do,' Millsy says confidently. '*The Shining* isn't her favourite book, it's her favourite movie – she likes the ambiguity of the movie and the way it taps into her own fears. I know that she hates rum. She got too drunk on it one time in, frankly, the most boring story about a person getting drunk I have ever heard in my life. And she doesn't like flowers, she hates flowers. It makes her sad when they die. And when she gets married she's going to have a plant in her pocket, and I don't know if I'll be lucky enough to be there, but it would be a huge mistake if you're there because you clearly don't know her *at all*.'

I feel my lips part as my jaw literally drops, just a little. We've only known each other for a summer but I feel as if Millsy knows me inside and out. And what he said about when I get married, well, at least I know that, after everything, he still wants to be in my life. I don't think I could live without him in it either. And he's definitely right about Lloyd. He doesn't know me at all, if he thinks I'm in love with him. He really hasn't changed a bit on the inside.

Lloyd, clearly bested by Millsy in a way he can't possibly argue with, lashes out at Millsy, hitting him in the face.

'Lloyd, what the hell?' I shriek. I've never seen him hit anyone before. I glance around to look for witnesses but it's just the three of us. I am horrified.

'Not the fucking face,' Millsy says. 'Why do people always go for the face? I'm on the verge of landing my first movie job and this clown hits me in the fucking face.'

He places his hand over his cheek to check the damage.

'Lucky you hit like a child,' Millsy points out.

'OK, Lloyd, you need to leave.'

'Gladly,' he says. 'You're not even worth it.'

Lloyd storms off in the direction of the exit, not the reception. I don't know where he's going; all of his stuff is still at my parents' place. I suppose he'll have to collect it at some point. I think I'll keep the hell away.

'That's fair,' I tell Millsy once we're alone. 'I'm probably not worth travelling all the way from Somerset for, infiltrating my family, starting on a man who could clearly beat the shit out of anyone if he wasn't so scared about damaging his face... Is it OK?'

'I'm lucky he slapped me instead of punching me,' Millsy says. 'Pathetic.'

'At least the part you're up for is mocap,' I remind him. 'But I am really sorry that he hit you. And do let me remind you that I absolutely didn't invite him here.'

Standing just outside the reception room, we're all alone, away from the excitement of the wedding, without Lloyd breathing down our necks. It's just us now. Just like it used to be. Except things can never really go back to how they used to be, can they?

Millsy runs his tongue across the front of his teeth, checking for damage.

'Does this mean you owe your cousin a slap?' he jokes.

'Oh, I would, but I'm back in her good books because I helped out with wedding stuff. Why don't I just give you my horrible portrait of her and we'll call it even?'

'Fair enough,' he says with a smile.

'Thanks for coming,' I tell him. 'I didn't think you would.'

Millsy shrugs it off.

'And I think you might have proposed to me, somewhere in the middle of what you said to Lloyd,' I tease jokily.

'That wasn't what that was,' he says with a laugh. 'But I did hear the part where he said that you don't feel the same way about me as I do about you and, honestly, that's fine. I miss you. I don't care if you want to be just friends, I just care that you're in my life.'

'That's all well and good but – wait, what?'

I'm caught off guard by his words. I can't help but cock my head like a dog confused by a high-pitched noise.

'If you just want to be friends that's fine by me,' he says. 'So long as you're in my life.'

'You want to be just friends,' I tell him.

'No, you do,' he replies.

'Wait, what? Let's just rewind a second. You're Joe "Millsy" Mills. Ladies' man. Doesn't settle down. Sleeps with anything with a pulse, as the story goes.'

'Do you really believe all that?' he asks me.

'Are you telling me that's not true?'

'Years ago, when I was young and stupid, the last thing I wanted was a girlfriend, but then, when Ruby got with Nick, I realised I was just a man in his thirties going out to bars, refusing to grow up. Is there anything sadder?'

'You essentially picked me up in a bar,' I remind him.

'I saw you sitting there alone and I felt sorry for you,' he says. 'Then, after we chatted for a bit, I realised that, not only did I like chatting to you, but you seemed like a bit of a loner too. OK, sure, I noticed you because you were beautiful, but can you honestly tell me you've seen this playboy Millsy you keep banging on about?'

'You thought I was beautiful and yet you immediately got me to change my hair colour,' I say.

'That's not true,' he insists. 'You wanted to change. I wanted to make you happy.'

'Don't think I didn't notice that the colour you picked out for me was the same colour hair your ex had.'

'She was blonde the last time I saw her – I told you at the time I almost didn't recognise her. You're really going to have to try a lot harder than this if you want to avoid falling in love so desperately.'

I smile.

'OK, last shot,' I start. 'When we were at my bosses' wedding, and I told you that you could flirt with whoever you wanted, and you immediately went off and hit on the bride...'

'You were so adamant that you wanted me to chat-up other women,' he tells me. 'So, I was walking to the toilets, and there was a girl walking past me, so I asked her if I could buy her a drink. My plan was to bring her back to you and hope that you realised that you didn't like me talking to other women. In hindsight, it was a crap idea, and I should have chosen someone other than the bride...'

'So when we slept together...'

'I thought that was it,' he replies. 'I thought that was us finally getting together. You thought it was just us hooking up?'

'I did,' I confess.

'Cara, for months now, it's been all about you. I haven't looked at other girls. I've stopped going out. I just want to spend my days with you, and my nights with you. I want you to go everywhere with me. I want you to stop me killing dogs. I want you ruining all my family parties – it will be nice to have someone to hate Jay with. Just think how much fun it will be when there's two of us. We could have framed him for the gender-reveal balloon thing!'

I laugh.

'Do you really think the two of us can be together?' I ask.

My usual hopeful feeling is bubbling up inside me but I'm too scared to let it take hold. I want to be with Millsy more than anything but... can we really be together?

'We *are* together,' he tells me. 'It just takes a while to realise sometimes.'

I've heard it said before that you finally find the one for you when you stop looking, or that you usually find your perfect person right under your nose all along. I feel as if Millsy ticks both these boxes. I wasn't looking for love with him when I met him, and I certainly didn't think I was going to find it. I don't think he did either though. Perhaps that's how you know when things are right. When they just effortlessly click into place.

'Does your face hurt too much to kiss me?' I ask him.

'My face will never hurt too much to kiss you,' he replies. 'Come here.'

Millsy picks me up, lifting me high in the air. As we kiss I wrap my legs around his waist and squeeze him tightly. You know when something just feels right? This feels right.

'Let's head back in,' Millsy says. 'I don't want to sound hysterical but, if my face is red, I might need to put some ice on it.'

'What happens next?' I ask him. 'With us, not with your face.'

'Nothing,' he says. 'We just carry on as we were, I guess, maybe we share a bed more often.'

'Just... life as normal?' I say. 'Sounds kind of boring for us.'

'Well, you know Fran's baby is going to be born any day, so there's going to be a christening soon.'

'And it will be Christmas before we know it – that usually involves a lot of parties,' I add with a smile.

'Imagine if I get the part in the movie and we get to go to the premiere – just think of the havoc we could wreak there.'

'Sounds great,' I reply.

'See,' Millsy says. 'We're going to be just fine.'

As we turn a corner Millsy grabs me and kisses me again, this time pinning me up against the wall.

'Oh, I've just put my hand in something wet,' he says, taking a step back.

We both glance next to us to see a large white wedding cake with a big, man-sized handprint pressed into the side of it.

'Oh, God, here we go,' Millsy says.

'Don't worry,' I reassure him. 'I have a plan...'

ACKNOWLEDGMENTS

Massive thanks to Nia and Amanda for being such a dream to work with. The entire Boldwood team is absolutely fantastic. I know how fortunate I am to be on board.

As always, thank you to everyone who takes the time to read and review my books, it means so much to me that you enjoy them. It's been so much fun revisiting Millsy, Ruby and Nick, who I first wrote about in my novel Truth or Date.

Thank you to my amazing family. Kim and Aud, you're both incredible. Joey and James, thank you so much for all your support. Thanks to my fiancé, Joe, as always, for *absolutely every-thing*. I love you all so much and I couldn't do any of it without you.

MORE FROM PORTIA MACINTOSH

We hope you enjoyed reading *The Plus One Pact*. If you did, please leave a review.

If you'd like to gift a copy, this book is also available as an ebook, digital audio download and audiobook CD.

Sign up to Portia MacIntosh's mailing list for news, competitions and updates on future books.

http://bit.ly/PortiaMacIntoshNewsletter

Discover more laugh-out-loud romantic comedies from Portia Macintosh:

Honeymoon For One

My Great Ex-Scape

ABOUT THE AUTHOR

Portia MacIntosh is a bestselling romantic comedy author of 15 novels, including *My Great Ex-Scape* and *Honeymoon For One*. Previously a music journalist, Portia writes hilarious stories, drawing on her real life experiences.

Visit Portia's website: https://portiamacintosh.com/

Follow Portia MacIntosh on social media here:

[f] facebook.com/portia.macintosh.3

[t] twitter.com/PortiaMacIntosh

[ig] instagram.com/portiamacintoshauthor

[BB] bookbub.com/authors/portia-macintosh

ABOUT BOLDWOOD BOOKS

Boldwood Books is a fiction publishing company seeking out the best stories from around the world.

Find out more at www.boldwoodbooks.com

Sign up to the Book and Tonic newsletter for news, offers and competitions from Boldwood Books!

http://www.bit.ly/bookandtonic

We'd love to hear from you, follow us on social media:

facebook.com/BookandTonic

twitter.com/BoldwoodBooks

instagram.com/BookandTonic

Manufactured by Amazon.ca
Bolton, ON

24328050R00153